A CATERED BOOK CLUB MURDER

Books by Isis Crawford

A CATERED MURDER
A CATERED WEDDING
A CATERED CHRISTMAS
A CATERED VALENTINE'S DAY
A CATERED HALLOWEEN
A CATERED BIRTHDAY PARTY
A CATERED THANKSGIVING
A CATERED ST. PATRICK'S DAY
A CATERED CHRISTMAS COOKIE EXCHANGE
A CATERED FOURTH OF JULY
A CATERED MOTHER'S DAY
A CATERED TEA PARTY
A CATERED COSTUME PARTY
A CATERED CAT WEDDING
A CATERED NEW YEAR'S EVE
A CATERED BOOK CLUB MURDER

Published by Kensington Publishing Corp.

A Mystery with Recipes

A CATERED BOOK CLUB MURDER

ISIS CRAWFORD

KENSINGTON
PUBLISHING CORP.
www.kensingtonbooks.com

KENSINGTON BOOKS are published by

Kensington Publishing Corp.
119 West 40th Street
New York, NY 10018

All Kensington titles, imprints and distributed lines are available at special quantity discounts for bulk purchases for sales promotion, premiums, fund-raising, educational or institutional use.

Special book excerpts or customized printings can also be created to fit specific needs. For details, write or phone the office of the Kensington Special Sales Manager: Kensington Publishing Corp., 119 West 40th Street, New York, NY 10018. Attn. Special Sales Department. Phone: 1-800-221-2647.

The K logo is a trademark of Kensington Publishing Corp.

Library of Congress Control Number: 2020943981

ISBN-13: 978-1-4967-1502-9
ISBN-10: 1-4967-1502-0
First Kensington Hardcover Edition: January 2021

ISBN-13: 978-1-4967-1504-3 (ebook)
ISBN-10: 1-4967-1504-7 (ebook)

10 9 8 7 6 5 4 3 2 1

Printed in the United States of America

*To my grandmother.
I wouldn't be here without her.*

A CATERED BOOK CLUB MURDER

Prologue

Lydia Baskerville cleared her throat. "I dreamt about you last night, Margo," she said, her voice loud against the hum of the air conditioner.

"I hope it was good," Margo Hemsley replied absent-mindedly as she concentrated on the square of canvas she was working on. She decided she needed to add a touch more light blue to the green she was using.

Lydia wrapped her shawl tightly around her shoulders. Even though it was hot outside, it felt like a meat locker in Margo's studio. Why Margo had to keep it like this was beyond her. "It wasn't good. It wasn't good at all."

Margo nodded. This was not new. Lydia's dreams never were. "So, I didn't win the lottery?" she joked.

Lydia frowned. "You were in danger."

Margo made clicking noises with her tongue as she considered the painting in front of her. She'd promised Steve and Irene she'd have it ready for their gallery by the end of next week. Now she was beginning to think she'd been overly optimistic.

Lydia switched topics for the moment, indicating the painting Margo was working on with a nod of her head. "That painting is quite the find," she observed.

"It certainly is," Margo agreed. She took a step back. The two women contemplated the oil on the easel.

"So," Lydia asked, changing the subject, "have you read the book for book club yet?"

Margo shook her head. A couple of the bobby pins holding up her unruly mop of ashy gray curls fell onto the floor. She picked them up, put them in the pocket of the flannel man's shirt she was wearing over her sundress, then combed her hair back with her fingers. "No, but I will before Tuesday."

"That's four days away," Lydia pointed out.

"I'm a fast reader."

Lydia frowned. "We read one Dorothy Sayers. I don't see why we have to read another," she groused.

"I agree. *The Nine Tailors* was enough for me," Margo said. Then she went back to studying the canvas she was working on.

"Although," Lydia conceded, "Sayers was daring for her time."

"She was," Margo responded. "But now she's just dated. Unlike Agatha Christie. I wonder why that is?" she mused.

"The language?" Lydia guessed. She rubbed her arms. The shawl wasn't helping much. "Don't you want to hear about my dream?" she asked, returning to the reason she had come here in the first place.

"To be honest, not really," Margo replied, eyes on her work. She liked Lydia; she was a friend, but she wished she would leave. It was hard to concentrate with Lydia yammering in her ear, and she needed all the time she could get. The buyer for the piece she was working on was flying in on Emirates next Friday, so it had to be ready by then. Margo sighed. People didn't realize how difficult it was to restore a painting, especially a painting that had been damaged in a fire.

Lydia told her about the dream anyway. "You were in trouble."

"So you said," Margo said.

"People are upset with you," Lydia told her.

Margo snorted.

"You need to keep your promises."

"That's what your dream said?"

"In so many words," Lydia replied.

"Interesting dream," Margo commented as she rested her brush on her easel and studied what she'd done. Then she thought about the other job she'd contracted for and wondered where she'd find the time to finish that one. She shouldn't have taken it on, but the money had been too good to resist.

"Did you hear what I said?" Lydia demanded.

Margo startled. "Of course," she answered, coming out of her reverie.

"No, you didn't."

"I most certainly did."

"Then tell me what I said."

Margo conceded that she couldn't.

Lydia let go of her shawl, extended her right hand, and laid it on Margo's arm. "Listen to me," she pleaded. "You're in danger. You really are."

"You keep saying that."

"Grave danger."

Margo raised an eyebrow as she looked at her friend. "Oh. Not just danger . . . grave danger," she said in a mocking voice.

"I'm serious."

"So am I."

Lydia removed her hand from Margo's arm and grasped her shawl again. "Listen, I know you don't believe in this stuff, but I'm usually right. Look at what happened to

Molly Edwards. I told her to be careful, and her house blew up from that gas leak. She's lucky to be alive."

"Lydia, her house blew up a year after you warned her," Margo couldn't help saying, although prolonging this discussion was the last thing she wanted to do.

"But it happened."

"Eventually."

"But it still happened. Dream time is different from real time."

Margo gave up. "Fine." *What was the point of arguing?* she thought.

"Please be careful."

Margo smiled at her. "I will. Sorry if I'm being curt. It's just that I'm on this tight deadline."

Lydia nodded. "I know."

"Don't worry," Margo told Lydia as she turned back to the painting. "Everything will be fine."

"I hope so," Lydia said, her tone dubious.

"It will," Margo reiterated as she studied the painting on the easel. "I promise."

And those were the last words Lydia heard Margo say.

Chapter 1

Bernie checked the clock on the wall of A Little Taste of Heaven. It was almost seven p.m., and Margo Hemsley hadn't picked up her order yet. She turned to her older sister. "This is the second Tuesday of the month, right?"

Libby cracked a roll of quarters into the register with a practiced flick of her wrist before answering. "As far as I know it is. Why?"

"Because Margo isn't here."

For the past five years, Margo Hemsley had had a standing order consisting of one small chocolate cake with mocha buttercream frosting, one small raspberry pie with whipped cream on the side, and a dozen peanut-butter chocolate-chip cookies, an order she would pick up at the shop and transport to the home of whoever was hosting the monthly meeting of the Longely Mystery Book Club.

Libby looked at the clock. "She's five minutes late."

"Exactly. She's always ten minutes early."

"Maybe she had car trouble," Libby hypothesized as she began waiting on Mike Crenshaw.

"You know what I appreciate about this place," Mike said to Libby as she boxed up his to-go order of fried chicken, dirty rice, and watermelon and feta salad.

Libby looked up. "No. What?"

"No kale."

"That's not true. We have a kale salad," Libby protested.

"Which I will never eat. I hate kale. My soon-to-be ex knows that, but she puts it in everything anyway. Why would she do that? Never mind. Don't answer," Mike said before Libby could say anything. Then he pointed to the strawberry shortcake in the display case and patted his belly. "And throw in a piece of that. I mean, what the hell. You only live once, right?"

"Right," Libby agreed as she pulled another takeout container from underneath the counter and cut a generous slice for him. "You're off schedule," she noted as she carefully transferred the slice to the container.

"How do you mean, Libby?" Mike asked.

"Well, you're a seven-fifteen in the morning Metro North guy. You never come in for dinner."

Mike laughed. "Dentist appointment." He made a face. "I have to get a new crown, so I decided to treat myself."

Libby added another piece of cake to the container. "In sympathy," she explained.

Mike smiled and nodded his thanks. "By the way, Margo's car is fine," he said.

"How do you know?" Bernie asked.

"Because I was picking up my vehicle from Azrias's at the same time Margo was picking up her Camry. I heard Phil tell her it was good to go and would be for another thousand miles or so. Then she'd need to get a new vehicle."

"Car shopping. Not my favorite thing to do," Bernie noted. Then she went into the back to finish cleaning up, leaving her sister and their two employees, Amber and Googie, to wait on the remaining customers. She looked at the clock again after she'd finished with the dishes in the sink. Seven-thirty. Margo had never been late in the five years she'd been picking up the order. Bernie reached for her phone and called her. There was no answer, so Bernie left a voicemail message.

Maybe Margo had gotten into an accident, Bernie mused. Or maybe she was sick. Maybe she'd gotten that stomach thing that was going around and was in the bathroom puking her guts out. Bernie hoped not as she grabbed one of the dish towels hanging from the wall-oven handle and spread it out on the counter so she could put the knives on it. She was very particular about how she treated them.

For one thing, they'd been her mother's, so they had sentimental value. For another thing, they were the tools of her trade: she was accustomed to their heft and balance, the way they felt in her hand. And for a third thing, they would be extremely expensive to replace. After she washed the four knives, she thoroughly dried them—if she didn't, they would rust—and laid them on the kitchen towel. Then she tried Margo again. Still no answer.

Bernie tapped her phone against her chin while she thought. She was probably being overly concerned, but on the other hand . . . She was in the middle of looking up the number for another member of the Longely Mystery Book Club when her cell went off. Betsy Glassberg was on the line.

"Has Margo come by?" she asked.

Bernie told her she hadn't.

"I'm worried," Betsy said. "She's forty-five minutes late."

"It's unlike her," Bernie agreed.

"And she isn't answering her phone," Betsy added.

"I know. I just tried calling her, too. Has anyone checked her house?" Bernie asked as she put the knives back where they belonged.

"Tom is driving over there now." Tom was Betsy's husband. "I don't suppose . . ." Betsy started to say, but Bernie finished her sentence for her.

"I could run the stuff over?"

"Yes. If that wouldn't be too much trouble."

"No trouble at all," Bernie said. "The shop officially closes in fifteen minutes anyway."

"The meeting is at the Westovers'," Betsy informed her. Their house was a little over ten minutes away.

Bernie told her she or one of her staff would be over in a few and hung up. Then she went out front and filled in Libby on what was happening. "So who is doing the delivery?" Bernie asked her sister when she was done. "You or me?"

"I will," Libby volunteered. She'd been planning on going over to her boyfriend Marvin's flat, and the Westovers' place was close by. "I just need to change into a clean shirt."

"And do something about the pants you're wearing," Bernie suggested.

"They're comfortable," Libby protested.

"They're hideous."

Libby looked down at them. What was so bad about paisley harem pants? "I wouldn't go that far."

"I would," Bernie told her. "Some fashions don't deserve to come back."

"Marvin doesn't care."

"He does. He's just too polite to say so. And even if he doesn't, you should."

"So what would you suggest, oh great fashionista?"

Bernie grinned. "I'm glad you asked. Wear the light pink sundress I gave you. Besides, it's too hot out for pants. You'll be more comfortable in a dress." She reached up, took off the thin gold chain she was wearing around her neck, and handed it to Libby. "Here. It goes with the dress."

Libby wanted to argue, but she couldn't. In her heart, she knew her sister was right. Twenty minutes later, she was on her way. The Westovers' house was in a development called Bubbling Brook, even though there never had been a brook, much less one that bubbled, on the property. A classic, three-bedroom, pale blue colonial with white shutters, there was nothing about it that called attention to itself. It looked like all the other houses on the block. Comfortable. A tad dowdy.

As Libby approached the Westovers' house, she noted that the driveway leading up to it was full. *The gang's all here; well, almost all the gang*, she thought as she parked Mathilda, the sisters' van, across the road. Then she grabbed the delivery and headed toward the Westovers' residence. The smell of honeysuckle enveloped her as she crossed the street. She was halfway up the porch stairs when Gilda Westover opened the door and stepped outside.

She had a cap of jet-black hair, wore aggressively large tortoiseshell glasses, and bright pink lipstick. Black was her favorite color, and tonight was no exception. She was wearing cropped black linen trousers, a black tank top, and white slides.

"You're just in time," she told Libby as she took Libby's package from her. "We're about to head out."

"Head out?" Libby asked. "I don't understand."

"To see if we can find Margo, of course," Gilda explained.

Libby nodded. Of course. "So, I take it Margo wasn't home."

Gilda shook her head, her face creased with worry.

"Not only wasn't she home, but her car wasn't in the driveway."

"Maybe she forgot," Libby suggested, feeling foolish as the words escaped her mouth.

Gilda peered over the edge of her glasses. "Seriously? We're talking about the person who never leaves home without her engagement calendar, the person who measures her life out in fifteen-minute increments."

Libby nodded. Gilda was correct. "Did Tom go inside Margo's house?"

"He couldn't. He doesn't have her key."

"Surely someone here does," Libby commented, gesturing toward the cars parked in the driveway.

"You'd think, but you would be wrong," Gilda replied. "Margo is a private person," she added by way of explanation, speaking louder so she could be heard over Lydia, whose voice was floating out of the open door.

"I warned her," Lydia was saying. "I told Margo. I went out of my way to tell her. Why didn't she listen to me? This is my fault. I should have tried harder."

Gilda rolled her eyes. "Lydia does tend to the dramatic," she observed.

Libby was about to say, yes, indeed she does, but she stopped herself in time. As her mother had warned and she had learned from painful experience, when you own a shop in a small town, it's a bad idea to say anything about someone else in public—even if it's positive—because it could come back and bite you in the behind.

"Do you need some help locating Margo?" Libby asked instead. After all, she and her sister had a pretty good solve rate when it came to this sort of thing.

Gilda shook her head and pulled up her pants. She'd had her stomach stapled six months ago and was still losing weight. "Thanks, but I think we've got this. We've read enough mysteries. I mean, how hard can finding her be? It's not like she's a secret agent or anything like that. We'll be fine."

Libby nodded, relieved. The moment she'd made the comment about helping, she'd regretted the impulse. After all, she hadn't changed her clothes to hang out with Marvin for nothing. "Well, keep me in the loop."

"I will," Gilda promised as the members of the LMBC streamed out of her house.

They're excited, not concerned, Libby thought as she watched Toni and Brad Musclow and Irene and Steven Offenbach head for their vehicles. *It's like they're going on a scavenger hunt or playing hide-and-seek.*

A voice behind her said, "I do hope she's okay."

Libby spun around. Lydia was standing in back of her. She'd put her salt-and-pepper hair up in a topknot and decorated it with a yellow rose from her garden. She took a step forward. Now she was close enough that Libby could smell the alcohol on her breath. "Why couldn't Margo have listened to me?" Lydia demanded. She blinked tears away. "Why doesn't anyone listen to me?" She raised her hands, then let them fall to her side. "All I want to do is help."

"I'm sure Margo is fine," Libby soothed.

"I wish I were sure," Lydia said. Then she turned and stumbled to her car.

Libby pivoted to Gilda. "I hope you're not going to let Lydia drive," she said.

"Absolutely not," Gilda answered. "The last thing we need at a time like this is an accident." And, with that, she ran off to intercept Lydia.

Five minutes later, the Westovers' driveway was empty.

Libby was about to get into Mathilda when she spied the package she'd brought lying on the top step. Evidently, in the confusion, Gilda had forgotten to take it into the house.

So much for good deeds, Libby thought as she went to retrieve it. *But on the bright side, Marvin and his crew would be happy.*

Chapter 2

The Next Day

It was ten a.m., and the morning scrum of customers at A Little Taste of Heaven had dissipated. Libby was leaning against the counter, sipping a cup of coffee and planning tomorrow's specials. She was wondering if she could get enough tasty local tomatoes to make gazpacho—recently they'd been flavorless, though, of course, it was still early in the season—or if she should make a cucumber and cantaloupe soup instead, when Betsy and Tom Glassberg walked into the shop.

"We need to speak to you," Tom said to Libby. "You and your sister," he amended. He was a short, chubby man with a deep voice. His wife, on the other hand, was as thin as a stick and six inches taller. The pair always reminded Libby of Jack Sprat and his wife, in reverse.

"Both of you," Betsy repeated for emphasis.

"It's important," Tom said.

Libby put down her coffee. "I assume this is about Margo," she said.

The Glassbergs exchanged glances. "Among other things," Betsy said.

Libby nodded, wondering what the other things were. "Can I get you coffee or something to eat first?" she asked, being polite.

"No, thanks," Betsy said, at the same time her husband said, "Don't mind if I do."

"I'll take a muffin," Tom said, ignoring his wife's evil eye. "Blueberry, if you please. No, make that a cinnamon bun. What?" he said to his wife. "I'm entitled once in a while."

"You had a pint of ice cream last night," Betsy reminded him.

"It was gelato."

"Even worse," Betsy said. She threw her hands in the air. "I give up. Have whatever you want."

Tim grinned. "Thanks. I think I will."

"Just don't expect me to take care of you when you have a heart attack."

"Go ahead," Tom said to Libby, who was hesitating.

Libby looked at Betsy.

"Give it to him," she said. "It's his body."

Tom patted his belly. "I'll start my diet after this."

Betsy snorted while Libby got the cinnamon bun out of the display case, put it on a paper plate, and handed it to Tom, along with a couple of napkins because the bun was sticky. Then she told Amber and Googie to call her if they needed her and motioned for the Glassbergs to follow her into the back room.

Bernie looked up from the mixer as everyone trooped through the prep-room door.

"They're here about Margo," Libby informed her.

"So, you still haven't heard from her," Bernie surmised after she'd shut off the mixer. There were two in the prep room: a commercial one that had a forty-pound capacity and the one Bernie was using now, which was considerably smaller, but much noisier.

"No, we haven't," Betsy told her. "We went out looking last night."

"That's what my sister said."

"But we didn't have any luck," Tom told Bernie.

"It's like she's disappeared off the face of the earth," Betsy observed.

"And gone into a black hole," Tom said.

"Hardly," Betsy replied.

"It's possible, Bets."

Betsy sniffed. "Anything is possible, but we're not in a science-fiction novel."

"She's just annoyed with me because I didn't leave any ice cream for her last night," Tom confided to Libby and Bernie. Then he took a bite of the cinnamon bun he was holding and smiled. "This is excellent. Absolutely delicious. Worth every single calorie."

"I'm glad you think so," Libby said, acknowledging Tom's compliment with a smile.

"We need your help," Betsy said, returning to the reason they'd originally come. "We want to hire you to find Margo. All of us do."

Bernie raised an eyebrow. "All?"

"The LMBC, the Longely Mystery Book Club," Betsy explained. "We're representing them. Plus, we're hoping there's something else you can take care of as well. For us."

"Let me finish what I'm doing, and I'll be right with you," Bernie promised them, turning the mixer back on with a flick of her thumb. Five minutes later, she'd finished making the dough for the chocolate croissants, covered the bowl with a cloth, and put the bowl in the cooler to allow the dough to rest. Then she brushed a few specks of flour off the top of her pink-and-white-checked gingham shirtdress, washed her hands, poured herself a cup of coffee from the carafe sitting on the corner of the prep table, and joined her sister and the Glassbergs in the office.

The office, which was small to begin with—or cozy, as Bernie and Libby's mother, Rose, liked to say—was made even smaller by the amount of clutter in it. Stacks of cookbooks and miscellaneous files were piled up along the bottom half of three walls, while the top halves were covered with cork bulletin boards full of reminders, schedules, to-do lists, and legal notices. There was just enough room for a desk, a file cabinet, and three chairs. Since the chairs were all occupied when Bernie came in, she perched on the corner of the desk. Everyone stopped talking.

"Have you asked the police to perform a wellness check?" Bernie inquired in the ensuing silence.

Betsy answered. "Yeah. I called when we got back the other night. An officer walked around Margo's house, but that was it. He said he couldn't go inside without a compelling reason—say, she had a heart condition or something. Which she doesn't. He said that maybe she'd just gone off for some reason and forgot to tell someone."

"Which I told him was totally unlike Margo," Tom interjected. "At which point, he said we should file a missing person's report if Margo wasn't back in twenty-four hours."

"Which is what Tom and I just finished doing," Betsy explained. "We were a little early, but they took it anyway. I guess this is what we pay our taxes for."

"I have to say Bets and I were shocked. The detective we spoke to said there really isn't a lot they can do," Tom replied after he'd taken another bite of his cinnamon roll. "He said he'd keep an eye out for Margo, but that was it."

Betsy leaned forward. "We wanted them to launch a full-scale search, but the detective said they couldn't do that unless we thought that Margo was either a danger to others or a danger to herself."

"Which she obviously is," Tom said. "Otherwise, she

wouldn't be missing. We keep calling, but the message goes straight to voicemail. I texted. No response. Obviously, something's really wrong. What the detective said makes no sense. No sense whatsoever. In fact, he was the one who suggested we come to see you. He said that you might be able to help us. I don't know why I forgot that you do this kind of thing."

"Did you speak to a guy called Clyde?" Bernie asked.

Betsy nodded.

"Just so you know, he's a lieutenant, not a detective. He's also my dad's friend," Bernie informed the Glassbergs. "And I think what Clyde was saying was that the LPD would launch an immediate search for Margo if she was suicidal or had dementia, or if she had a life-threatening disease of some kind and needed treatment."

"Or she was a minor," Libby added.

"That's ridiculous," Tom scoffed.

"Not really," Libby interjected. "Statistically speaking, most people who go missing show up again after a couple of days, usually a little worse for the wear."

"Not Margo," Betsy declared. She leaned forward. "What if Margo doesn't show up? What if Margo's in danger?" Betsy asked. "She could be." Betsy raised her hands, then let them fall back into her lap. "I mean, for all we know, she could be lying in a ditch somewhere, a victim of a carjacking. Or maybe she was kidnapped."

"It's more likely that she got into some sort of accident," Bernie gently suggested.

"I called the hospitals in the area last night," Betsy replied. "They don't have anyone there by that name."

"Or matching her description," Tom added.

"The accident, if there was one, could have happened someplace else," Bernie said.

"I'm surprised they talked to you at all, what with the HIPAA law and everything," Libby commented.

Tom patted Betsy on the shoulder. "My wife can be very convincing."

Betsy beamed. "I really can be. Actually, I lied and told them Margo was my sister." Then she frowned as she thought of the other possibilities she'd been contemplating. "Margo could be unconscious," Betsy said. "Or, worse, she could have amnesia and not know who she is. Imagine how scary that would be. Or she could be in a fugue state and have taken a plane somewhere and then seven years later"—Betsy snapped her fingers—"bang! She comes out of it with no idea where she is or how she got there or what she's done." Betsy shivered. "I can't imagine how awful that would be. All those years of your life gone. Just like that. We have to find Margo before it's too late."

"I don't think that kind of thing happens very often," Libby felt constrained to point out. "It may happen in mystery novels, but it's pretty rare in real life."

"But it does happen," Betsy insisted.

"Yes, it does," Bernie agreed. "But a more likely scenario is that Margo might have had an unexpected emergency and her cell phone isn't working, so she can't call you."

"But surely someone around her would have a phone she could use," Tom objected.

"Maybe she doesn't remember your numbers," Libby said. "I'm embarrassed to admit I don't remember anyone's anymore."

"That's true," Betsy conceded. "I don't either."

"Me either," Tom admitted. "I used to know everyone's, and now"—he patted his wife's shoulder again—"I just know Betsy's."

"That's so sweet," Betsy said, and she leaned over and gave Tom a peck on the cheek. He blushed.

"There's another possibility as well," Bernie said, coming up with yet another scenario. "Margo could have met some guy and be hanging out with him. You know, having a lost weekend."

Tom snorted. "You wouldn't say that if you knew her."

Betsy laughed and shook her head. "No way," she agreed. "Tom's right. That would never happen."

Bernie raised an eyebrow. "Never?"

"Never," Betsy repeated firmly.

"*Never* is a strong word," Bernie observed.

"Okay. Then let's say it's highly unlikely," Betsy conceded.

Bernie got up, leaned against the door frame, and took a sip of her coffee. Sitting on the edge of the desk was just too uncomfortable. "Tell me what you did when you went over to her house and checked on her," she said to Tom.

"Sure," Tom replied. "No problem. I rang the bell several times. No one answered. Then I walked to the back to see if her car was there, which it wasn't. I tried the doors, but they were all locked, and lastly I walked around her house and looked in the windows where the shades weren't pulled down, but there was nothing to see. She wasn't there. Of course, she could have been in another room."

"Did you talk to her neighbors?" Bernie inquired.

Tom shook his head. "I couldn't. The houses on either side of her were dark. No one was home."

"Did you knock on their doors to check?" Bernie asked.

Tom shook his head again.

"Leave them a note?" Libby asked.

Tom looked chagrined. He scratched his cheek. "I probably should have. I'm sorry, but it just didn't occur to me."

"How about Margo's family?" Libby asked. "Did you speak to them?"

Tom turned to his wife. "I don't think she has any. Do you, Bets?"

Betsy shook her head. "Not living. She's an only child,

and both her parents are dead. Maybe she has some cousins or aunts and uncles around someplace, but if she does, I don't know who they are. She certainly never talks about them."

"How about her friends?" Bernie asked.

"We're her friends," Tom said. "I mean, our group is."

"I'm sure she has other friends," Libby observed. "Has anyone spoken to them?"

This time Betsy answered. "If Margo does—and I'm not saying she doesn't—we don't know who they are. She's never mentioned them. Like I told your sister, she's a very private person."

"I never heard her talk about anyone like that, either," Tom noted, confirming his wife's statement.

Libby leaned forward. "What does Margo talk about?"

"You mean in general?"

Libby nodded.

Tom thought for a moment, then said, "Mostly her work, galleries, the mystery we're reading, movies, restaurants. That sort of thing. You know, the usual."

Betsy sighed. "I mean, now that I think about it, I realize how little we do know about Margo. It's embarrassing. It's scary, really, all things considered."

"Do you think that's true for the other members of your group as well?" Bernie asked.

"I assume so," Tom said, finishing the last of his cinnamon bun.

"Absolutely," Betsy remarked. "I don't see why they would be any different than us."

"Can I ask where everyone went when they were looking for Margo?" Libby inquired, remembering how everyone set off in their vehicles last night.

"From what they told me when we spoke, the Westovers, the Musclows, and the Offenbachs drove around, checking out places they thought Margo was likely to be at," Betsy answered, "while Tom and I made phone calls once he got back from her house."

"And Lydia?" Bernie asked.

"Oh, she went with the Westovers. Gilda insisted," Betsy said. "She had had way too much to drink."

"That's for sure," Libby said.

Bernie took another sip of coffee, reflecting that she liked this blend. It was lighter, and somehow lighter seemed better in the summer. She asked her question again. "Where did everyone go?"

Betsy thought for a moment before replying. Then she said, "The benches down by the river, the shopping mall over in Riverhead, the framing shop on Croydon Street, and the dog park."

"Margo has a dog?" Bernie asked, wondering who was taking care of it if she did.

"No," Betsy said. "She just likes to watch them."

"And then what happened?" Libby prompted.

This time Tom answered. "Nothing. When no one could find her, everyone went back to their houses. I guess we all hoped she would show up later."

Betsy leaned forward. "By the way, Gilda sends her apologies about leaving the stuff you brought over on the porch steps. It's just that with all the excitement . . ."

Libby lifted a hand. "It's fine. Totally understandable."

"We'll pay."

"No need. I donated it," Libby informed her. Well, in a sense, she had. Marvin, his dad, and their office staff had been extremely grateful.

"I mean, this behavior is not like Margo," Betsy said. "Not like her at all."

"So you said," Bernie replied.

"She is, as the British like to say, a person of regular

habits," Tom confirmed. "Not that the police seemed to care. They just said they'd take it under advisement, whatever that means."

"Which is why we are so concerned," Betsy said, exchanging glances with her husband.

"Give it to them," Tom said.

"Give us what?" Libby asked.

"This," Betsy said, reaching into her bag—Bernie noted it was a Hermès—and coming out with an envelope. "This is from all of us," she said, handing it to Libby. "To get you started. We went to the bank right after we left the police station. I hope it's enough."

Libby opened the envelope up and peered inside.

"That's a fifteen-hundred-dollar retainer, and there's more where that came from, if you need it," Tom told Libby as she took the money out. "Please say yes."

Fifteen hundred dollars would certainly come in handy, Bernie thought as she took another sip of her coffee. *Workman's comp was due next week.* "What do you think, Libby?"

Libby put the money back in the envelope. "I think we'll be happy to look for Margo."

Betsy smiled. "Thank heavens. I can't tell you how relieved this makes me feel."

"But," Libby continued, "I'm also thinking that maybe you'd like to give this another day or two before we start."

Betsy and Tom shook their heads.

"We want both of you to get to work immediately," Betsy said. "I just can't shake the thought that something is very, very wrong."

"Are you sure?" Libby asked.

"I've never been more positive of anything in my life," Betsy told her.

"In that case," Libby said, "we'll need the phone number for the Musclows and Lydia." She turned to Bernie. "I think we have everyone else's."

"We do," Bernie replied.

"Not a problem," Tom said, taking out his phone. "I'll text them to you now. So, what's your first step going to be?"

"Go over to Margo's house. Knock on her door. See if she's home."

"I already told you she's not," Tom said.

"Just to make sure she hasn't come back," Libby explained. "Then we'll talk to her neighbors."

"I hope you have better luck than we had," Betsy noted.

"Me too," Bernie said.

"I should have broken a window and gone into her house," Tom said suddenly.

"That wouldn't have been a great idea," Bernie said. "You could have gotten yourself arrested."

"I understand, but what if Margo has fallen and broken her hip and she can't get up?" Betsy exclaimed. "You know. Like in the ad. What if she's writhing on the ground in agony, calling out for help, and nobody can hear her? What then? Just the thought makes me shudder. Or what if she's been attacked by a serial killer, and he's tied her up and is torturing her to death? What about that?"

"I think you're letting your imagination go into overdrive," Bernie gently suggested.

Betsy looked abashed. "You're right. I probably am. I suppose this is what comes from reading too many mysteries. But things like that do happen," Betsy protested. "Not that often, but they do happen. Even in a place like Longely." She brought her hands up in a gesture of supplication. "Please find our dear friend. I was so worried I couldn't sleep last night."

"It's true. She couldn't, which meant I couldn't, either," Tom testified.

"Please," Betsy said again. "I implore you. Just do whatever you have to do to find Margo."

"We'll certainly give it our best shot," Bernie promised.

Tom beamed. "Terrific."

"Thank you. Thank you so much." Betsy choked back a sob. "This is such a relief. We didn't know who to turn to." She exchanged another glance with her husband. Tom nodded again. "There is something else you might be able to help us with as well," Betsy said. "Margo was working on restoring two portraits of a woman by Thomas Eakins."

Libby raised an eyebrow, "Eakins?"

"An American painter," Tom clarified.

"We have a buyer," Betsy explained. "So if you have to go into Margo's house and happen to see them . . ."

"We'll call," Bernie assured her.

Betsy smiled and thanked her.

Five minutes after the Glassbergs left, Bernie was on the phone with Clyde.

"I'll take a chocolate cream pie as my commission for recommending you for the job," he said as soon as he heard Bernie's voice on the other end of the phone.

Bernie laughed. "How do you know why I called?"

"My powers of brilliant deduction. In fact, make that two pies: chocolate cream and lemon meringue."

"Those are old-fashioned, fifties-style choices," Bernie observed.

"That's because I'm an old-fashioned, fifties kinda guy," Clyde replied. "I'll be around this evening to pick them up."

"We'll have them ready," Bernie promised. "Is there anything Libby and I should know about Margo?" She'd found that the trick to locating someone was knowing as much as you could about them.

"Not that I can think of," Clyde reported. "She's clean as a whistle. Doesn't even have a jaywalking ticket."

Bernie was surprised. She never bothered to wait for the light to cross. "Jaywalking's illegal? I had no idea."

Craig chuckled. "Well, now you do. By the way, I just finished calling the hospitals in the area on the off chance Margo was admitted, but they had no one there by that name. I also forwarded a description to them so that if she shows up, I'll hear." Then Clyde stopped speaking, and Bernie heard yelling coming over her phone.

"Gotta go," Clyde said quickly. "We got a problem." And he hung up.

"Did Clyde have any words of wisdom to contribute?" Libby asked when Bernie put her phone down.

"Nope," Bernie said. "We're on our own." Which is how she liked it. Libby not so much.

Chapter 3

Two hours later, on their way back from a paper-goods run to Costco's, Bernie and Libby pulled up in front of Margo Hemsley's house on Bank Street. They'd tried calling her cell phone on the way to and from Costco, but the same thing that had happened to the Glassbergs had happened to them. Their calls had gone straight to voicemail.

"So, what do you think?" Libby asked Bernie as she surveyed the lilac-colored, two-story colonial with the bright red door and the dark purple window frames.

"I think she needs to repaint her house."

"Well, it certainly stands out. I'll give you that." All the other houses on the block were beige, gray, or white. "But that's not what I meant," Libby went on.

Bernie continued to study the house. "Why would she do this?"

Libby shrugged. "Actually, I don't think it's that bad."

"It's pretty bad."

"Any thoughts?"

"On another color scheme?"

"On what we're about to do."

"Just follow the plan," Bernie said as she stopped the van in front of Margo's house.

Libby got out and rang the bell. There was no answer, not that she'd expected one. She tried again anyway, just to make sure. Still nothing. Libby turned and shook her head. Bernie motioned her back to the van.

"On to canvassing the block," Libby said after she'd climbed back into Mathilda.

Bernie nibbled on her lower lip while she surveyed the street. Margo lived in one of the older sections of Longely. The houses there had been built in the fifties and sported ample lawns, large trees, and mature hedges that ensured privacy. Margo's house sat on a corner lot that backed up onto a vest-pocket park. The driveway snaked around the house on its way to Margo's garage.

The neighbor with the best view of Margo's home lived directly cross the street, while the other neighbors had their views partially to completely blocked by the over-grown hedge surrounding Margo's house.

"I'm thinking," Bernie waved her hand to indicate the street in front of her, "that our chances of finding out when Margo left her house yesterday are not great. She can come and go without being seen by ninety percent of the people on this block. Our best shot at finding out when she left her house is talking to the people that live over there." She pointed to the house across the street. "Unfortunately, they don't seem to be home."

"Neither, for that matter, does anyone else on the block," Libby observed. "I guess people are still at work or their kids are still at day care."

Bernie sighed. It was a pattern she was seeing more and more. "Where are the yentas when you need them?" she lamented. "We might have to come back this evening."

"Hopefully not," Libby said.

"Ditto that," Bernie said, thinking of the plans she'd made. "I guess we'll find out soon enough," she added, putting the van in park. "At least it's a nice afternoon," she commented as she turned off the van's ignition. It had been an abnormally cold, rainy spring, and she was happy for the warmth and sunlight, although it had gotten really hot, really fast—not that she was going to complain. "You want to take the left side of the road, and I'll take the right?" Bernie asked her sister.

Libby nodded. "Works for me," she said after she'd opened the van door.

"Here goes nothing," Bernie said.

"Hopefully, not literally," Libby replied, turning toward her sister. "You know, Clyde is probably right. Margo is probably off somewhere having a great time and she'll turn up in a day or two a little worse for the wear."

"Let's hope so," Bernie answered as she got out of the van. The smell of freshly cut grass made her smile. She took a minute to straighten the pale pink silk sheath she was wearing and then walked toward the closest house and rang the bell.

Libby crossed the street and knocked on the door of the house that had the best view of Margo's place. No one answered. She tried again. When she got no response, she moved on to the house next door. But no one was at home there, either. It took four houses before Libby got a response.

"You're not the cable guy," the woman who answered the door observed. She appeared to be in her early twenties, and Libby thought she looked as if she was on her way to or had just come from work.

"Nope." And Libby explained why she was there.

The woman frowned. "You're talking about Margo Hemsley, right?"

"Right," Libby replied.

"Wow." The woman pursed her lips. "She doesn't strike

me as the type that ups and disappears. At least that's my impression, although honestly I don't know why I'm saying that."

"That's what everyone else says, too," Libby replied.

The woman smiled. "It's nice to know I'm not alone."

"How well do you know her?"

"Not really well at all. You know, just to say hello and good-bye to. That sort of thing. I didn't see her yesterday, but then I catch the seven forty-one into the city, and I usually don't get off the train until six-thirty at night, which puts me home around six forty-five at best or seven at worst."

"Can you tell me when was the last time you did see her?" Bernie asked. She'd crossed the street when she'd seen the door to 179 open.

The woman adjusted her topknot while she tried to recall. "I'm pretty sure it was a couple of weeks ago. I was going past Margo's house when she backed out really fast. She almost hit me. She apologized afterward and said she'd been daydreaming. Maybe she was in an accident."

"Let's hope not," Bernie said. "What kind of car does she drive?" Bernie asked, seeking to confirm what Crenshaw had told them.

"A white Camry. It's got a dent on the passenger door from her last accident. Like I said, she's a terrible driver. I can't imagine what her insurance rate is like."

"Is there anything else you can tell us?" Libby asked as a large ginger tabby padded up the porch steps, rubbed against the woman's legs, then marched through the open door into the house.

The woman shook her head. "I'm sorry, but I'm really not around that much. As I just said, during the week, I leave early in the morning and get home in the evening, by which time I'm completely bushed, and on the weekends I'm down in Brooklyn visiting my boyfriend. I'm just home now because I'm waiting for the cable guy." She took her phone out of her skirt pocket and checked it. "Who is already three-quarters of an hour late. What else is new? Why no one can come when they say they will is beyond me."

Bernie gestured to the houses on the block. "Is there anyone here we should talk to? Anyone who is friends with Margo?"

The woman fingered the string of pearls around her neck while she thought. "No one comes to mind," she said. "The most likely person would be Amanda Gornig. She's in the gray house with the white trim." She pointed to a house two doors down on her side of the street. "She usually has a day off during the week—I forget which one—so there's a chance she could be home."

"So Margo has no friends here that you know of except for Amanda Goring," Libby stated.

"I don't know if Amanda is friendly with her, either, but if Margo was friendly with anyone, it would be Amanda. Those two have been here longer than anyone else." The woman brushed her bangs to the side, then shook her head. "I moved here four years ago from Oakland, and I can count the number of times I've spoken to Margo. She's just not very friendly."

The woman was about to say more, but the cat came out of the house, and she paused to give it a pat on the head. "Give 'em hell, Charlie." she said as he jumped off the porch and disappeared into the shrubs. "Go get those voles."

She looked up. "Now, where was I? Oh, yes," she said, continuing. "As I was saying, we have these neighborhood get-togethers every month—nothing fancy, just pizza and beer—and once in a while, someone does a movie night or a beer tasting, but Margo never comes to any of those—at least, not when I've been there. Maybe she's shy. I really don't know.

"What I do know is that I and most of the other people on the block wish she'd repaint her house, although it *is* a good landmark. I'll say that for it. I always tell people we're four houses down from the lilac house with the purple windows and the red door. You really can't miss it."

Bernie laughed as she handed the woman her card. "No. You certainly can't."

The woman looked at it and smiled. "You guys own A Little Taste of Heaven?"

"We do," Libby said. "You should come by."

"I keep meaning to. Now I definitely will. I hear you have great takeout and fabulous desserts."

Bernie and Libby both grinned.

"We do our best," Bernie told her.

The woman smiled back. "Sorry I can't be of more help with Margo," she said. "But if I think of anything, I'll give you a call. I hope you find her or that she turns up. She seems like a nice lady."

"I hope we find her, too," Bernie said.

The woman extended her hand. Bernie and Libby shook it. "My name is April, by the way—April Reardon." And, with that, she went inside her house and closed the door.

"Well, at least we got another customer, if nothing else," Bernie said.

"Possible customer," Libby corrected. Then she and Bernie trooped over to Amanda Gornig's house, stepped onto her porch, and rang the bell. It played the first bars of the *William Tell* overture. A moment later, Amanda Goring answered the door.

Bernie put her in her late forties to early fifties. She was wearing a pair of Bermuda shorts, a stained white T-shirt, pink Crocs on her feet, and a pink floppy-brimmed sun hat pulled down on her head, which made it hard to read her expression.

"Yes?" she said as she took off her gardening gloves and laid them on the arm of the rocking chair next to her.

"April Reardon said you might be able to help us," Bernie told her.

Amanda frowned. "With what?"

"Margo Hemsley."

"What about her?"

"She seems to have gone missing," Libby told her.

"Seems?" Amanda repeated. "Either she has or she hasn't."

"It's not quite that simple." And Bernie explained what was going on. "So," Bernie continued when she was done with her explanation, "we were hoping you could give us some information that will help us find her."

Amanda took off her hat and ran her fingers through her hair. It was too short, emphasizing the smallness of her head in proportion to her body. "I can't," she replied, putting her hat back on.

"Can't or won't?" Bernie asked.

"Can't," Amanda said without pausing to think about it. "I really have very little to do with Margo."

"Even though you've been neighbors for a long time?" Libby asked.

"Even though we've been neighbors for a long time," Amanda echoed. "Don't get me wrong. She's a nice lady. We'll borrow a cup of sugar from one another if we need to, but we don't sit around and chat about old times—or about new times, for that matter. She's always working, and she doesn't like having people in her studio. When she first moved in and I heard what she did, I was really interested—I like art, you know—and I asked if I could see her studio, but she kept putting me off until I finally gave up. She's someone who keeps herself to herself, as my grandmother liked to say." Amanda encompassed the block with a gesture. "At least, around here she does. As far as I know, she isn't friends with anyone in the neighborhood."

"That's more or less what April said," Libby informed Amanda.

Amanda nodded and flicked a leaf off the front of her T-shirt. "I would say that's a fairly accurate assessment."

"I don't suppose you have a key to her place?" Bernie asked.

Amanda snorted. "What do you think?"

"I think probably not," Libby replied.

"And even if I did, I'm not sure I'd give it to you."

"I understand," Bernie said. "I'm not sure I'd give it to us, either."

Amanda laughed. "Only because she's so particular about it. I suggested to Margo that we exchange keys when she first moved into her house." Amanda made a clicking sound with her tongue. "You would have thought I'd suggested killing her firstborn—not that she has a firstborn."

"Do you know anyone she's close to?" Bernie asked.

Amanda shook her head. "Not really. I'd say that the mystery book club she belongs to comes closer to fitting that description than anything else. Sorry I can't be of more help," Amanda said. "Is there anything else?"

Bernie and Libby shook their heads.

Amanda began pulling on her gloves. "I guess it's time to get back to weeding," she said. "The dandelions await."

"Here," Bernie said, holding out A Little Taste of Heaven's card.

"Sorry, but I'll just lose it," Amanda told them, refusing the card. Then she turned around and went inside her house, shutting the door firmly behind her.

"You think she knows more than she's telling?" Libby asked her sister as they walked back down the porch steps.

"No, I don't," Bernie answered.

"Neither do I," Libby said.

She and Bernie spent another fifteen minutes knocking on the doors of the remaining houses on Bank Street, with no luck. Of the three people who were home, two didn't know who Margo Hemsley was, and one knew her by sight but had never talked to her.

"So much for that," Libby said as they walked back to their van.

"I guess Margo's house is next on the agenda," Bernie remarked as she stopped to admire the flowering cherry tree in front of April Reardon's house. "Maybe there's something in there that will tell us where Margo went."

"Or maybe we won't have to go in," Libby replied, and she pointed to a red truck pulling out of Margo's driveway.

Chapter 4

The truck rounded the corner and disappeared before either Bernie or Libby had time to see who was driving it or get the license plate number. However, both sisters took note of the deep dent in the middle of the bumper. Other than that, there was nothing much to distinguish it from any other red Dodge pickup truck on the road.

"Maybe whoever was in the truck was dropping Margo off," Libby suggested as she took a tissue out of the pocket of her khaki shorts and blew into it. Whatever was floating around in the air was really bothering her allergies.

"One can only hope," Bernie said, reaching for her phone.

"Who are you calling?" Libby asked.

"Betsy Glassberg, to see if any of the LMBC crowd owns a red pickup truck."

"They would have called us if one of them had found Margo and was bringing her back," Libby replied, following her sister's line of thought.

"True. But it never hurts to check." And Bernie made the call.

"None of us have one, but maybe the truck left tire

marks," Betsy suggested excitedly when she heard what Bernie had to say. "Maybe you can take a cast of the treads."

"Good idea. Unfortunately, I don't have my cast-taking materials with me," Bernie replied. She was somewhat bemused by the suggestion.

Betsy laughed. "I guess I'm reading too many mystery stories. In those, the detective would be able to deduce what kind of tire it is just by looking."

"And it would be the kind of tire that's only found on a 1950s Studebaker," Bernie answered.

"Exactly. Well, keep me informed."

"Will do," Bernie promised.

"So?" Libby asked when her sister didn't say anything.

Bernie tucked a lock of hair back behind her ear. "Apparently, none of the LMBCers have a red truck."

"One possibility eliminated," Libby said. "I'm not surprised. I figured them for a hybrid-sedan kinda crowd."

"That's what Betsy said," Bernie informed her sister.

"Maybe someone else dropped Margo off," Libby suggested as she and her sister crossed the street.

"If so, I hope she had a good time doing whatever she was doing," Bernie said, thinking of the possibilities.

"Me too," Bernie agreed as she rang Margo's front doorbell again. Maybe she had been dropped off. But after a second ring, Bernie was forced to conclude that either Margo hadn't been or that she was in no condition to answer the door. Next, Bernie lifted the cover of Margo's mailbox, took out the mail, and looked through it.

"Anything interesting?" Libby asked.

"Nope." Bernie showed Libby. "Just junk mail." Then she replaced the flyers and started looking around for a hidden spare key. But if there was one, she couldn't find it. "Time to check the back," Bernie said as she started down the red-brick path that led to the rear of the house. The bricks were uneven. Some had sunken into the earth, while others had heaved up or disappeared, and Bernie had to keep her eyes on the ground as she walked so she wouldn't twist her ankle.

"I don't see how you can walk in those things," Libby told her sister as she watched Bernie teetering down the path in her four-inch stilettos.

"With practice," Bernie answered, although she had to admit she would have been better off wearing flats. "Lots of practice." Then she stopped at the side door, climbed the step leading up to it, and tried that doorknob. It too was locked. "Just checking," she explained.

Libby gestured to the door. "Hey, Bernie, I think the color of the side door matches your dress."

Bernie looked at her dress, then she looked at the door. "Not really. The pink I'm wearing has blue undertones, while the pink on the door has orangey undertones."

Libby snorted. "Well, excuse me."

"I can't help it if I have a good sense of color."

"And I don't?"

"You said it, I didn't."

Libby put her hands on her hips. "How can you say that?" she demanded.

"Simple." Bernie pointed to the shirt Libby had on. "Look at what you're wearing."

"What's wrong with what I'm wearing?" Libby squawked.

"Besides the fact that your docksides need new heels and your cargo shorts are too big?"

"Yes. Besides that."

"Well, I guess the color of your shirt is okay if you're a crossing guard or a construction worker."

Libby looked down. "I think the shirt looks summery," she protested.

"It's neon green," Bernie replied.

Libby crossed her arms. "What's wrong with that?"

"If you don't know, I can't explain it."

"Works for me."

"Color is interesting, though," Bernie mused, going off on a tangent.

"How so?" Libby asked, glad to get off the topic of her clothes.

Bernie explained. "For example, in China, white is the symbol of death, while here white is the color of purity. Take Margo's house, for example." Bernie waved her hand to encompass it. "Its colors render it extremely visible."

"You can say that again," Libby agreed.

"And yet, whenever we've seen Margo, she's always been wearing neutrals or pastels."

"What's your point?"

"My point is that there's a dichotomy here. The bright colors for the house versus the colors she chooses to wear. There's a definite lack of continuity."

Libby rolled her eyes. "Oh, please. Talk about making a big deal over nothing."

"Margo's an artist, Libby. Colors are important to her."

"If you say so, Bernie," Libby replied. "But I can tell you one thing Margo doesn't like," Libby remarked when they reached the backyard a moment later.

"What's that?" Bernie asked.

"Gardening."

It was true, Bernie thought, surveying the scene in front of her. The laurel hedges that separated Margo's yard from the vest-pocket park were overgrown, the grass needed to be mowed, and the top of the picnic table beneath the maple tree was covered with bird poop.

"The ferns love it, though," Bernie observed, pointing to a group of them clustered underneath the tree.

"What are you thinking?" Libby asked, catching the speculative gleam in her sister's eyes.

"I'm thinking fiddlehead ferns," Bernie said. Harbingers of spring, they were delicious lightly sautéed in a pan with good olive oil, chopped garlic, and leeks, and sprinkled with sea salt. "We should do a 'Welcome to Spring Day' next year and serve them then."

"We don't have time to go foraging," Libby objected.

"I think we can get them from Walter's farm."

Libby thought for a moment, then she said, "In that case, next year we can serve them by themselves, or we can make them part of a spring-vegetable ragout. Baby fava beans, peas, leeks, garlic scapes, maybe Boston lettuce or baby spinach, and garlic. Sauté everything together quickly, and serve the ragout with some freshly grilled French bread and good butter. Maybe throw in a couple of sautéed artichoke hearts and/or mushrooms. Morels? No," Libby said, answering her own question. "Too expensive. Maybe shitakes or plain brown bellas."

"Either way sounds delicious," Bernie said.

"It does, doesn't it?" Libby agreed. "In fact, maybe we can make a vegetable ragout a steady menu thing. You know, root vegetables in the winter . . ."

"And pumpkin and white beans in the fall and something with corn and tomatoes in the summer," Bernie said, finishing Libby's sentence for her.

"And we could sell the ragout as a side or a main dish," Libby suggested.

Bernie nodded. "With or without added protein. I like it. I think it'll work." These days, she and Libby were trying to work more veggie and vegan dishes into their menu without getting too health-storish.

Libby smiled. "I like it, too."

"Really," Bernie observed, "what's not to like."

"Nothing," Libby said. Then she indicated the back-yard with a nod of her chin. "Margo's own little wilder-ness patch."

"*Unkempt* is the word that comes to mind," Bernie said. She brushed away a fly that had landed on her shoulder. "Or maybe Margo did this on purpose because she likes her privacy."

"Well, she sure got it," Libby allowed. The density and height of the hedges effectively blocked the view of Margo's house from either the house next door or anyone using the vest-pocket park. "I just hope there's no poison ivy in here," Libby said, thinking back to what had happened to her on the last case they'd worked.

"Poison ivy doesn't grow in the shade," Bernie said, even though she had no idea whether that was true or not. Then she quickly changed the subject. "But the good thing about the hedge," she said, nodding to it, "is that the neighbors won't be able to see what we're going to do."

Libby didn't answer. Instead, she pointed to a shoe lying in the grass, right next to the stoop. "That doesn't look good."

"Maybe, maybe not," Bernie agreed as she went over and picked it up. The shoe, a size seven black ballet flat, had scuff marks on its toe and a heel that needed to be replaced. "There could be lots of explanations."

"For instance," Libby pressed.

"For instance, Margo's dog dragged it outside."

"Does Margo have a dog?" Libby asked.

"Not that I know of," Bernie admitted. "Okay. Then she could have lost it going up the steps."

"How do you lose a shoe, Bernie?"

"You can if you're stumbling up the stairs and you're really drunk," Bernie told her sister as she put the shoe back where she found it.

"Ah, like the time in high school when you came home from Johnnie O's party," Libby said.

"What a long memory you have," Bernie commented as she contemplated Margo's back door. It looked as if it was going to be simple enough to open. "Here goes nothing," she said as she walked toward it. For once, Libby didn't say anything about what she was about to do, and Bernie could guess why. "It's the shoe, isn't it? That's why you're not giving me grief."

Libby nodded.

"It probably doesn't mean anything," Bernie said.

"Probably," Libby agreed, thinking about what Betsy had said about Margo lying inside the house, alone and injured, and hoping that wasn't the case. She gestured to the back door. "I wonder if that's the entrance to Margo's studio?"

"It is what it is," Bernie chirped as she started up the three cement steps that led to the back door.

Chapter 5

"What does that even mean?" Libby grumped. She hated that phrase. It was beyond irritating.

"It means I don't know," Bernie told her as she pointed to the middle step, the edge of which was crumbling. "Be careful you don't trip," she cautioned.

"Margo should get that fixed before someone breaks their neck," Libby said, flicking aside a small ball of concrete with her left foot. "I wonder if she doesn't have the money to fix up her house or she just doesn't care."

"Considering that the house looks freshly painted, I'll go with she doesn't care," Bernie answered as she rang the doorbell. There was no sound. "It's not working," Bernie informed Libby as she knocked on the door instead. The door swung open.

"Wow," Bernie announced.

"Interesting," Libby observed. "Especially since Tom said it was locked when he tried it."

"This could be good," Bernie said.

"Or not," Libby observed.

"Let's be positive. Maybe Margo is back. Maybe whoever was in the red truck did drop her off," Bernie said as she studied the lock. It didn't appear to have been tampered with, and the door gave no evidence of being forced. Which meant that whoever had opened the door had used a key or lock picks. She was hoping it was the former as she stepped inside Margo's house. The smells of paint and turpentine greeted her.

"Margo's studio," Libby observed, stating the obvious, as she joined her sister.

"I bet this is an add-on," Bernie said, surveying the room.

It was spacious, with light pouring in from the large windows on the left and the skylight in the ceiling. The pale green walls were crowded with a combination of photos, watercolors, a few oils, and some pen-and-ink sketches jostling for space with one another. A big wooden table in the middle of the room was buried under newspapers, stacks of drawing tablets, unread junk mail, half-empty seltzer bottles, an empty press pot, a couple of sixteen-ounce mugs, and a scattering of empty candy wrappers.

On the right side was Margo's easel, which contained an oil of a herd of goats grazing on a hillside overlooking a river.

"I bet that's the Hudson," Bernie said, commenting on the oil.

"When it was still clean," Libby replied as she surveyed the rest of the furnishings, which consisted of a zero-gravity chair, an old yellow-tweed sofa, a surprisingly neat desk, and an old gray metal file cabinet. She pointed to the sheet, blanket, and pillow on the sofa. "It looks like Margo sleeps here."

"Hopefully, she's asleep in her bedroom," Bernie said, and she started calling out Margo's name.

But Margo didn't answer. The only sound Bernie and Libby heard was the chirp of a robin sitting on a tree branch outside the window and the tick of a clock on the studio wall.

"Maybe she's passed out," Libby suggested.

"Or taking a shower," Bernie said, even though she didn't hear water running through the pipes.

"I guess we'll find out," Libby said as she and Bernie advanced into the kitchen. "Margo," Libby called out again. "It's Bernie and Libby."

There was no answer. Bernie and Libby exchanged glances.

"I hope she's okay," Bernie said.

Libby nodded. "Me too."

They peeked into the living room and the dining room. Margo wasn't there. Next, they climbed the stairs to the second floor, calling out Margo's name as they went, hopefully alerting her to their presence, because they didn't want to startle her. But Margo wasn't in any of the three bedrooms or the two bathrooms.

"So much for the red truck theory," Bernie concluded as she and Libby walked back down the stairs to the first floor.

"At least she's not lying dead in the bathtub," Libby said, thinking of what Betsy had said earlier.

"There is that," Bernie agreed. "So who opened the door?"

"Maybe Margo came back and left again," Libby suggested.

"Maybe," Bernie said. "But why?"

"Because she forgot something."

"Or," Bernie said, "maybe she is being held against her will, and that person took her key and came back here and got whatever it is they got."

Another idea occurred to Libby. "Maybe Tom was lying about trying the back door. Maybe it's been open all this time."

"Why would he do that?" Bernie asked.

"Maybe lying is the wrong word," Libby allowed. "Maybe he got flustered. Maybe he thought he had checked all the doors. People do strange things when they're stressed."

"Yes, they do," Bernie said. It was time to go back over the house. "Hopefully, we'll find something that will point us in the right direction."

"Hopefully," Libby said, following her sister into the kitchen.

"It seems as if Margo left in a hurry," Bernie declared as she eyed the dirty dishes in the sink, the quart of milk on the kitchen table, and a plate with congealed, half-eaten scrambled eggs on it.

"It does, doesn't it?" Libby replied, thinking of the rest of the house, which, in contrast to the studio and the kitchen, was as neat as the proverbial pin, as Bernie and Libby's mom liked to say—whatever that meant. "But," she added, "there are no overturned chairs or broken dishes."

Bernie nodded. "Suggesting she left under her own volition."

"Unless someone was pointing a gun at her," Libby said.

"Someone she knew. Someone she'd open the door for," Bernie hypothesized as she opened and closed kitchen cabinets.

"What are you hoping to find?" Libby asked.

Bernie shrugged. "I don't know," she confessed as she walked into the living room. It didn't provide any answers; neither did the dining room. Both rooms were furnished with Shaker furniture, rag rugs, and American folk art and looked as if they were ready for a shelter magazine shoot.

"Nice," Libby said as she studied the uncluttered surfaces and polished wood.

"Very nice," Bernie commented. She pointed to a painted chest that served as a coffee table. "That's worth quite a bit if it's real."

"It's pretty," Libby said. She took another look around the living and dining rooms and then went back upstairs. Bernie followed.

The bedrooms were almost as tidy as the living and dining rooms, except that the bed in Margo's bedroom wasn't made, and there were a couple of pairs of sneakers on the floor and three pairs of jeans tossed over a chair.

Bernie opened Margo's closet door, while Libby looked through Margo's dresser drawers. Everything looked in order, and without knowing what was supposed to be there, it was impossible to tell if anything was missing, although at first glance Libby and Bernie decided it didn't look as if anything was.

They tackled the bathrooms next. Again, nothing seemed to be missing. If Margo had packed anything, it wasn't obvious, since Margo's toothbrush and toothpaste, hairbrush, shampoo, and cosmetics were still in the bathroom.

"She didn't take this," Libby said, holding up a quart-sized plastic bag filled with TSA-approved travel-size cosmetics.

"So odds are she wasn't planning on being away," Bernie said. "There's no indication that she packed anything."

Libby closed her eyes for a moment and thought. "Maybe Margo got an emergency call and ran out of the house, expecting to be back," she said, coming up with another scenario.

"And then something happened to prevent that," Bernie said. "The question is what?"

"An accident is the most likely answer."

"In that case, it had to have happened somewhere else. Otherwise, her name would have been listed on one of Clyde's databases."

"Unless Margo gave the authorities another name."

"Why would she do that?" Bernie demanded.

"I don't know. Because she was doing something she shouldn't? For all we know, Margo might be sitting in jail."

"I hope not," Bernie said as she opened the door to the attic. "Maybe there will be something of interest up here."

But there wasn't. There wasn't anything in the basement, either, just a lot of junk that needed to be thrown out.

"At least we know Margo isn't here," Libby said as she and her sister walked back into Margo's studio.

"She isn't here now," Bernie said. "But did she come back earlier, or did someone else?"

"Well, if she did come back, she didn't take anything with her," Libby said. She gestured to the studio. "This is where she spent most of her time," she observed.

"Agreed," Bernie said, and then she and her sister got down to their second job, looking for the portraits of a woman Betsy and Tom had asked them to get for them. They had told Bernie and Libby that a client was coming soon and they wanted to show the paintings to him.

"I don't see them," Bernie said, referring to the Eakins portraits.

"Maybe Margo took the paintings with her," Libby said.

"Or maybe the man in the red truck took them," Bernie said.

"Is that like the Man in the Yellow Hat?" Libby asked, referring to one of the main characters in Curious George.

Bernie laughed. "Mom's favorite." And she and Libby kept on looking. When she was sure the paintings weren't there, she called Betsy and told her they couldn't find them.

"They have to be there," Betsy cried.

"Well, I'm sorry, but they aren't," Betsy told her.

"For God's sake, look again. The paintings aren't that large. Maybe they're in a closet."

But they weren't. They also weren't in Margo's desk or underneath the pile of papers on it, or in the file cabinet sitting by the desk, or in the three black-leather portfolios lying on the upper shelf in the closet, or under the piles of papers on the large oak table, or under the sheet and pillows on the sofa—not that there was any reason they should be.

Fifteen minutes later, Bernie called Betsy back and gave her the bad news.

Chapter 6

Two Days Later

It was a little after two o'clock on a rainy, dreary Thursday afternoon when April Reardon walked into A Little Taste of Heaven. By now, the afternoon rush had subsided, and there were only two customers in the shop. Libby watched as April closed her umbrella and put it in the umbrella stand by the door.

"I should have come here sooner," she said as she inhaled the odors of butter and yeast and cinnamon and cardamom.

Libby smiled. April smiled back.

"Well, you're here now, and that's what counts," Libby told April when she got up to the counter.

"I remembered something," April told her.

Libby stopped filling the salt shakers, leaned forward, and waited for April to continue.

"And," April said a moment later, "since I have a doctor's appointment down the block, I thought I'd kill two birds with one stone: try your chocolate croissants, and tell you about this question Margo asked me." April shrugged.

"It's probably nothing, but the question struck me as weird. Or, rather, it didn't strike me as weird when Margo asked me it, but considering what's happened . . ." And April's voice trailed off.

Bernie came up behind Libby and washed and wiped her hands on a paper towel. She'd been filling up a tub with the salmon salad she'd made twenty minutes ago. "Go on," she urged, giving April an encouraging smile.

April unsnapped her raincoat. "As I said to your sister, it's probably nothing," she reiterated, "but last week as I was coming back home, Margo flagged me down and asked if I knew where a place called Myer's End was."

Libby wrinkled her nose. She'd never heard of the place before.

"And did you?" Bernie inquired.

April nodded. "It's the old name for Myer's Landing."

"The swamp?" Bernie asked. If she remembered correctly, the place April was referring to was located in a deep valley some fifteen miles or more away on the northwest border of Longely County. "The place with the giant hogweed? The place they were talking about on the evening news?"

April nodded. "That's the one. The only reason I know where it is, is because I used to have a friend who lived near there."

"I thought they drained that place," Amber said, speaking up. She'd been listening to the conversation while she was cleaning the counter.

"The county wanted to." The swamp was a source of the occasional flare-ups of equine encephalitis that occurred during the summer. "But they couldn't," April informed her. "There are short-eared owls and pygmy rattlesnakes in there, and they're both endangered species."

"Lovely," Libby murmured, thinking of the rattle-snakes.

"I got to thinking that it's an odd place for Margo to have asked me about," April continued.

"It is, isn't it?" Bernie agreed.

"I mean I can't think of any reason Margo would want to go out there."

Libby hazarded a guess, "Bird-watching?"

April laughed. "She's not exactly the outdoors type. At least, I don't think she is."

Margo hadn't struck Libby as that, either. "I don't sup-pose she told you why she wanted to go there?" Libby asked April, hoping that she had said something, but guessing she probably hadn't.

April shook her head. "She just said she didn't know where it was."

"It didn't show up on her GPS?" Bernie asked.

"I don't think she had a GPS," April said. She went on. "After I gave her directions, she thanked me and went back inside her house, and that was the last time I saw or heard her."

"Is there anything else that you recall?" Bernie asked.

"Nope." April smiled apologetically. "I hope this helps. I don't see how it will, but I thought I should tell you anyway."

"You never know what will end up being important," Libby reassured her. "Thank you for telling us. We appre-ciate it."

Bernie broke into the conversation. Another question had occurred to her. "Does Margo have a gardening ser-vice? Or maybe she is having some work done on the house?"

April laughed. "Well, if she has a gardening service,

they're doing a pretty bad job. And as for having work done on her house . . . how to put this? I don't think Margo likes to spend money on that kind of stuff, but on the other hand, she *did* pay to get her house painted, so I could be wrong. Can I ask why you want to know?"

Bernie explained about the red truck.

"Sorry, I can't help," April told her, "but like I said before, I'm not usually home on the weekdays. This week has turned out to be the exception." And with that, April turned her attention to the display case. "God, everything looks so good," she exclaimed.

"It is," Libby told her. "Now, what else can I get you besides a chocolate croissant? Some coffee? A strawberry rhubarb tartlet? A brioche?"

"I don't know if I can choose," April lamented. "It all looks and smells so wonderful. I feel like I've died and gone to heaven."

"I'll make it easy for you," Bernie told her, and she grabbed a pastry box from under the counter. "How about one of everything? Our treat."

"I couldn't," April protested feebly.

"Sure, you can," Bernie told her. "Now, how do you like your coffee?"

"Black with two sugars."

Bernie nodded. "You want the croissant now?"

"Please."

"I'm giving you the fattest one," Bernie informed April as she picked one out of the front of the display case, grabbed it with a pair of tongs, placed it in a square of tissue paper, and handed it to April.

April took a bite. "Oh my God," she cried after she swallowed, "this literally melts in your mouth."

"It's the butter," Libby said. "Lots and lots of butter.

The kind we use has a high butterfat content. In for a penny, in for a pound, right?"

"Don't tell me," April cried. "I don't want to know."

"Well, the croissant may not be good for your waistline, but it's definitely good for your soul," Bernie told her.

April sighed with pleasure as she took another bite. "The chocolate in this is wonderful."

"It's seventy percent dark, from Brussels," Libby informed her.

April finished the croissant while Bernie filled a box with pastries for her to take home. "Good luck at the doc's," Bernie said as she handed the box to April.

"Luckily, I'm going to weigh in before I eat these," April said, referring to the box of pastries Libby was handing her. She took her cup of coffee in the other hand, thanked the sisters again, and headed out the door.

"What do you think?" Bernie asked her sister while she watched April get into her Mini Cooper.

"About what April told us?"

Bernie nodded.

"There's nothing up in Myer's Landing."

"That's what makes it worth checking out. Anyway, this is the only lead we have."

"It sure isn't much of one," Libby pointed out, thinking of the rattlesnakes. "If they're smaller, does that make them less venomous?"

"The rattlesnakes? I think it makes them more poisonous, actually."

"Terrific."

"But I think the rain will keep the snakes in their den."

"You know it or you think it?"

Instead of answering, Bernie looked at the clock on the wall and said, "If we leave now, we could be back in time for the evening rush."

"I suppose we really should go, shouldn't we?" Libby remarked, resigned to her fate.

"Do you realize how big that place is?" Sean asked, putting down his newspaper, when Libby and Bernie came upstairs to tell him what they were going to do.

"So you're saying we shouldn't go?" Libby said, setting a tray containing a bowl of strawberries and a smaller bowl of heavy cream on the coffee table.

"I'm saying it's a long shot," their father replied, as he leaned over, took a ripe red strawberry, and ate it. "Fresh picked?" he asked as the flavor of strawberry, the flavor of summer, filled his mouth.

Bernie nodded. "Lisa just brought them in. Listen," Bernie continued, "I know doing this is a long shot, but we have to do something."

"I suppose you do," Sean allowed, eating another strawberry. They were sweeter than candy.

"Do you still think Margo's off someplace having a good time?" Libby asked her dad.

"Given what you found at Margo's house, I'd say the odds of that are diminishing rather quickly."

"I think so, too," Bernie said, frowning.

"Of course, there is another possibility," Sean suggested. "Margo could have taken the Eakins paintings and left the door to her house open to make it look as if someone else did it," he hypothesized as he dipped a third strawberry into the bowl of heavy cream and popped the cream-clad fruit into his mouth.

"Too complicated," Bernie said.

"Maybe, maybe not," Sean responded. "People do strange things. Very strange things."

Bernie couldn't help smiling. "Once a cop, always a cop," she observed.

"I'm not going to deny it," Sean said as he made room on his lap for his cat, Cindy. "Come for some cream, have you?" he asked her as she licked up a drop that had fallen on his khakis.

Half an hour later, after changing into long-sleeved shirts, long pants, socks, and hiking boots, the sisters started out for Myer's Landing.

"Be careful out there," Sean cautioned them as they were leaving the flat. "And stay on the path. There's quicksand."

"Is that a metaphor for life?" Bernie asked,

"Ha ha. No. It's a fact," Sean told her.

"Quicksand?" Libby squeaked. "I thought that stuff only existed in fifties adventure movies."

"Nope. It exists right here in Longely."

Libby shuddered.

"Personally," Bernie said, "I'm more worried about getting a tick bite."

"That too," Sean replied. "Don't forget the insect repellent."

"Did you ever get sucked in?" Bernie asked her dad.

"To the quicksand? No. But Clyde almost did. Ask him about it the next time he comes over."

"Good place to get rid of a body," Bernie noted.

"It is," Sean agreed. "Fortunately, that never happened on my watch. Or if it did, I don't know about it."

And on that note, the two sisters kissed their dad good-bye and went downstairs. On the way to their van, they stopped in the shop and made themselves mozzarella and tomato sandwiches on freshly baked olive bread, poured big to-go glasses of iced ginger tea, and put some Bing cherries in a Tupperware container to take along as well.

"At least, we'll have something to eat if we get lost," Libby noted as they walked out to the van.

"We're not getting lost," Bernie said. "That's why GPS was invented."

But, of course, that's not the way things worked out.

Chapter 7

The roads were clear of traffic, and it took Bernie a little less than twenty minutes to drive out to the swamp. The area was a New York State Wildlife Management Area, and there was a tourist information hut constructed of logs at the entrance. Bernie stopped and got out. The door to the building was open, but no one was inside. A large table over to one side held a leather-bound notebook with a pen attached and a neatly typed sign next to it, instructing visitors to sign in.

Bernie scanned the page in front of her. It was half full. Margo's signature wasn't there, not that that necessarily meant anything, Bernie decided, as she read the newest entries. The latest one, written five days ago, was from a Robert Joyce from Boston and read, *Nice to know places like this still exist*, while the next-to-last one, written one week ago, was from a Wyatt Bender from Staten Island who wrote that he'd seen two possums and a doe and her two fawns on his drive through the area.

Out of curiosity, Bernie leafed through the three pages before them as well. Most of the entries, Bernie noted, fell into two camps: The people visiting came either from New

York City or from out of state. Evidently, no one from Westchester had visited, or if they had, they hadn't bothered to sign in.

Interesting, Bernie thought, as she turned her attention to the other materials on the table. Next to the sign-in book sat stacks of printouts concerning hunting, fishing, and trapping rules and regs; warnings about the dangers of giant hogweed plants; ways to avoid rattlesnake bites and what to do if you get bitten; and reminders that this was a trash-in/trash-out area and that no camping was allowed.

Who would want to? Bernie wondered, as she moved on to the piles of brochures situated next to the printouts, all of which touted local area attractions. Last but not least, sitting off to the left on the table was a pile of glossy brochures with a TAKE ME sign written in red. Bernie did as instructed and got back in the truck.

"There's a sign-in book in there," Bernie informed Libby.

Libby turned her gaze from the window. "And, let me guess, Margo isn't in it."

"That doesn't mean she wasn't here."

"And it doesn't mean she was."

"True." And with that, Bernie changed the subject. "According to this," she said to Libby, reading from the brochure, "there's sphagnum moss and swamp lilies growing here, as well as hummocks with white birch and cedar."

"What is a hummock?" Libby asked.

"Some sort of small island," Bernie told Libby after she'd looked the word up on her phone. "Also, the area is inhabited by white-tailed deer, raccoons, possums, and skunks, as well as a host of other small mammals. The brochure also says to be careful of ticks and to stay on the designated paths."

Then Bernie showed Libby the map printed on the last page of the brochure. Libby took it and studied it for a moment. The swamp area was represented by an irregular, light-green rectangle with three black squiggly lines running through it. The lines represented roads. A legend on the bottom of the page gave the area's dimensions, which Libby had to squint to read because the print was so tiny.

"I didn't realize this place was so big," she observed as she gave the brochure back to Bernie.

"Over four hundred square acres big," Bernie said, repeating what she'd read.

Libby turned her head and went back to studying the landscape. *It was not*, she thought, *a friendly-looking place.* "I don't get it. Why the hell would Margo come up here?" she wondered out loud.

"I don't know. Maybe she was sketching something or taking pictures," Bernie guessed.

"She restores paintings. She doesn't paint them."

"She could do both."

"I guess she could, at that," Libby allowed.

"Or she could have been bird-watching," Bernie suggested. "Evidently, this place gets visitors from all over the country." Bernie looked at the map again and sighed. It was rare in this neck of the woods to find such a large, empty space. If it weren't for the two protected species, she was sure there would be an apartment complex here right now.

"This is ridiculous," Libby complained. She waved her hand, indicating the area in front of her. "I mean, where do we begin?" Then she answered her own question before Bernie could. "I guess we could call and see if any of the rangers on duty—are they called rangers?—"

"I think so," Bernie replied.

"—have seen Margo. I wonder if they have surveillance cameras."

"I haven't seen any, if they have," Bernie said. "Maybe they have some set up farther into the wildlife area." Then she tapped the map again with a scarlet fingernail. "According to this, there are three entrances to this area, and we came in through the major one," she said.

"And your point is?" Libby asked.

"My point is that if Margo did come up here, she probably used Route Twenty, just like we did, since we're both on the same side of town."

Libby swatted at a fly that was buzzing around the van's interior. "Meaning?"

"Meaning that narrows down the area we have to search a little."

"A very little."

"What are we looking for anyway?" Libby asked.

"Honestly, Libby, I have no idea."

"Great, because neither do I."

"A trip through here will be interesting, though," Bernie said, playing the cheerleader. "Maybe we'll see a short-eared owl or some deer. That would be cool."

"Just as long as we don't see a pygmy rattlesnake or a skunk, I'm good," Libby responded as she rolled up her sleeves and used the back of her hand to wipe a bead of sweat off her forehead.

"Or giant hogweed. Don't forget that," Bernie said, and she gave Libby the map. "Tell me where I'm going."

Libby squinted at the map. The print was tiny. "You don't happen to have a magnifying glass on you, by any chance?"

"I don't even have one off me." Bernie hit her forehead with the flat of her hand. "Duh, no. I have something better," she said, reaching into her tote and getting her cell out. She went to Google and typed in Myer's Landing Wildlife Management Area, but nothing came up. "Damn," she said.

"What?" Libby asked her.

Bernie showed her her cell.

Libby read the message in the upper-left-hand corner. "No service. I guess we'll have to do this the old-fashioned way."

"I guess we will," Bernie agreed as she put Mathilda in gear. "Here goes nothing."

"You can say that again," Libby told her sister as they started into the park. "This all looks the same to me," Libby complained after they'd gone a quarter of a mile. She was looking at a flat expanse of marshy plants.

"Try reading the map," Bernie suggested.

"I am trying, but it isn't exactly user-friendly," Libby said as she brought it closer to her face. *Could they have made the legend any smaller?* she wondered. "Are you sure there wasn't a larger map in the visitor's center?" Libby asked.

"Positive," Bernie told her.

"Okay. But I'm not promising anything."

"Good thing you didn't," Bernie said fifteen minutes later, after Libby had admitted she had no idea where they were. The fact that Bernie's cell phone still wasn't getting any service didn't help matters.

"I will say one thing, though," Libby allowed as Bernie pulled over to the side of the road and put Mathilda in park. The air was full of birdsong and the hum of insects. The town of Longely seemed a long ways away. "It is peaceful out here. Maybe Margo came here for inspiration and then she couldn't find her way back," said Libby, proposing a new theory.

"Let's hope not," Bernie said as she suddenly realized how hungry she was. She'd had an early light lunch of cottage cheese and red and black raspberries, and nothing to eat since then. "Libby, hand me one of those sandwiches," she said, indicating with a nod of her chin the small wicker picnic basket they'd brought. "We might as well eat," she said as she took the sandwich Libby handed her and began to unwrap it.

The sandwich was slightly warm from being in the sun, so the mozzarella had softened a bit, and the tomato and garlic had worked their way into the bread. Bernie took a bite. First came the slight tartness of the tomato, then the creaminess of the cheese, the saltiness of the olives, the feel of the olive oil that Bernie had used on the bread instead of mayo, and the slight heat from the coarsely ground pepper.

"How can anything so simple taste so good?" Bernie asked. It was a rhetorical question, but Libby answered it anyway.

"It's the ingredients," Libby replied. "With something this simple, you don't have anything to hide behind."

"True," Bernie said as she poured tea from the thermos they'd packed into a cup and took a sip. Then she sat back and watched the sun dancing over the clusters of reeds and the birds diving down into the marsh.

"What's that?" Libby asked, pointing to a long-legged bird with a long, thin beak.

"That, I believe, is a great blue heron," Bernie said as she took another bite of her sandwich.

"I've never seen one before," Libby commented as she watched the bird wade into the brackish water, stick his head down, and come up a second later with a small fish in his beak. "It looks as if he got lucky," Libby noted as the heron flew away.

"I wish we could say the same," Bernie said, finishing her sandwich and opening the Tupperware container full of cherries. After she ate a few and spit the pits out the window, she picked up the brochure Libby had put down and tried to figure out where they were. "Didn't we make a left here?" she asked, tapping a point in the black line snaking through the green on the map.

Libby shook her head. "I think we made a right."

"Are you sure?"

"Pretty sure," Libby said, taking a last bite of her sandwich. Then she folded up the reusable sandwich wrapper and put it back in the picnic basket.

"Fifty percent sure? One hundred percent sure?"

"Maybe seventy percent sure."

Bernie looked around. "It wouldn't hurt to have a few signs around here."

"For the snakes?"

Bernie didn't say anything. She was thinking. "If we go east, we should be able to get out of here."

"Which way is east?"

Bernie pointed.

"Are you sure?"

"Reasonably sure."

"And if it's not?"

"What's the worst that can happen?"

"I'm glad you asked," Libby said. She'd been giving the matter a lot of thought since they'd entered the wildlife preserve. "I'll tell you what's the worst that can happen. We can drive around until we run out of gas, and then we'd have to get out and walk, at which time we'll fall down into a nest of rattlers and get bitten. Then we'll lie there writhing in agony until the park rangers find us or we die."

"Works for me," Bernie said as she finished her iced tea and screwed the thermos top back on. Then she put Mathilda in drive and started forward. "Maybe they'll erect a plaque in our memory."

"I thought you were going to turn around," Libby said.

"I will when I get to a place where I can turn." Bernie

indicated the road in front of them. "This road is so narrow I'm afraid that if I try to turn here I'll slip off into the bog."

Five minutes later, Bernie was still looking for a turnoff. As she drove, she passed a momma duck and her string of babies paddling around in the marsh. Then she stopped for a flock of geese that had decided to cross the road. Bernie honked, and they all stopped and stared at her before continuing on. Bernie's honking startled the other birds feeding there, and they all rose up in a cloud.

"What are those?" Libby asked, pointing to several birds that were now hovering in the sky. "They're very large."

"I think they're buzzards," Bernie said. "Turkey buzzards."

Libby turned to look at Bernie. "Are they like regular buzzards?"

"I imagine so," Bernie said.

"Don't buzzards eat dead things?" Libby asked.

"I believe they do." Bernie bit her lip, thinking of the implications. "They're probably feeding off a dead deer or possum or raccoon."

"Probably," Libby agreed, hoping that was the case, even though she knew in her heart of hearts that it wasn't.

"I guess we'll find out," Bernie said, and she took her foot off the brake and began driving again, going more slowly because she didn't want to see what was waiting for her.

The dirt road snaked this way and that, going off into unexpected directions, none of which were shown on the map. It took Bernie longer to arrive at the scene than she had expected. When she got there, five turkey buzzards flew up, squawking at the intrusion, then landed again.

"There," Bernie said, pointing to the hood of a partially submerged white car.

"Margo's car is white, isn't it?" Libby asked as Bernie shut the van off.

"Yes, it is," Bernie said. She opened the van door and got out, leaving the keys in the ignition. "She owns a white Camry."

Libby cursed as she got out of the van. "God, that's awful," she noted, referring to the foul odor lingering in the air.

The sisters exchanged glances. They had smelled that smell before.

"It could be a deer," Bernie repeated.

"Or something smaller," Libby said. "Remember the smell when that mouse died in the walls?"

Bernie nodded and unbuttoned her shirt as a trickle of sweat worked its way down her back. It was hot in the sun. The two sisters slowly walked to the side of the path and peered down. They spotted the car immediately. It had sunk down and was sitting with its tires covered in the muck. No one was in the vehicle, but the driver's-side door was wide open. A woodpecker was exploring the interior. Bernie couldn't help thinking that the vehicle reminded her of the giant white alligator at the natural history museum in San Francisco.

Libby pointed to the vehicle. "Whoever was in the car must have gotten out," she hypothesized as she unbuttoned her shirt and used its hem to wipe away the drops of sweat that were beading on her forehead and falling into her eyes.

"Maybe he or she made it to the road and managed to get picked up," Bernie suggested, but there was no conviction in her voice.

As she took a step off the roadway, she could hear a plop, followed by another one, as two frogs jumped into the water. A small turtle stared up at her as she parted a clump of tall grass, lumbering away as Bernie stepped into it. The grasses brushed her cheeks, and a swarm of insects buzzed around her face. She swatted at them and took another step.

"Be careful of the snakes," Libby called.

"Thanks," Bernie said. "I'll try and do that." Her next two steps took her clear of the high grass.

"Anything?" Libby asked.

"Not yet," Bernie replied. "I take that back," she said almost immediately. She could see something not too far away. At first, she'd thought it was part of a partially submerged, broken-off tree branch floating in the brackish water, but now that she was closer, she realized she was seeing the back of a person, a person wearing a tan shirt.

"Is it Margo?" Libby asked.

Bernie slapped at a mosquito. "I can't tell."

Libby took a couple of steps to the left and peered into the water. Now that her sister had pointed it out, Libby could see the body, too. It was lying facedown. Two of the turkey buzzards that had taken off had come back down and were sitting on its back, pecking at the nape of the neck, while the other three buzzards hopped around the silty water a short distance away, waiting for Bernie and Libby to leave. A large bullfrog jumped on the body, sat there for a moment, and jumped off.

"Are you going to check?" Libby asked.

"Unless you want to," Bernie replied.

"I wouldn't want to deprive you of the pleasure."

"Please. Be my guest," Bernie told her.

"No. No. You're there already," Libby answered.

Bernie couldn't argue with that because she was. She sighed and took another two steps. She could feel the ground underneath her feet give slightly. Oh my God! Quicksand? *Get a grip*, she told herself, as her heart began hammering in her chest. No. If she were standing in quick-sand, she would be sinking, and she wasn't. She let out the breath she didn't know she'd been holding and took another step, gingerly putting her weight on her forward foot. The ground held, so she took another two steps. By now, the water was over her ankles and was creeping up to her calves, making her glad she'd worn her oldest pants and sneakers.

"I didn't think there'd be this much water," Libby said.

"Neither did I," Bernie said. But they'd gotten a lot of rain in the last months, turning this part of the swamp into a shallow lake. By now, she was near enough to the body to hear the hum of the flies that had settled on it. When she got closer, she turned her head away, took a deep breath, then turned back and reached out to the body. The flies on it rose en masse as Bernie turned the corpse's head toward her.

"Well?" Libby asked. She couldn't see. Her view was blocked by her sister.

Bernie straightened up, took a couple of steps back, turned toward her sister, and let her breath out. "It's definitely Margo," she said. "No doubt about it."

Chapter 8

It was a little after eight on a sultry Tuesday evening, and the remaining members of the Longely Mystery Book Club, plus the Simmons sisters, were seated in Harry and Gilda Westover's living room sipping the iced lemon verbena sun tea that Gilda had made and eating the peach blueberry cobbler that Bernie and Libby had brought with them.

As Bernie stirred a lump of sugar into her tea, she noted that the large, well-proportioned living room led into a dining room, which, in turn, led onto a screened-in porch. The walls of the house were painted a soft, light green, while the furniture was comfortable and unremarkable, as opposed to the paintings hanging on the walls, which were remarkable.

"From our gallery," Harry Westover had explained when Bernie and Libby had paused to study them. "They're all from the Hudson River School," he'd added.

"They're marvelous," Libby had exclaimed, thinking of what the Hudson Valley had looked like in the mid-nineteenth century as opposed to now. The farms and the vast stretches of forest were gone, having given way to homes and roads. She wasn't sure it was an improvement.

Harry had smiled. "Yes, they are quite wonderful. And just think, fifty years ago they were giving these paintings away."

"You could have bought them at garage sales," Tom Glassberg noted.

"Value is all in the eye of the beholder," Irene Offenbach observed.

"Not really," her husband replied. "Look at the golden ratio. The same proportions exist in the cave paintings of Lascaux and the Greek sculptures. That argues for a universal standard."

Irene was about to reply, but before she could, Betsy Glassberg intervened. "Please," she said, "let's not get into this art thing again."

"You're right," Irene demurred, taking a seat on the armchair next to the sofa.

A moment later, Libby sat down as well. She realized it had been a little over a week since she and her sister had found Margo. This was the first time they'd all gotten together since then. Looking around, Libby couldn't help reflecting on the fact that, despite their differences in appearance, how similar this group of people gathered in the living room were.

All of them were either interested in the arts or made their living from it. All of them were comfortable financially. All of them were in their late forties to mid-fifties. And all of them looked as if they hadn't had a good night's sleep in weeks. Libby was wondering what, if anything, that might have to do with Margo's death when there was a rumble of thunder and an arc of lightning lit up the sky. Irene jumped.

"Oh my God," she said, laughing as she put a hand to her breast. "That startled me."

"A perfect night for a murder," Brad Musclow observed.

"I wish you wouldn't say that," his wife, Toni, told him. "It's one thing to read about it, but it's another thing when it happens to one of your own."

"And then there were nine," Steve Offenbach murmured before he took another sip of tea. A short man, he sported a neatly trimmed beard, a seersucker jacket, a dark navy-and-white, polka-dotted bowtie, and a pair of khaki Bermuda shorts.

Irene corrected him. "You mean *And Then There Were None*."

"I'm not talking about the Agatha Christie book," Steve responded. "I'm talking about the fact that, with Margo gone . . ."

"Murdered, like Toni said," Betsy Glassberg replied.

"We don't know that," Steve objected.

"I think we do," Betsy said. "It's obvious Margo was killed."

"If you'd allow me to finish," Steve said, raising his voice.

"By all means," Betsy answered. She took a bite of the peach blueberry crumble, swallowed, and complimented Bernie and Libby on it before telling Steve to go ahead.

"Thank you." Steve nodded and continued. "As I was saying, with Margo gone, there are nine of us now."

Gilda interrupted. "I still can't believe it," she said as she tucked a strand of hair behind her ear. Tonight she was wearing white sandals with a black, sleeveless sheath.

Toni Musclow put her plate down on the coffee table and leaned forward. Dressed in full-on Prada and Missoni, she was one of the more fashionable members of the group.

"I agree with Bets. I don't care what the police say," she told everyone. "You'd have to be crazy or stupid, or both, to think that Margo's death was an accident."

Betsy Glassberg clapped her hands as another bolt of lightning lit up the sky. "I couldn't have said it better myself, Toni."

Toni nodded her thanks as Lydia cried, "I warned her."

Everyone in the room turned to look at her. Lydia was sitting on an oxblood-colored leather armchair by the fireplace. Bernie could see that Lydia's lower lip was trembling.

"I saw what happened in the dreams I had," Lydia continued. "They foretold everything. Everything." Lydia held back a sob. "And I told Margo. I went to Margo the day before she . . . she . . ." Lydia closed her eyes. "There was water. I saw water. I"—Lydia took a deep breath and continued—"and I tried to warn her, but she wouldn't listen to me. She wouldn't pay attention. She was concentrating on her work . . . you know . . . the way she always did. Her art. That's all she ever cared about."

"She cared about us," Irene said, in a voice meant to be comforting.

Lydia made her hands into fists. "Margo should have listened." Her voice was loud and full of anger. "She should have listened to me. If she had, she'd still be alive today."

Libby watched everyone in the group exchange uneasy glances.

"Now, Lydia," Toni said soothingly.

"It's true, Toni," Lydia cried, sinking back into the chair. "It is. I know you think I'm crazy, but I'm not." Lydia sat back up. "Margo visited me last night."

"If you say so," Steve said.

"I do." Lydia raised her voice in the face of Steve's skepticism. "I saw her," Lydia insisted. "She was standing in the doorway, and she said to me, 'I should have listened to you.' And then she said, 'I want whoever did this punished. I want you to find them and punish them. Don't let my death go unavenged.'" Lydia bit her lip. "And then I woke up. I was cold, so cold. I had to take a hot shower to warm up."

Harry Westover levered himself out of the armchair he was sitting in, walked over to where Lydia was sitting, reached down, and patted the top of Lydia's head. "Now, now," he said, "no need to get so upset. We're all on the same page with this, even if Margo didn't visit us. That's why we're all here. Isn't that right, everyone?"

"Definitely," Betsy and Irene said together.

Instead of answering, Tom Glassberg took another bite of Libby's and Bernie's blueberry peach crumble, chewed, and swallowed. "Excellent," he told the sisters when he was done. "I especially like the touch of cardamom."

"Thanks," Libby said.

"You're welcome," Tom replied, dabbing at his mouth with a napkin. Then he put the napkin down on the end table next to the chair he was sitting in and addressed Lydia. "Too bad none of us have your talent," he told her.

Lydia stiffened. "It's a curse, not a talent," she informed him.

"My mistake. I don't suppose Margo let you in on the name of her killer, by any chance? It would save us time, not to mention a lot of money, if she did."

Lydia's face turned crimson. "Don't mock me!"

"I wouldn't dream of it," Tom responded, his voice full of sarcasm.

Lydia hit the arm of her chair with the flat of her hand. "You're doing it right now," she said.

"Am I?" he replied, his face expressionless.

Lydia was about to reply, but Brad Musclow got there first.

"He doesn't mean anything, Lydia."

Lydia sniffed. "Yes, he does, Brad. He can't stand the fact that I have this power. He never has."

Tom snorted and took a sip of tea. "You're right, Lydia. Have it your way. I'm dying of jealousy," he replied as he swirled the ice cubes in his glass.

"Why don't we skip the personal attacks and get down to business?" Brad suggested. "After all, we're not here to fight."

Everyone nodded their heads again.

Brad looked each person in the eye, "So, we're agreed?" he asked.

"Yes," everyone said in turn.

"Good." Brad extended his hand to Tom. "Do you want to speak for the group, or should I?"

Tom shook his head. "Go ahead. Be my guest. It's all yours."

Brad smiled. "Excellent," he told Tom as he turned to Bernie and Libby. They were both sitting on rush-bottomed, claw-foot chairs brought in from the dining room. "We, all of us," and Brad made a circular motion with his fingers to include everyone sitting in the room, "want to hire you to find out who killed Margo. After all, if it hadn't been for you, she never would have been found."

"We don't believe what the police are saying," Betsy added. "Margo was killed. This wasn't an accident. Someone lured her out there to that godforsaken place. Either that or they broke into her house and dragged her out. And stole the Eakins," Betsy added. "Don't forget that. The police don't seem to care about that, either. I tried to tell the detective who spoke to me and Tom about the theft, but he didn't care. He didn't care at all. I mean, he said he did, but he never wrote anything down in his book. Never asked any follow-up questions. I don't think he realizes how much money those paintings are worth."

"Yeah," Irene said, backing Betsy up. "Margo could

have interrupted a burglary. She could have gone down to her studio and startled the burglar and he shot her."

"There was no blood," Steve reminded Irene. "And no bullet wound."

"I'm speaking metaphorically," Irene told him.

"I'm not," Steve said. "If what you're saying is the case, then how did the perp get Margo to the swamp? I spoke to the police, and they said that, according to the coroner, there wasn't a mark on her body."

"Maybe the perp tased her or held a cloth suffused with ether over Margo's mouth," Irene replied. "Did the police look for fingerprints on her skin? Sometimes you can get an impression using Scotch tape."

"I don't believe they did," Bernie said.

"They should have," Irene exclaimed.

"I'm afraid it's too late now," Libby informed Irene.

"They should never have allowed Margo to be cremated," Betsy stated.

"I don't think they had much choice," Bernie replied. "Especially after her death was ruled an unfortunate accident."

"It's what she wanted," Libby informed them. "She left written instructions and prepaid."

"How do you know that?" Tom demanded.

"My boyfriend," Libby explained. "His dad owns the funeral home."

There was a moment of silence while everyone digested that piece of information. Then Toni spoke.

"All I know," she said, "is that Margo would never have gone to that place on her own. Never in a million years."

Gilda nodded, her large hoop earrings going up and down, punctuating her head's movement. "Absolutely. She hated places like that. She didn't like bugs or snakes or anything that crawled or crept. She was strictly an indoors type of gal."

"Margo didn't hike or bird-watch or do any of the kind of stuff that you'd do in a place like that," Irene said.

"Myer's Landing," said Bernie, supplying the name.

"They can call it whatever they like," Irene replied fiercely. "To me, it'll always be the place where Margo died. Did the police check the surveillance cameras?"

"There aren't any for the police to check," Libby told her. She and her sister had talked to the park rangers.

"Figures," Irene replied. Then she said, "Plus, Margo didn't drink. Maybe a glass or two of wine with dinner or an occasional Irish whiskey . . ."

"Jameson's," Steve said, interrupting.

". . . but that was it," Irene continued, picking up where she'd left off. "Am I right?" she asked, looking around at the members of the LMBC. They all murmured their assent. "So, she never would have gotten drunk and gone out to that place and driven off the road and drowned, like the police are saying she did."

Everyone in the room, except for Bernie and Libby, nodded in agreement again.

Betsy pulled her floral-print skirt back down around her knees and continued. "Irene's correct. That's completely unlike Margo," Betsy noted. "She never had more than two drinks, and if she felt tipsy, she would have called an Uber. Margo was always very careful about that sort of thing. Her parents were killed by a drunk driver, so the fact that she would have driven drunk is inconceivable. She was a cautious driver. She always stayed within the speed limit. She never even did rolling stops. In fact, because of what happened to her parents, she didn't like to drive. She hated going somewhere she didn't know. When we went to the Eastview Mall, Toni or I would pick her up."

"So, what do you think happened to Margo?" Libby asked, addressing the question to the group in general.

Betsy replied as another clap of thunder sounded. "This is what I think. I think someone dragged Margo out of her house, drove her car to the swamp, forced her to drink enough alcohol to render her unconscious, and then dragged her into the swamp, put her face in the water, and left her to drown."

"Or someone could have killed Margo and put her body in the freezer for a day to throw everyone off," Harry suggested.

Irene frowned. "Why would they do that?" she asked.

"Like I said, to throw everyone off the track, of course," Harry replied.

"Don't be ridiculous," Toni retorted.

"I'm not," Harry replied. "It was in the mystery we read a couple of months ago."

"That's why what we read is called fiction," Toni told him. "Think about it. If you're going to do that, why not keep the body in the freezer? Why leave it where they did for someone to find?" Toni asked.

"Maybe whoever did it wanted the body found? Maybe they had to empty out the freezer?" Harry suggested.

"We're talking about Margo here," Irene cried, "not some corpse in a mystery we're reading for book club."

"I think in this case, our reading could help," Harry replied stiffly.

"No, it can't, Harry," Irene said. "Reality and fiction are, by definition, different. One thing has nothing to do with the other."

"How can you say that, Irene?" Harry demanded. "Of course, it does. Fiction is based on reality, which is why we know things that other people don't. In fact, if we weren't all so busy I'd say we should investigate this ourselves."

"Are you saying we're suspects?" Steve interjected.

"Of course not. Why would you say that?" Harry demanded.

"I didn't," Steve told him. "But you did."

"I most certainly did not," Harry countered.

"Maybe not directly," Steve answered. "But you sure as hell implied it when you said we know a lot about killing people."

Harry gave a small, disgusted shake of his head. "Oh, please. Your inferences never cease to amaze me."

Betsy clapped her hands before Steve could answer. "People, can we please stop arguing?"

"We're not arguing," Harry told her. "We're discussing."

"I don't care what you call it," Betsy said to Harry. "Stop doing it. We need to focus. This is important."

"I was just introducing possibilities," Harry protested, a hurt look on his face. "Possibilities are the foundation of all good detective work."

Lydia interrupted. "I told her. I did," she insisted.

"I know you did," Betsy said gently. "And I'm sure that Libby and Bernie will follow up on what you saw—that is, if they're willing to take this case." Betsy turned toward the sisters. "Are you?"

"What if the police are right?" Bernie asked her. "What then?"

"They're not," Lydia cried out, unable to contain herself.

"But if they are?" Bernie persisted.

"Then we'll deal with that when the time comes," Betsy said. "Either way, it will be money well spent. At least we'll know what happened." She turned to the group. "Isn't that right?" she asked them.

"Yes," everyone except Lydia said.

"Well, Lydia?" Steve said. "Are you in or out?"

"In, of course." Lydia told him, straightening her shoulders and sitting up. "How can you ask that question?"

"I just wanted to make sure," Steve explained.

"Good." Betsy took a quick sip of her tea before turning to face Libby and Bernie. "So," she asked the sisters, "will you take the job? We'll pay you, of course."

"What do you think?" Bernie asked Libby.

"If that's what everyone wants," Libby said, although she was still on the fence about what had happened to Margo. She could see the investigation going in either direction.

"It is," Betsy replied. Bernie and Libby watched her get up, go into the hallway, and come back with her pocketbook. Then she reached inside and came out with an envelope and handed it to Bernie. "There's a four-thousand-dollar retainer in there. And if that's not enough . . ."

"Hopefully we'll be able to close this out pretty quickly," Bernie told her.

Betsy stuck out her hand and Bernie shook it.

"Alright, then," Bernie said. "Libby and I will start tomorrow. Just remember, we can't promise anything."

Gilda answered. "We know that," she said. "We're just asking you to try. That's all."

Chapter 9

It was a little after ten p.m. by the time Bernie and Libby walked into RJ's. By then, the rain had stopped, leaving behind a grassy scent in the air and water droplets dripping off the trees. An owl was hooting off in the distance. As the sisters entered, Bernie could see that the bar was practically empty, not that Bernie was surprised. The place was packed in the fall, winter, and spring, but it usually wasn't very busy in the summer, and even less so on a weekday night.

Tonight, there were a handful of regulars at the bar and four people playing pool over in the back corner, but the red leather booths were empty, and the jukebox sat silent. Tonight, you could hear the click of the cue on the balls whenever someone took a shot.

"Look, it's the girl detectives," Brandon called out as Bernie and Libby came through the door.

They curtsied.

"Thank you, thank you. No need for adulation," Bernie said, curtsying again as two of the regulars sitting at the bar clapped and Libby's boyfriend, Marvin, swiveled in his seat and lifted the glass of beer he was drinking in a salute.

"So, what did the LMBC want?" Marvin asked as Libby and Bernie sat down next to him. "Wait. Don't tell me, let me guess. They want to hire you."

"Do they?" Brandon said as he pulled two wheat beers and put them in front of Bernie and Libby, along with a basket full of pretzels. "Tell us. Inquiring minds want to know."

Bernie pointed at Marvin. "Give that man a cigar. You are one hundred percent correct. They just hired us to find out who killed Margo."

"Interesting," Mike Crenshaw observed. He was sitting two barstools over. It had taken Libby a minute to realize who it was. Michael Crenshaw was a regular customer of theirs, but usually she and Bernie saw him in a suit and tie. Tonight, though, he was wearing jeans, a black T-shirt, and a green baseball cap perched on his head. "I thought the police decided Margo's death was an accident," he said.

"They did," Libby told him, "but the book club members don't agree with that assessment."

Mike shook his head. "People believe what they want to believe."

"Ain't that the truth?" Brandon commented. As a bartender, he'd become adept at sympathetic but meaningless comments.

Libby had a vague recollection of Mike Crenshaw saying something about Margo the day she'd gone missing. "You know . . . knew her, right?"

Mike picked up a handful of pretzels and popped them into his mouth one by one. "Not really. Just to say hello to."

Now Libby remembered. "That's right. You said something about running into Margo at the garage."

"Yeah. She was picking up her vehicle. Hard to believe."

"What's hard to believe?" Libby asked.

Mike shrugged. "Just that, one minute, Margo's here and we're talking, and the next minute she's gone." He snapped his fingers. "Poof. Just like that." Then he looked up at the clock on the wall. "Jeez. I didn't realize what time it was. I have to get going." And he gulped down the rest of his drink and laid a twenty on the bar. "Keep the change," he told Brandon, who nodded his thanks.

"I hope we're not chasing you out," Bernie told Mike.

Mike smiled and shook his head. "Nope. It's just time to go home and get ready for tomorrow."

"I wonder why you never hear about co-ed book clubs," Marvin mused as Mike walked out the door into the summer night.

"The Longely Mystery Book Club is co-ed," Bernie pointed out.

"I know. That's what got me thinking. But that's the exception," Marvin replied. "Most book clubs are made up of women."

"Because women read," Libby said.

"Or maybe," Brandon said, "the book is just an excuse for women to get together, gossip, and drink wine . . ."

"And men . . ." Bernie began.

Brandon laughed. "Don't need an excuse. They have sports. And beer."

"You might be right there," Bernie agreed.

Brandon put his elbows on the bar and leaned in toward her. "So, the Longely Mystery Book Club thinks that Margo was murdered?" Brandon asked.

"That seems to be the general consensus," Bernie informed him.

"But you don't agree?" Marvin said, picking up on the tone of Bernie's voice.

Bernie ate the slice of orange in her beer, put the peel on a napkin, and folded the napkin in half. "You know, I'm

not really sure. Let's just say, I think the police are probably right, but there are several things that bother me about
what happened to Margo, so, no, I don't think things are
cut-and-dried."

"Such as?" Marvin inquired.

Bernie answered. "Like the fact that, according to the
members of the Longely Mystery Book Club, Margo's behavior went counter to the way she usually acted. She was
a very scheduled person, or, as they used to say in the good
old days, 'she was a woman of regular habits.'"

"You're saying Margo pooped at the same time every
day?" Brandon asked.

"Cute," Bernie told him as Marvin and Libby laughed.

"Don't encourage him," Bernie admonished them, but
she was smiling while she said it.

Libby took a sip of her beer and put it down. "Me?
Never."

Bernie snorted. She ate a pretzel and continued. "As I
was trying to say, when Margo picked up her order, she
was always ten minutes early. You could make book on
that. In the five years she's been doing it, I have never, ever
known her to be late. Or change her order, for that matter.
She always wanted the same thing, although, on reflec-
tion, the part about her not changing her order may have
had something to do with the other book club members.
Ergo, the fact that she didn't pick up her order, that she
didn't make alternative arrangements, that she didn't let
anyone know she couldn't do the pickup, that she disappeared without a word to anyone—all of that makes me
suspicious."

"I would have thought that would have made the police
suspicious as well," Marvin observed.

"You would have thought, and you'd be wrong," Libby
replied. "They put Margo's conduct down to, and I'm

quoting here, 'She flipped out.' As in something happened—they don't know what—and Margo got upset, and
started drinking, and drove herself out to the swamp, and
once she got there, she had an accident, drove off the road,
and drowned." Libby leaned forward. "Personally, I think
if it was a guy that this had happened to, the police would
have taken it a little more seriously, devoted a little more
time to an investigation. And then, of course, there's the
shoe." And she explained.

Marvin ran his finger around his glass. "I was surprised
the coroner finished up as fast as he did. Usually, they like
to keep the body in cases like this. We got Margo and cremated her about a week after you guys found her," he
said, referring to Bernie and Libby.

"And then her cousin scattered her ashes over the At-
lantic," Bernie said, filling in Brandon on the rest of the
story.

"Distant cousin," Marvin clarified. "Four times removed,
whatever that is. Evidently, it was what she wanted," Marvin explained. "The strange part is that Margo told me she
didn't know her cousin existed until recently. Ancestry.com
brought them together."

"I'd rather be buried," Libby said.

"I'd rather not be dead," Brandon said.

"Well, there is that," Libby agreed.

"Any other reasons you think Margo may have been
killed?" Brandon asked, returning to the topic at hand.

"Several things, actually," Bernie replied. "First of all,
according to Margo's friends, she didn't like bugs of any
kind. That's number one. And number two: Margo didn't
drink, except for an occasional glass of something now
and then, because both her parents were killed in a drunk-
driving accident . . ."

"That sucks," Brandon noted.

"It definitely does," Bernie agreed, continuing on with her narrative. "And yet here Margo is, ending up in Myer's Landing, bug heaven, a place she had no reason to go to or would ever want to go to, blitzed out of her mind. What the hell was she doing there? According to her friends, this was someone who spent most of her time in museums and art galleries."

"Maybe she was meeting someone there for"—Brandon wiggled his eyebrows and leered—"a little fun."

"Yeah," Bernie said, "the swamp is where I would want to get laid instead of a nice hotel room with air-conditioning, clean sheets, and a shower."

"Your wish is my command, my lady," Brandon said, and he bowed. "I'll run home and get my can of bug repellent."

"How romantic," Bernie said. "I don't know how I can refuse."

Brandon grinned. "You can't." He switched topics. "Did anyone tell the police what you just told me?"

Libby nodded. "Betsy said she did."

"And what did the police say?"

"The detective, a guy called Andredi, wrote it down in his notebook, thanked her for the information, and told her he'd be back in touch."

"And then?" Marvin asked.

"And then nothing," Libby told him.

"What does your dad's friend Clyde, the one who is still on the force, say?" Marvin asked.

Libby shrugged. "He said he's seen stranger things. He said people aren't as consistent as we like to think they are."

"Interesting," Marvin said. He checked the time. "It seems later than it is."

"Not to me it doesn't," Brandon replied. He studied the room. "Maybe I'll close early tonight. There's no one here anyway."

The man who had been sitting next to Mike Crenshaw looked up from his phone. "I resent that," he told Brandon. "I'm here, in case you haven't noticed." He pointed to the two other men sitting at the bar. "And so are Andy and John."

"Don't worry, Sid," Bernie assured him. "Brandon's kidding. He's not going anywhere."

"He better not," Sid said.

Marvin finished his beer and asked Brandon for another one. Then he turned to Bernie. "You said several things made Margo's death problematic for you. You named three. Are there any more?"

Libby answered for her sister. "Yeah. The red truck, the missing sketches, the shoe in the grass, and the opened door."

Marvin raised an eyebrow.

Libby explained. "When we went to Margo's house, the back door was open, but when Tom went to Margo's house the night she didn't show up, the back door was locked. At least that's what he said."

"So, Margo came back, got something, and left again? Is that what you're saying?" Marvin asked.

Bernie ate a pretzel. "That's one explanation. Another is that the person who killed her took her key and went back in to get something."

"Possibly it was the person driving the red truck that we saw pulling out of Margo's driveway," Libby added. "Maybe they came in and took the Eakins." She shook her head. "If we'd gotten to Margo's house a little earlier, we might have caught him or her."

"Did you tell the police?" Marvin asked Libby.

She nodded. "What do you think? We told my dad, and my dad told Clyde, and Clyde told Andredi." Libby shrugged. "He was not impressed. He said it 'wasn't compelling,' whatever that means."

"Maybe he's right," Brandon noted. He straightened up, took the towel off his shoulder, and wiped down the counter, after which he got Bernie another beer.

"Did Margo ever come in here?" Bernie asked Brandon. Brandon shook his head. "At least not when I was here. Anyway, you just said she didn't drink."

"True," Bernie said, "but some people come in and don't drink. They have a soda and hang out with their friends."

"Well, Margo wasn't one of those," Brandon answered.

"But you do know her, right?" Libby asked.

"Of course, I do. I know everyone in Longely."

"That's a bit of an exaggeration, isn't it?" Bernie teased.

"Not really," Brandon countered. "If I don't know them personally, I know about them," he declared. "Margo is the one who painted her house those weird colors. Let me tell you, her neighbors were not pleased when they saw what she'd done."

"Was anyone particularly angry?" Libby asked.

"You mean angry enough to kill her?"

Libby nodded.

Brandon laughed. "Hardly," he said. "Who would kill someone over a paint job? You'd have to be nuts to do that."

"Some people are," Libby observed.

Brandon thought for a minute. "I'd say the people I'm talking about were miffed. Yes. *Miffed* would be the word I'd use."

"Who are we talking about here?" Bernie wanted to know.

"April Reardon and Sam Huntington." Brandon tapped his fingers on the counter as he reconsidered what he'd said. "Maybe *miffed* isn't the right word. Maybe *puzzled* is. Yes, they couldn't understand Margo's color choice."

"Besides that, what else have you heard about Margo?" Bernie asked him.

"Not much," Brandon admitted. "Certainly nothing juicy."

"I know one thing about her," Sid said, joining the conversation from four seats away.

Bernie, Libby, Marvin, and Brandon turned toward him.

"What's that?" Libby asked.

"Buy me another beer, and I'll tell you."

"Don't be a putz, Sid," Brandon told him.

"It's okay," Bernie said to Brandon, "give it to him."

"Before I tell you," Sid clarified.

"You're kidding," Brandon huffed.

Bernie made a calming gesture. "It's fine. I think I can afford the six bucks."

Brandon shrugged. "Your call," he said.

"Make it a Sam Adam's Summer Ale," Sid said.

Brandon snorted but did as instructed.

"Margo likes expensive cars," Sid said when the glass was in front of him.

"How expensive?" Libby asked.

"Expensive expensive," Sid told her.

Bernie turned toward him. "And you know this how?"

"Jason is my friend."

Bernie gave him a blank stare. "Jason who?"

"Jason Sitwell."

"Sid, who is Jason Sitwell?" Libby asked.

"He works over at Freelander's," Brandon said when Sid didn't answer. "Isn't that right?"

Sid nodded.

"Really?" Bernie said, thinking of the vehicle she saw in the muck, the vehicle that Margo had been thrown out of.

"Really," Sid said.

"Because she sure wasn't driving anything fancy whenever I saw her."

"That's because she keeps them in Freelander's storage space."

"Freelander has a storage space?" Brandon asked.

"In back of the strip mall that houses the vet and the pizza shop."

"You mean Julius Plaza?"

Sid nodded emphatically. "That's exactly where I mean."

Bernie gave Libby a meaningful look. "I think it's time to start looking for a storage space for our old Austin Healey, don't you?"

"Austin Healey?" Libby repeated, a note of puzzlement in her voice. Did they have a car she didn't know about?

"Yes, the one dad got from Aunt Edna," Bernie said, kicking her sister in the shin. "Remember?"

"Oh, that one," Libby agreed, trying not to flinch. "How could I forget?"

Marvin perked up. "You have an Austin Healey?" he asked. "Wow. Where is it?"

"It's coming next week," Libby lied, mindful of the fact that Sid was listening in on the conversation. If there was one thing she'd learned from living in a small town, it was to keep one's lies consistent.

Chapter 10

"I can't go," Sean said to his daughters as he took another bite of the grilled-cheese sandwich Libby and Bernie had just brought upstairs for a mid-morning snack.

"What do you mean, you can't go?" Bernie demanded.

"Just what I said," he told his youngest daughter,

Then he savored another bite of his sandwich. The texture of the slightly toasted baguette, the rough crumb, and the chewy crust, contrasting with the oozy goodness of the melted mozzarella, the spiciness of the Italian basil, and the kick of the freshly ground pepper were good for the soul.

He reflected that this sandwich was one of those things that was sublime in the right hands and awful in the wrong ones, which only went to prove what his wife had always said: that the simplest things were the hardest to make well. Practically anyone could throw together an edible chili, but to make perfect scrambled eggs took a high degree of skill.

"But, Dad . . ." Bernie objected, her voice trailing off as she considered what she wanted to say.

Sean startled. "Sorry," he said, called back to the

present. He broke off the tiniest piece of his sandwich and held it out for Cindy the cat, who gently took it out of his hand. "What were you saying?"

"Why can't you go?" Libby asked, jumping into the conversation. "You like doing this sort of thing."

Sean looked up at his daughter. "That's not the point. I can't go because I arrested Tommy Chung on a felony auto-theft charge ten years ago and nabbed him on a chop shop beef three years before that. I wasn't his favorite person then, and I'm pretty sure I won't be now."

Libby wrinkled her nose. "Who is Tommy Chung?" she asked.

"The guy you want to speak to." Seeing the look of puzzlement on his daughters' faces, Sean amplified. "The guy who owns Freelander's. He bought it from Ron Freelander a couple of years ago. Somehow, given our past history, I don't think Chung is going to tell me anything about Margo and her cars—even if there's anything to tell."

"You think we're going on a fool's errand," Bernie challenged.

"I didn't say that," her father replied.

"No, but you implied it," Bernie said.

Libby stopped eating her sandwich as an idea crossed her mind. "Oh," she said. "Do you think Chung will know who we are?" This possibility had not occurred to her before.

Sean broke off another piece of his sandwich and fed it to his cat. Then he answered Libby. "I wouldn't be surprised," he responded. "But even if he does, he might not feel as strongly about you as he does about me. In answer to your question, Bernie, go see him. It's worth the time. After all, you don't have much else."

Bernie answered. "True. Aside from the red truck and the missing paintings . . ."

"Which," Sean observed, "practically speaking, are dead ends . . ."

"For the moment anyway," Libby agreed.

Bernie finished what she was saying. "We have April Reardon and Sam Huntington not liking the paint job on Margo's house."

"Which is a pretty thin motive for killing someone, if you ask me," Sean opined. "Of course, people have killed other people for a cigarette butt."

Bernie sighed. "I know we don't have a hell of a lot to work with at the moment, which is why we're hoping you can reach out to Clyde again . . ."

Sean interrupted. "Reach out? Please. What are you? A lawyer?"

"Fine," Libby said. "Can you call him . . ."

Sean nodded. ". . . and?"

"Invite him over."

"So you can grill him on why Detective Andredi"— Sean gave the word detective a sarcastic twist—"came to the conclusion he did?"

Bernie grinned. "Exactly. Tell him I'll make him a strawberry shortcake this time."

"The one with biscuits?"

"The one with biscuits," Bernie told her dad. "After all, that's the way Clyde likes it, isn't it?"

"Yes. You know, you and your sister are going to bear the responsibility for the Longely Police Department's weight gain."

"Clyde is bringing the pies we're giving him into the station house?" Libby asked.

Sean nodded. "What's left of them. Well, he can't bring them home," Sean explained, seeing the puzzled look on his daughters' faces. "His wife has him on a diet."

"His wife always has him on a diet, poor guy," Bernie murmured.

"You can say that again," Sean said as Bernie and Libby kissed their dad good-bye.

Then they both headed out the door and downstairs to the shop. There the sisters checked in with Googie and Amber, their counter people, to make sure they didn't need anything before they left.

The shop was almost empty, which was the norm, 9:30 to 11:45 being the interval when the morning rush was over and the lunch scrum hadn't begun. By now, Libby and Bernie had finished their morning tasks, which included but were not limited to preparing the corn, tomato, salmon, cucumber, and avocado salad they were featuring for lunch, baking the walnut and carrot muffins they were serving with the salad, and getting a jump on the seafood chowder, the three-color vegetable lasagna, and the cheesecake A Little Taste of Heaven was showcasing for dinner that evening.

It had just finished raining, and the sun had come out when they walked out the door. The sky was a bright blue, the grass was an intense green, and drops of water glinted from the blades of grass and the leaves of the trees. In short, it was a picture-perfect day—for once.

Bernie took a deep breath and let it out. "Nice," she said, inhaling the odors of fresh-cut grass and the faint brackish smell of the Hudson River a little over a mile away as she and her sister headed for their van. "It would be a good day to play hooky," she noted wistfully. "Maybe go to the beach."

"It would be nice, wouldn't it? But I think right now this is about as good as we're going to get," Libby replied as she opened the driver's-side door and got in.

Considering the time of day, Libby figured it would take

them between ten and fifteen minutes to get to the garage, which was located on the outskirts of Longely, across the street from a strip mall that hosted a nail salon, a yoga studio, a gift shop, and a resale shop specializing in high-end clothing.

"Turn right, turn right now," Bernie said to Libby as she was about to go by the garage.

Libby took a hard right, and they screeched onto the blacktop in front of the shop. Freelander's had been in business for twenty-five years and looked exactly as one would expect a garage to look—except for the types of vehicles parked out front.

"I think we're a little out of place here," Libby said to Bernie as she pointed to the two Teslas, the three BMWs, and the dark green MG in the parking lot, waiting to be serviced.

"Just think rich thoughts," Bernie replied.

She didn't care about cars—she'd much rather have a Chanel suit—but she had to admit she wouldn't mind owning the MG, not that that was ever going to happen. At least, not in this lifetime. And on that thought, Bernie opened Mathilda's door and got out.

Even though she knew it was silly, especially considering what her dad had said, she'd dressed for the part in strappy white sandals, a peach polka-dotted sheath, and her white Prada summer bag. At Bernie's insistence, Libby was likewise arrayed in a pink gingham sundress and a pair of white jeweled sandals, both items courtesy of Bernie's closet. After all, as Bernie had told Libby, there was no harm in trying. Maybe their dad was wrong. Maybe Chung didn't know who they were. Which would make things a hell of a lot easier.

Libby pulled at her shoulder strap as she and her sister walked toward the door.

"Stop it," Bernie hissed.

"I can't help it. The strap's too tight."

"It's fine," Bernie said. "We're the same size."

Libby snorted. "We are so not," she told her sister as they walked inside.

"Yes," the guy behind the counter said. "What can I do for you?"

Pleasant-seeming was the word that came to Bernie's mind. He looked to be in his midtwenties and was of medium height and medium weight, with brown hair and eyes. The only distinguishing thing about him was his milky right eye.

"Are you Jason Sitwell?" Bernie asked.

"I am."

"Sid said you might be able to help my sister and me out," Bernie told him. Maybe, with a little luck, they wouldn't have to deal with Chung at all.

"If I can," Jason said.

Bernie began the story she'd concocted. "My aunt died . . ."

"Sorry to hear it," Jason said.

"Thank you. And she left us an Austin Healy."

Jason whistled. "Nice thing to be left."

Bernie grinned. "My sister and I think so, too."

"You need to have it looked at?"

"That too, but what we need at the moment is a place to keep it. I heard you store vehicles."

"We don't," a voice said from the back room. "You've been misinformed."

Tommy Chung, Libby guessed, as a tall, good-looking man stepped out front.

Chapter 11

Tommy Chung walked over to the front desk, patted Jason on the shoulder, and told him to take a coffee break. Then, as Bernie and Libby watched, he opened the register and took out a five and a ten. "You like Starbucks, don't you?" he asked Jason.

"Yeah," Jason answered. "I do."

"Good." Chung handed him the fifteen bucks. "Run down and get me a large . . ."

"You mean venti," Jason told him.

Chung glared at Jason, and Jason stopped talking. "As I was saying," Chung continued, "get me a large black coffee with two sugars and a couple of packages of those chocolate-dipped graham crackers, and get yourself whatever you want as well."

Bernie reached in her bag. "Hey," she said to Jason, having suddenly realized she was in dire need of caffeine, "if I give you some money, can you get my sister and me two small cappuccinos with a sprinkle of cocoa and cinnamon on top?"

Jason looked at his boss to see if he could. Chung shook his head.

"You'll be gone by the time Jason gets back," Chung

informed Bernie before turning back to Jason. "Well," he said to him, "what are you waiting for? Get your ass in gear and get out of here."

"That's not very polite," Bernie remonstrated as Jason scurried out the door.

Chung pointed to Jason. "To him?"

"Him too. But I was thinking of us. That's no way to treat potential customers."

Chung watched Jason get into an old Civic, then turned to Libby and Bernie and said, "You're right. It's not. But since you're not customers, it doesn't matter." He readjusted the collar of his pale pink polo shirt. "Obviously, you didn't hear what I said, so I'll repeat it for you."

"Oh," Bernie said, "my sister and I heard what you said. We're just not paying attention to it."

"Cute."

Bernie smiled her most winning smile.

Chung was not impressed. "Whatever you want, I don't have it."

"How do you know?" Libby asked.

"Trust me, I know," Chung answered.

"You're passing up a major opportunity here," Bernie said.

Chung laughed. It was not, Bernie decided, a nice laugh.

"I'm willing to take that chance," he said. Chung looked down at his phone and back up. "I'll tell you what I'm going to do. I'm going to save us all a lot of time and dancing around each other and tell you how it's going to go. You're Sean Simmons's daughters, which means I'm not talking to you on general principles. About anything. And in case you're wondering how I know who you are—as in whether I've kept tabs on you and your dad—I haven't. Not that it would be hard to do, with you owning the store and all, but there was a picture of you two in the local rag a couple of weeks ago with a caption underneath explaining how the two of you found Margo Hemsley in the swamp."

"Oh, yeah." Bernie had forgotten about that. "And the place is called Myer's Landing."

"Do I look like I care?" Chung said, waving his hand in dismissal. His phone pinged. He looked down at it, typed something, then looked the sisters up and down, letting his eyes linger on their bodies.

"Like what you see?" Bernie demanded.

"Not bad," Chung allowed. "Lucky for the two of you, you guys take after your mother in the looks department," he stated. "I'd hate to see you with your dad's nose."

"It's Roman," Libby said.

"It's large," Chung replied.

"So you believe in visiting the sins of the fathers on the sons . . . daughters?" Bernie asked.

Chung snorted. "That's very biblical of you."

"Seriously," Libby said. "We haven't done anything to you."

Chung frowned, the fake bonhomie gone. "But your father has."

Now it was Bernie's turn to snort. "He was doing his job."

"Is that what he told you?"

"You mean, he wasn't?" Bernie demanded. "It's not his fault that he was good at his job and you weren't good at yours."

"Really," Chung said.

"Yes, really," Bernie said.

Chung put his hands on his hips and leaned forward. "Where do you get that from?" he demanded.

"Obviously, if you were good at stealing, you wouldn't have gotten caught twice," Bernie pointed out.

"Besides, we're nothing like him," Libby said, deciding to change the conversational course.

"Not true," Chung told her.

"How are we like him?" Libby asked.

"Yeah. In what way?" Bernie inquired.

Chung thought for a moment and said, "Maybe I was wrong. Maybe you're not. After all, you guys play detective, which I imagine is why you're here now. Only that was your dad's job. You guys are amateurs. This is your . . . what is the word I'm looking for?" Chung tilted his head and pretended to think. He snapped his fingers. "Wait. I've got it. Hobby. Yes, *hobby* is the word I'm looking for."

"We help people out," Bernie said stiffly.

"If that's what you want to call it," Chung told them.

"What do you call it?" Bernie wanted to know.

Chung smirked. "I call it being nosy. You know what they say: curiosity killed the cat . . ."

". . . but satisfaction brought it back," Bernie said, finishing the rhyme.

"How do you know we're here about Margo, anyway?" Libby demanded. "We never said we were. We could be here about the Austin Healey."

Chung sniggered. "Right. Of course, you are. You think I'm stupid?" Chung continued. "You think I don't hear things?"

"Like what," Libby asked.

"Like get out of here," Chung said, and he looked at his phone again. "I'm done talking to the two of you."

"Works for me," Bernie said, and she grabbed her sister by her arm and started pulling her toward the door. "Come on, Libby. Let's go. This is obviously a waste of time."

Chung threw his hands in the air. "Duh. Finally, she gets it."

When she got to the door, Bernie turned. "My dad was right," she told Chung. "You are a jerk." And she hurried outside.

"What was that about?" Libby asked Bernie once they were outside, Libby practically running to keep up with her sister as Bernie headed for Mathilda. "I don't get what the hurry is."

"Simple," Bernie answered. "It just occurred to me that since Jason was willing to talk to us, why are we wasting our time on Tommy Chung? If we're lucky, maybe we can catch Jason at Starbucks."

Libby nodded her approval. "And maybe he'll talk to us there."

Bernie opened the van door. "Exactly."

"You do have your moments," Libby allowed.

"Nice of you to say so," Bernie said, getting into the driver's seat as Libby hopped into the van.

She put the van in gear and zoomed out of the parking lot before Libby had time to put her seat belt on. There was only one Starbucks in the immediate area, and it was less than five minutes away, unlike two others that were fifteen- and twenty-five-minute drives from Freelander's. Bernie was hoping Jason was still there, which was a good possibility, since the place was usually both packed and understaffed, so service tended to be glacial. Bernie was praying that would be the case now.

Chapter 12

"**I** think we're in luck," Bernie said, surveying the parking lot.

It was filled with vehicles crammed into every possible nook and cranny, so Bernie dropped Libby off at the door with instructions to find Jason, while she looked for a parking space. Fortunately, the parking gods were smiling; a moment later, someone pulled out and Bernie maneuvered the van into the vacant spot. It was a tight fit, and she had just enough room to open Mathilda's door partway and inch her way out.

When Bernie walked inside, she could see the place was even busier than usual. For a moment, she felt a brief pang of envy. A little more business to fill in the gaps at A Little Taste of Heaven wouldn't hurt. As she watched everyone patiently waiting to get their caffeine fix, she decided she didn't need a cappuccino after all. It wasn't worth the wait.

There was a long line of people standing in front of the ORDER HERE sign, a large cluster of customers waiting to pick up their orders, and an even larger number of folks hunting for a place to sit down, since all the seats seemed to be taken by people reading, talking on their phones, or working on their laptops. After looking around for a minute, Bernie spotted Libby. Partially hidden by a display rack of tea tins, she was sitting at a corner table, over by the window, across from Jason.

"Not in a hurry to get back, I see," she said to Jason once she'd threaded her way to their table.

Jason colored. "Just taking a break," he mumbled, ripping open a third packet of sugar and stirring it into his coffee.

"I can see why you would need one," Bernie said. "Your boss can't be very nice to work for."

"He's okay," Jason told her in a voice that lacked conviction. He put the lid on his coffee cup and reached for his boss's drink. "I shouldn't be talking to you," Jason said, starting to get up.

Bernie put a hand on Jason's shoulder and gently pushed him back down into his seat. "Your boss won't know."

Jason shook his head. "You'd be surprised what he knows."

"He won't know if you don't tell him," Libby assured him.

Jason looked down at the table and bit his lip.

Bernie took her hand off his shoulder and sat down next to him. "Look around. Is there anyone here your boss knows?"

Jason did as instructed. "I don't think so," he said after he'd scanned the crowd.

"Alright then," Libby told him. "It's not a problem."

"It is a problem because Mr. Chung knows a lot of people," Jason protested, "and I don't know who he knows. Someone could see me and tell him." Then another idea occurred to him. "And what if Mr. Chung comes looking for me?" Jason asked. "What then?"

"He won't come looking for you," Libby assured him. "He'd have to close the shop, and even if he did—worst-case scenario—so what? We ran into each other by accident. We're just talking, about cars in general. It's not a big deal."

"It will be to him," Jason predicted. "Mr. Chung would never buy that story. He doesn't like not being listened to."

"I see," Bernie said, studying Jason's face. He'd developed a small twitch under his left eye. "Why are you scared of him?"

"I'm not," Jason protested.

"You sure seem as if you are to me," Bernie told him.

"And me too," Libby said. She smiled at him. "Tell us what's going on," she urged.

"Nothing, really," Jason said. "It's just that Chung has a real bad temper, and I don't like being around when he loses it."

"Does he lose it a lot?" Bernie asked.

"Enough," Jason replied. "He's really easy to piss off."

"Has he ever hit you?" Libby asked gently.

Jason shook his head. "Nothing like that. But he's very loud when he's mad. And, like I said, he gets mad a lot."

"And he's big," Bernie added. "There is that."

Jason glared at her. "I know I'm skinny," he told her. "You don't have to rub it in."

"That's not what I meant," Bernie assured him. "I'm sorry you took it that way."

"It's okay," Jason allowed after a minute had passed. "He always calls me Little Man. It gets to me after a while."

"Jason, is there anything else about Chung my sister and I should know?" Bernie asked.

Jason answered immediately. "Yeah. He's got these sketchy friends. I think he was in jail or something. At least, that's what one of the guys who works at the shop told me." He shrugged. "I guess, when it comes down to it, it's just easier not to piss Chung off," Jason explained. He was about to say something else when his phone pinged. He took it out and looked at it. Then he showed it to Bernie, who in turn showed it to Libby. Libby read the text. *Where the hell are you, Little Man? You'd better get your ass back here now.* It was from Chung.

"Nice," Libby said, handing Jason's phone back to him. He put it in his pocket and started to get up again.

This time, Bernie didn't stop him. Instead, she and Libby got up as well and followed him out to the parking lot.

"We just want to know about Margo Hemsley's cars," Bernie told him as they walked him over to his vehicle, a beat-up old Civic with a dented front bumper.

"I don't know what you're talking about," Jason insisted as he got his keys out of his pants pocket.

"Your friend Sid says different," Libby said.

"Well, he's wrong," Jason told her.

Bernie reached into her pocketbook and came out with her wallet. "Listen," she said, "all we want to know is what kind of cars Margo had and whether she stored them with you guys. That's it. And whatever you tell us stays with us."

"We promise," Libby said.

"Why do you care anyway?" Jason asked.

"Because it might lead to something else," Bernie explained.

"Like what?" Jason asked.

"Like the fact that she was murdered," Libby answered.

Jason made a face. "You really believe that?" he asked.

"That's what we're getting paid to find out," Libby replied.

"She was a nice lady," Jason said.

"Exactly," Bernie replied as she drew out five twenties and fanned them out. "I've got a hundred bucks that can be yours if you tell us what we need to know."

"Just like in the detective stories," Jason observed as he reached out his hand for the cash.

"Now, now," Bernie said, drawing her hand back. "You tell me first, and then I'll give you the money, just like in the detective stories."

Jason looked around the parking lot. He didn't see anyone he knew. "Fine," he said, opening the Civic's door.

Bernie and Libby waited.

"Fine, what?" Libby asked when the silence had gone on longer than it should have.

"I don't know why Mr. Chung is making such a big deal about this anyway. It's not like it's a state secret or anything," Jason whined. "Everything is such a big deal with him. It's not like he's doing anything illegal or anything like that."

"The vehicles," Libby prompted.

"Margo Hemsley has three in storage. A Jag, a Rolls, and a Lexus."

Bernie whistled. "Not bad. Not bad at all."

"I know," Jason said. "That woman really had a thing for cars. Most women don't. At least, not like that, not the ones I know anyway."

"So the vehicles are in storage over at Chung's place?" Bernie repeated.

Jason nodded. "That's what I said." And he reached for the money.

"Not so fast," Bernie told him. "Where is this place?"

"You can't get in," Jason told Bernie quickly. "Chung's got cameras and stuff set up all over the place."

"I didn't say we were going to try and get in," Bernie said. "I just want to know where Margo's vehicles are being stored."

Jason swallowed. Bernie noticed his left foot was going up and down.

"Because?" he asked.

Bernie crossed her arms over her chest. "Because I do, Jason. That's reason enough. You want your money?"

Jason nodded again.

"Then tell me."

"Okay. Fine. I was just trying to keep you out of trouble," he muttered.

"What I think is that you're trying to keep yourself out of trouble," Libby observed.

"What's wrong with that?" Jason demanded.

"Chung's not going to know you told us," Bernie reassured Jason.

Libby pointed to Bernie. "And don't worry about us. My sister and I can take care of ourselves."

"You don't know Chung," Jason told Bernie, as he drew a half circle on the blacktop with his right foot.

"And you don't know us," Libby told him.

Bernie studied Jason for a minute. He was looking at a spot on the ground. *He's trying to decide*, she thought, as she held up the hundred dollars and said, "Do you or do you not want the money? If you don't want to tell us, that's okay. We'll just walk away."

Jason looked up. He took a deep breath and let it out. "One-fifty," he proposed. "Make it one fifty, and we have a deal."

"One fifteen," Bernie said. "And that's it."

"I'll take it," Jason said. He watched as Bernie took another fifteen dollars out of her wallet. He swallowed. "Alright. Don't say I didn't warn you. Chung's place is located behind Pepino's Pizza Palace."

Bernie and Libby nodded. They both knew Pepino's. It was run by a Russian guy and his son.

"The one in Julius Plaza?" Bernie asked, just to make sure.

"Their chicken wings are really good, but their pizza isn't so great," Libby noted. "The couple of times I've bought a slice, the crust was soggy, and there wasn't enough cheese."

"Their garlic knots are pretty good, though," Jason told her. "They use real chopped-up garlic and butter. Definitely worth the trip."

"Thanks," Libby said. "I'll bear that in mind."

"I hate to interrupt," Bernie said, "but where exactly is this place?" She didn't remember seeing any structure there that looked as if it could accommodate one vehicle, let alone three.

Jason told her. "There's this dirt road—well, it's really more of a path—on the right side of Pepino's. It's the back way. Follow the path, and you'll get to where you want to go."

"What about the front way?" Libby asked.

Jason shook his head. "Too visible. Honestly," he said in response to Libby and Bernie's skeptical expressions.

"If you say so," Bernie said, and she gave Jason his money and thanked him.

"You won't be thanking me if Chung catches you," Jason warned as he got into his vehicle. The next minute, he was out of the parking lot, driving down Colvin Avenue faster than he should have been.

"Curiouser and curiouser," Bernie murmured as she watched him go.

"That Margo owns those vehicles or the place where they're being stored?" her sister asked.

"Both," Bernie replied. "Definitely both."

Chapter 13

As it turned out, the information Jason had given Bernie and Libby about Chung's auto-storage unit being monitored was correct.

"Look at those," Bernie said, pointing to the four cameras semi-hidden in the maple trees on either side of the path. "Jason wasn't kidding."

"It makes one wonder," Libby said,

"Yes, it does," Bernie agreed. "Either Chung is paranoid, or he has something to hide, or both."

She and her sister were standing halfway down what was little more than a deeply rutted path to the one-story, cinder-block structure down below. One look and Bernie had decided to park Mathilda in the lot in front of the pizza place and proceed down on foot, because even if she could maneuver their van down the steep path, there was a good chance she wouldn't be able to get Mathilda back up. The path was too muddy from all the rain that had fallen in the last few days.

"And there are probably more cameras we can't see," Bernie added. "In fact, I'd make book on that. You'd think this place was Fort Knox."

"Not to mention tick central," Libby said, noting the long grass on either side of the path and wishing she was wearing long pants. "I wonder if Chung is storing anything else in there as well."

"Good question," Bernie replied. "Given his security system, it wouldn't surprise me if he were. But getting a car down here"—she indicated the path to the building with a sweep of her hand and shook her head—"I don't know. It looks pretty iffy to me."

"Jason did say this is the back entrance," Libby reminded her sister.

"Yeah, well, this one is not exactly tailor made for vehicles. It would be quite the job getting them in and out of here, especially low-slung ones."

"Do you think Chung is watching us now?" Libby asked, indicating one of the cameras with a nod of her head.

"The idea had crossed my mind," Bernie told her.

"Maybe it's time to leave," Libby said, picturing Chung getting into his car and racing over—and doing what? Maybe nothing. Probably nothing. But she didn't want to find out.

"Yeah. We've pretty much seen everything there is to see anyway," Bernie agreed. "At least for the moment. Although," she reflected after another minute had gone by, "it would be interesting to see what the front of the building looks like, where the main entrance is, never mind what's inside of it."

Libby gave her sister the stink eye. "Don't even think of breaking in."

"I wasn't," Bernie protested, even though she had been entertaining the idea. "I was just expressing an opinion."

"Because this is way, way above your pay grade."

Bernie put her hand on her chest. "I'm hurt. Deeply hurt."

Libby snorted. "Of course, you are." Then she changed the subject. "Really," she said, studying her surroundings for the second time, "unless you'd heard about it, you'd never know this place exists."

"No, you wouldn't," Bernie replied. "Maybe that's the idea," Bernie observed as she followed her sister back up the hill, pausing now and then to pull one or the other of her heels out of the dirt it had become lodged in. Thank heaven, she wasn't wearing her new Chanel mules. "And then there's the question of why Margo's vehicles are here instead of her garage. She certainly had room for them in there." She reconsidered. "Well, maybe just two. No. One."

Libby brushed a sumac branch away from her face. "Because she was hiding them? Because she didn't want anyone to know they existed? At least, that would be my guess."

Bernie came up with another option. "Or because they're extremely valuable and there's better security here at Chung's place."

"This may also be true," Libby agreed. "Maybe Margo bought them as an investment," Libby posited. "I read a Rolls Phantom was auctioned off for four million recently."

Bernie whistled.

"I know," Libby said. "Crazy, right?"

"Margo doesn't look like someone who has that kind of money," Bernie noted as she waved away a wasp that was flying around her head.

Libby thought about Margo's house and her clothes and car. "Maybe she's one of those people who don't spend any money on themselves and invest it all."

"Frugal," Bernie interjected.

"Then they die, and you find out they owned two million dollars' worth of real estate and lived in a tiny bungalow," Libby continued.

"Like dad's Aunt Margaret," Bernie said. "Except she didn't live in a bungalow; she lived in the basement of a two-story house and rented out the upper floors."

"Then it turns out she was worth three million, which she willed to some museum in Illinois."

"A railroad museum. Yeah," Bernie said. "Who knows? Or Margo could have bought Facebook or Apple stock when it first came out. She'd be a millionaire many times over by now if she had. I'll tell you one thing, she sure didn't get that kind of money from her job. Or," Bernie continued, another idea occurring to her, "Margo could have inherited money. She could be a trust-fund baby."

"I wonder if the people in the Longely Mystery Book Club would know?" Libby slapped at a mosquito. By now, she and her sister had reached the parking lot.

"That should be easy enough to find out," Bernie said, and she took out her cell and called Gilda Westover. When Gilda answered, Bernie put her on speaker phone and asked about the cars.

"What cars?" Gilda inquired, sounding puzzled.

Bernie explained. There was a moment of silence, then Gilda said, "Are you sure?"

"Pretty sure," Bernie told her, thinking of her source.

"Well, it's news to me, if it's true," Gilda said. "Margo ran around in that beat-up Camry of hers for a reason. She couldn't afford to get another car. She was hoping she could get the Camry to last for another year." There was a slight pause, and then Gilda continued. "There must be some mistake. Has to be. You must be talking about someone else. Margo would never own a Lexus or a Jag, let alone a Rolls. She hated anything that showy. I don't know where you got your information, but whoever told you this is lying to you. Definitely lying. You should check them out."

"I'll do that," Bernie promised, as she shifted her cell to her other hand. "Another question. Did Margo have family money?"

"No," Gilda said. "Absolutely not. Her mom and dad owned a candy store in the Bronx off of Pelham Parkway. Margo went to school on a scholarship. Her parents couldn't have afforded to send her. And they would never have sent her to art school anyway. Too frivolous. And then, of course, they died."

"Was there insurance money?" Bernie inquired.

"Not as far as I know," Gilda replied.

"Margo own stocks? Bonds?" Libby asked. "Was she good at playing the market?"

Gilda laughed. "Hardly. Margo didn't know a put from a call. The only thing she was interested in was art. That's what she lived and breathed. She didn't have stocks or bonds or lots of money. And she didn't want any, either. She was perfectly content with the way things were, the way her life was going. More than content, actually. She had her work and a few good friends, and that was enough for her. She didn't want anything else. What you're saying is ridiculous." And, with that, she hung up.

"Gilda seems pretty sure of herself," Libby remarked as Bernie slipped her cell back in her bag.

"Yes, she does," Bernie replied. "But perhaps Gilda doesn't know Margo as well as she thinks she does."

"Also a possibility," Libby allowed. "But leaving Gilda's reaction aside . . ."

"We come back to why would Margo be hiding those cars."

"Same answers as before." Bernie tapped her nails on her thigh. "Because she doesn't want anyone to know she has them, or because they're too valuable to keep in her garage, or both."

"Which brings us back to our main question: Where did the money to purchase them come from?"

"Where indeed?" Bernie repeated. "Margo is certainly turning out to be . . . interesting. There was definitely a lot more going on with her than her friends knew about."

"Which might be what got her killed," Libby said.

Bernie nodded. "I'm thinking we missed something when we were at Margo's house. We should go back and take another look-see."

"Agreed. But before we do, let's have a brief word with Yuri. Maybe he knows something about Chung's building," Libby suggested.

"Not to mention buy some chicken wings," Bernie said.

"And try his garlic knots," Libby added. "Don't forget that." In her mind, there was no such thing as too much garlic.

Pepino's Pizza Palace was empty, and Yuri was leaning against the counter, watching the news on TV, when Libby and Bernie walked in. Yuri smiled when he saw them. "This is an unexpected pleasure."

Libby and Bernie smiled back.

"What brings you over to this side of town, ladies? Can I get you a couple of slices? I just made a fresh pie with pepperoni and sausage."

"Thanks. That sounds good, but we'll take a dozen grilled wings and a couple of garlic knots instead," Libby told him.

"We ate lunch a little while ago," Bernie explained.

"It's okay," Yuri said. He threw twelve half-cooked wings on the grill. "You won't hurt my feelings. I know my pizza isn't up to your standards, but people seem to like it. Business is good." He shrugged his shoulders. "Go figure." He chuckled. "Who would have thought a guy from Ukraine, who never had a slice of pizza when he was a kid, would end up owning a pizza shop?" He nudged a wing toward the middle of the grill with the edge of his tongs. "Now, what can I do for you lovely ladies, besides get you something to eat, that is?"

Libby told him.

Yuri shook his head. "Sorry. I know Chung owns that building, but that's about it. It was here when I bought this place. The realtor told me some guy had built it for his son; he wanted to make soap or something, but he couldn't get the necessary permits, so that was that. A couple of years ago, I tried to buy it off Chung. I thought it would make a good warehouse, but Chung didn't want to sell."

"Did he tell you why?" Libby asked.

"Nope." Yuri took two garlic knots and put them on a plate, then he turned the wings and brushed them with a mixture of olive oil, lemon juice, red pepper flakes, and parsley. "He just told me he wasn't interested."

"Anything else?" Bernie inquired.

"About the building? Not really," Yuri told her. "Occasionally, I see SUVs going up and down that path Chung calls a road. He doesn't want to fix it." Yuri frowned. "Says he doesn't want to spend the money. I'm surprised he hasn't gotten stuck on it." He pointed to himself. "I sure wouldn't drive my car down there, that's for sure. But then Chung usually is driving his old Range Rover, so I guess it doesn't matter. That vehicle's a beast."

"Does he go down there a lot?" Bernie asked.

Yuri scratched his neck while he thought. "Not very

often. Why should he, when he can come in through Applewood? But it's not like I'm looking out the window, watching. You know what it's like in this business."

Bernie and Libby nodded. They did.

Yuri continued. "Most days, I hardly have time to breathe, let alone take in the view. And I'm not here all the time, either. We close at eight and open at ten. We do a big lunch business," he explained, catching Libby's quizzical expression, "but there's not much going on here after six."

Then he turned and plucked the wings off the grill with the metal tongs, plopped them down on a paper plate, and put them on the counter. Libby reached into her bag for her wallet, but Yuri shook his head. "Don't be silly. They're on me," he said.

"Come in for coffee and a cookie or a muffin next time you're on our side of town," Libby told him.

Yuri grinned. "I hear your cinnamon rolls are excellent."

"They're not bad," Libby allowed.

"Good. And sorry I couldn't be more help."

"It was a long shot," Bernie said.

"These look great," Libby added, pointing to the wings.

Then she and Bernie thanked Yuri and sat down at one of the tables to eat. The wings were perfect. Slightly charred on the outside, with crisp skin, tender meat, and a slight kick from the red pepper flakes, while the garlic knots were soft and buttery.

"This was excellent," Libby told Yuri after they'd finished. "Really, really good."

Yuri grinned. "My pleasure. And if I hear anything, I'll let you know."

Bernie thanked him, threw the plates away, and wiped her hands on a couple of napkins, after which she and Libby headed out the door.

"Those were good chicken wings," Libby said when they got outside.

"Yes, they were," Bernie agreed. "They were good enough to merit a return trip."

"Maybe we could make them in the shop," Libby mused. "It would be an easy add-on. There's practically no prep time involved."

"True. But," here Bernie held up a finger, "even factoring that in, we still don't have the manpower. We'd have to hire an extra person to man the grill, not to mention the fact that we'd have to reconfigure the kitchen to be able to fit the grill in."

"We could fry the wings."

"Grilling is what makes them so good," Bernie pointed out.

"We could use the grill for other things," Libby suggested.

"I suppose we could," Bernie conceded.

"Like grilled-cheese sandwiches and hamburgers and fried eggs," Libby said.

"Agreed," Bernie replied, "but then we'd have to put in a new fire-suppression system."

"I hadn't thought about that," Libby admitted, thinking of the cost.

"We can do the math on our way back to Margo's house."

Libby made a face. "And I thought we were done."

"This is why we get paid the big bucks."

"Uh-oh," Libby said, putting her hand to her mouth.

Bernie turned toward her sister. "What's uh-oh?" Bernie asked.

"You're not going to like this," Libby warned.

"Like what?"

"I locked the back door on the way out."

"At least you remembered before we got there," Bernie said. She looked at her watch. They had just enough time to run back to the flat, grab her lock picks, and return to Margo's place.

Chapter 14

Fifteen minutes later, Bernie and Libby were back at Margo's house.

"I'm glad Dad wasn't home," Libby observed.

"Me too," Bernie said, thinking of what he would have said about the endeavor they were about to embark on.

Except for the hum of a lawn mower off in the distance, the neighborhood was quiet, the empty houses standing sentinel over the street. The wind had picked up, rustling the leaves of the aspen and maple trees. Dark clouds were scudding across the sky. It looked as if a storm was coming.

The neighbor's dog two doors down barked as Bernie drove up Margo's driveway and parked the van as close to the back door as possible. She figured that way no one would be able to see them from the street. In the park, a soccer game was going on in the far corner of the field, the shouts of the players and spectators floating in on the breeze.

Two squirrels chittered at Bernie and Libby from the branch of an overhead oak as the sisters got out of the van. Once again, Libby noted the long grass and the disheveled laurel hedge.

"I think we can deduce that no one is mowing the grass or keeping the hedge in check," Libby observed as she got out of the van and started for the back stairs.

Bernie followed. "This is why we're brilliant detectives," she replied as she climbed the stairs.

"Why?" Libby asked.

"Because we notice things like that," Bernie said, fumbling in her bag for her set of lock picks. She found them and pulled them out. "Here we go," she said as she chose a pick and inserted it into the lock. It didn't work. She tried another. That one didn't work, either.

"Are we losing our touch?" Libby asked sweetly.

Bernie sniffed. "Hardly," she replied as she inserted the third pick in the lock, tried to turn it, and failed.

"I hear the third time's the charm," Libby chirped. "Evidently, they were wrong."

"Evidently," Bernie said through gritted teeth. She was not amused.

The remaining two picks didn't work. Bernie frowned. First her hair dryer had broken, then she'd used salted instead of unsalted butter in the peach blueberry galette, and now this. It was definitely one of those days.

"You should have kept Brandon's," Libby observed.

"Possibly," Bernie allowed. She shook her head. She couldn't figure out why these weren't working. She examined the lock. There were no scratches on it, nor were there any marks on the doorframe. "I suppose we could always break a window," Bernie mused.

Libby held out her hand. "Let me try."

"Really?" Bernie asked.

"Yes, really," Libby replied.

"What happened to the 'we shouldn't be doing this' mantra you always fling at me?"

"It's better than breaking a window," Libby pointed out.

Bernie shrugged. "I suppose you're right. That's so dé-classé."

"Not to mention obvious," Libby said as Bernie switched places and handed Libby the lock picks. "Be my guest." Then she watched as Libby picked one at random, inserted it in the lock, and wiggled it around.

"Son of a bitch," Bernie cried as she heard the telltale click.

Libby buffed her nails against her shirt. "When you've got it, you've got it."

"Beginner's luck," Bernie grumbled as Libby returned the set to her.

"If that's what you want to think," Libby replied smugly.

"We'll see what happens next time," Bernie told her.

"There's not going to be a next time," Libby replied. "I'm doing what Mom always said to do. I'm quitting while I'm ahead." Then she turned back to the door. "Here we go," she said as she pushed it open and stepped inside Margo's studio. Bernie followed, closing the door behind her.

For a moment, neither of the women said anything. They were too stunned. This was not what they'd expected. This wasn't the way things had looked the last time they'd been here. Sometime between then and now, someone had ransacked Margo's house.

Finally, Libby said, "Whoever is going to clean this up certainly has their work cut out for them."

"An understatement if there ever was one," Bernie observed. Then she added, "Margo wouldn't be happy to see this."

"No, she wouldn't. She'd be completely devastated. Unfortunately, that's not her problem now," Libby noted as she took in the full magnitude of the scene in front of her.

Paints, charcoals, and pastels were scattered over the floor, leaving a kaleidoscope of colors in their wake. All the cabinet drawers had been taken out of the cabinet, dumped, and piled on top of each other on the floor. The blank canvases that had been stacked neatly against the wall were strewn around the floor, as were the pictures that had been hanging on the wall. In addition, someone had slit open the seat cushions that had been on the sofa in the room's far corner.

"I guess we're a little late to the party," Bernie observed.

"I guess we are. Whatever party this was," Libby said. Then she added, "And I, for one, am glad we are. I wouldn't like to meet whoever did this." She thought of Chung.

"I wonder if Chung had anything to do with this?" Bernie asked, echoing her sister's thoughts. "Maybe that's why he was acting the way he was."

"Could be," Libby replied. "And then there's the man in the red truck. I wonder if he figures into this."

"He could. Maybe he's working for Chung," Bernie replied.

"Well, he's definitely not cutting the grass or trimming the bushes," Libby observed. There were too many possibilities, she thought, which was precisely the problem. She took a couple of steps forward and stopped. "I wonder if whoever did this found what they were looking for?"

"I wonder what it was they were looking for?" Bernie said. She tapped her fingers on her thighs while she considered the debacle in front of her. First the vehicles, and now this. It was becoming apparent to her that there was a lot more to Margo than met the eye.

"I wonder how they got in," Libby said, interrupting Bernie's train of thought.

"I imagine the same way we did. They didn't break a window."

"Either that or they had a key," Libby suggested, opening up another set of possibilities.

"That too," Bernie answered. She shook her head as she took in the scene in front of her. "We should take off our shoes before we go any farther," she suggested. "The last thing we need to do is leave shoe prints."

"I don't know if bare feet are any better."

"I have just the thing," Bernie said, remembering the pairs of flipflops she'd left in the van from her last few pedicures. She was back a moment later and handed a pair to Libby, who put them on, leaving her shoes on a clean spot by the door. "And you said pedicures were a waste of time."

"No. I said I didn't like people I didn't know touching my feet."

"That's not what you said," Bernie protested.

"Fine," Libby replied, although she was positive that's exactly what she'd said. She changed the topic. "Whoever did this was pretty thorough," Libby observed, carefully walking around the edge of the floor, trying to keep clear of the paint and pastels as she went into Margo's kitchen.

Things were just as bad in the kitchen. The oven door was open, as were the doors of the refrigerator and the freezer. Ice cubes melted on the floor, and the contents of a quart of milk swirled on the linoleum, around a blob of mayonnaise. Everything was out of the kitchen cabinets and either on the floor or the counters. There was a mound of flour dumped on the counter and a smaller mound of sugar next to it, followed by a ripped bag of panko bread crumbs scattered over everything. For some reason, the bread crumbs reminded Bernie of sand, making her wish she was in Montauk or Cape May or Santa Cruz.

The rest of the house wasn't much better. All the pieces of upholstered furniture had been cut open, their insides ripped out; beds had been overturned and gutted, closets emptied, the contents of drawers and medicine cabinets dumped out. Bernie reflected that whoever had done this had taken their own sweet time. They hadn't been worried that someone would come along and interrupt them.

Chapter 15

"I don't think they, whoever they are, found what they were looking for," Bernie said to Libby as they headed back downstairs, where it was slightly cooler, the heat of the day having collected within the walls of the house.

"What makes you say that?" Libby asked.

"Because, otherwise, whoever did this would have stopped. But they didn't. They started in the studio, went into the kitchen, proceeded to search the rest of the downstairs, then went upstairs and tried their luck there." Bernie thought of the bedrooms. The destruction seemed to get worse with each successive room; the cuts to the mattresses and the chairs were longer and deeper. It was as if the person or persons doing the looking became more frenzied, or perhaps the word was *frustrated*, as they went.

Libby chewed on the inside of her cheek. "Whatever they were looking for had to be small enough to fit in a bag of flour or be taped to the back of a painting," she observed, thinking of what she'd seen.

"Or sewn into the inside of a sofa cushion," Bernie noted.

"Which leaves a wide range of possibilities," Libby said. She sighed. "So, if I were Margo, where would I hide something?"

Bernie shook her head. She didn't know. "She read all those mysteries. Maybe she got an idea from one of them."

"Maybe," Libby said. "In truth, whatever it is could be anywhere. It could be in a safe-deposit box, for all we know. For that matter, it could be in the glove compartment of the Rolls Margo is storing at Chung's."

"But it's probably here," Bernie said. "At least, the person doing the searching thought it was here."

"Maybe that's because whoever tossed the house didn't know about Margo's vehicles."

"That too is a possibility," Bernie conceded. "After all, no one else seems to." She corrected herself. "At least Gilda didn't."

"You think Gilda's lying?"

"No, I don't," Bernie replied, after thinking over her answer to her sister's question. "I have no reason to think that. On the other hand . . ."

"You never know," Libby said, finishing her sister's sentence for her.

Bernie nodded. "Exactly." It was a lesson she and her sister had learned the hard way.

"Well, I'll tell you one thing," Libby said. "We're not breaking into Chung's storage facility to find out."

"Not without some heavy-duty stuff," Bernie agreed before she reached for her phone and called Betsy. "If you wanted to hide something, where would you put it?" she asked Betsy when Betsy picked up.

"Why are you asking?" Betsy replied. She sounded bemused.

Bernie explained.

"That's terrible," Betsy exclaimed, "Margo would be beyond upset. I don't understand."

"Neither do we," Bernie confessed.

"Gilda told me about the cars," Betsy continued. "You think you know someone . . ." Her voice trailed off. Bernie waited. She heard Betsy take a deep breath and let it out. "I have to tell you, I was never good with the mystery part of mysteries. That's why I like to read them. They always surprise me." *Great*, Bernie thought, as Betsy continued. "But usually in the books we read, the weapon is hidden in plain sight, like in a can of ground coffee that's stored in the freezer."

Bernie thought of the famous leg of lamb episode in *Alfred Hitchcock Presents* in which the wife kills the husband with a frozen leg of lamb, then roasts it and serves it for dinner.

"Agatha Christie was Margo's favorite author, if that helps," Betsy told her. "She always liked the classics. Except for Sherlock Holmes and Dorothy Sayers. She didn't like them at all."

"Ask Betsy what Margo's favorite book was," Libby instructed Bernie. She'd been following the conversation.

Bernie did.

"I'm pretty sure it was *Death on the Nile*," Betsy replied. "But I don't see how that will help you much. I don't think anyone hid anything in that book, although I could be wrong."

"What was the last book the group read," Bernie asked Betsy.

"*The Witch Elm* by Tana French. Margo thought it was pretty good."

"I did too," Bernie told her.

"Ditto," Betsy said. Then she added, "Maybe whoever did this was after the Eakins as well."

"Doubtful. After all, they weren't here the first time Libby and I looked," Bernie reminded her.

Betsy sighed. "God, I wish I knew what Margo did with those paintings. Margo was always so responsible, too. What happened to her?"

"That is the question you hired us to answer, isn't it?" Bernie replied.

"Betsy still asking about the Eakins?" Libby asked after Bernie had hung up.

Bernie nodded. "I wonder how much those paintings are worth?"

"Enough," Libby said, who'd googled them. And she told her sister what she'd found out. She fanned herself with the edge of her hand. "What do you think happened to them?"

Bernie shook her head. She didn't have a clue.

"Maybe there's a secret panel or passageway some-where and Margo hid whatever it was in there," Libby suggested, thinking of what Betsy had said to her sister.

Bernie grimaced. "Because fifties houses come with them, just like fog-shrouded mansions on deserted islands do?"

"She could have had one made," Libby pointed out, thinking of panic rooms. "People do."

"I guess it wouldn't hurt to look," Bernie allowed, even though she doubted that was the case. But then she hadn't thought that Margo would be the type of person to own three expensive cars, either.

Twenty minutes later, Libby was ready to concede de-feat. She and her sister had tapped the walls, turned the handle on the thingamajig that opened and closed the fire-place damper, looked for discrepancies between outer and inner spaces, seen if any of the dresser drawers had a false bottom, investigated the attic crawlspace, and gone over the basement and garage with a metaphorical fine-tooth comb. They'd come up dusty and empty-handed. Now they were outside getting ready to get into Mathilda.

"That was a waste of time," Bernie remarked, as she watched a robin dive-bomb a chipmunk. The chipmunk scurried into a hole in the large maple whose leaves were shading the better part of Margo's backyard.

"That robin must have a nest up there," Libby observed as she prepared to get into Mathilda.

"I wonder," Bernie said, recalling what Betsy had said about *The Witch Elm*. If she remembered correctly, the book had featured a hidey-hole in a tree. Maybe Margo had taken a clue from the book, in a manner of speaking.

Chapter 16

"What if we're not looking in the right place?" Bernie said to Libby.

"I think we've exhausted all the possibilities here."

"Maybe not." Bernie tapped her fingernails against her thigh. "What would be the least likely place you would think Margo would hide something?" Bernie asked her sister.

"Australia. The Galapagos."

"Someplace a tad closer to home."

"I don't know."

Bernie grinned and indicated the knothole next to the one the chipmunk had disappeared into. Either one would make a good place to stash something.

"Are you talking about those thingies in the tree?"

"Knotholes. They're called knotholes."

"Whatever they're called, they're pretty high up the tree trunk," Libby observed. "Like maybe ten feet."

"Which is what ladders are for," Bernie retorted as she felt a couple of raindrops on her head. Great. The storm was coming.

"Do you see a ladder?" Libby asked, looking around

the back of the house. "It wouldn't exactly be inconspicuous." In order to reach the knothole, Margo would have had to use a tall ladder. There hadn't been one in the basement, and the only thing in the garage was a folding step stool. "Plus, I can't picture Margo climbing up a ladder that high, much less getting it over there. Those things are heavy."

"Maybe she had help. Or maybe she was desperate. It's amazing what you can do once the adrenaline kicks in," Bernie pointed out.

"We should go before it starts pouring," Libby said as she watched her sister walk over to the tall clumps of weeds growing along the fence that marked the property line between Margo's backyard and the park.

"You can wait in the van if you want," Bernie told her sister she waded into the weeds. "I just want to take a quick look. Maybe Margo stored a ladder back here somewhere." As she took another step through the grass, a swirl of tiny gnats swarmed up in front of her. There was nothing there. Just more weeds and a few stunted scrub trees.

"Come on," Libby urged. "Let's go." She pointed to the black cloud overhead. "It's going to pour. We can come back another time."

"By then it may be too late. Maybe the people who searched Margo's house will get the same idea I did and come back."

"Unlikely," Libby stated.

"But possible," Bernie said as she made her way over to the rusted chain-link fence. There was a clap of thunder. *Libby is right*, Bernie decided. *It really is going to come down*, she thought as she watched the soccer players heading for their vehicles.

She was about to head for Mathilda when she heard a

rustle by her foot. Looking down, she saw something disappearing underneath a stunted fern. *Probably a field mouse*, Bernie thought. Then she realized that the background behind the fern was black, blocking her view of the park. An object of some sort? She reached out her hand and touched it.

She felt plastic, soft plastic, and something hard underneath it. Then she saw black and a small ribbon of red. She smiled. It was a garbage bag—actually two, no, three of them. Heavy-duty ones. Margo had used them instead of a tarp. Bernie pulled, and the garbage bags slid off, revealing a tall ladder.

"I found it," Bernie called back to her sister as she struggled to untangle the ladder from the weeds that were growing around it. By now, it was raining harder, the drops bouncing off of Mathilda's windshield. "Come and help me."

"And get wet?"

"Fine, Libby. Be that way. See if I care. Stay in the van," Bernie told her, and she returned to what she'd been doing.

"Works for me," Libby said, her voice lost in a rumble of thunder. She didn't like getting wet to begin with, but she especially didn't like rain pelting on the top of her head. "Let's wait. This should pass soon," she replied, alluding to the storm. "Anyway, there could be lightning. You don't want to be on a ladder when there's lightning."

"The operative word is *could*," Bernie replied as she kept on tugging at the ladder. Libby sighed. She wasn't going to go help her sister. There was no reason she should. That's what she told herself as she got out of the van and headed in Bernie's direction. Guilt. She wished she wasn't so susceptible to it. But she was. And her sister knew it, too. It really sucked.

"You owe me," Libby said to Bernie as Bernie freed the ladder. "You owe me big-time."

"Natch," Bernie told her as she and Libby lifted the ladder up and carried it over to the tree. "God, this thing is heavy," Libby complained as she and her sister unlatched the ladder, opened it up, and placed it as close to the knotholes as they could get it.

There was another clap of thunder.

"You really are nuts," Libby told Bernie.

"So you've always said," Bernie told her as she took off her shoes and started climbing. The ladder wobbled underneath her when she was on the seventh rung. "Libby," she cried.

"I'm doing the best I can," Libby told her as she sneezed and blinked water out of her eyes.

"Do better," Bernie said. She took a deep breath and took another step while Libby leaned in and braced the ladder against the tree.

"You should come down," Libby told her sister. "The ground is uneven. I don't know how much longer I can hold this thing."

"It'll be fine," Bernie said, and she kept climbing. "This should do it," she said as she reached the second rung before the top. She stretched out her hand. Nope. Too far away. She climbed onto the final rung. This will work, she decided, as she reached out her hand again. Her fingers touched the rim of the knothole, the bark rough and pebbled underneath her fingers.

She was thinking that she'd better be right when a chipmunk stuck his head out of the knothole next to the one Bernie was touching and chittered angrily at her. Bernie stared at him, and he stared at her. Then he ducked his head back into the knothole.

"He's probably getting reinforcements," Libby said.

"Cute."

"You know, he could have a family in there. An extended family."

"Always so optimistic."

"Realistic," Libby corrected. "I understand rabies shots aren't very pleasant, even if there are fewer of them now than there used to be."

Bernie wiped a couple of raindrops off her cheek. She had a brief vision of a chipmunk hanging off each finger. "Fine." She pointed to a long stick lying a couple of feet away from Libby. "Hand me that, would you?"

"Ah-ha."

"Ah-ha, what?"

"So I'm right."

"Yes. You're right. Satisfied?"

"Satisfied enough." And Libby walked over to where Bernie had pointed. She was picking up the stick when Bernie yelled for help.

"The ladder's falling," Bernie cried.

Libby looked up. Her sister was hugging the tree limb as the ladder swayed from side to side. "Oh, dear."

"Oh, dear? Is that all you have to say?" Bernie demanded.

"How about, hang on. I'll be right there."

"Make it fast," Bernie told her, hugging the tree limb more tightly. It was so thick she could barely get her arms all the way around it. Then she wrapped her legs around the ladder's side rails to try to stabilize it.

Libby ran. "I told you this was a bad idea," she said to her sister as she grabbed the ladder and steadied it.

"Yes, you did," Bernie allowed as she started climbing down. She held out her hand. "Stick, please."

"Don't I even get a thanks?"

"Thanks. Now can I have the stick?"

Libby held the stick out, and Bernie reached out, grabbed it, and started back up the ladder. "Here goes nothing," she said when she reached the second rung before the top. Then she reached over and inserted the stick into the first hole. She heard something—she couldn't identify what—and felt the stick jump in her hand. She was so surprised she let go of it.

"What's going on?" Libby called up.

"I don't know," Bernie said as she picked up one end of the stick and carefully drew it out. "Holy crap," she said, looking at what was on the end of the stick. Then she showed it to Libby.

"I told you," Libby said.

"You were talking about chipmunks, not traps."

"Close enough."

"How can you say that?"

"I just did."

Bernie decided it was time to change the subject. "I'll tell you one thing. Margo wasn't fooling around."

"That's for sure. I thought those things were illegal."

"They should be," Bernie said, looking at the trap. It had split the stick in two. Made for small mammals, it was spring-loaded, designed to hold and crush tiny limbs. She shuddered, thinking about what it would have done to her hand, let alone a squirrel or a chipmunk, as she put the stick half without the trap stuck to it back in the knothole and moved it back and forth and from side to side. When she was sure there was nothing else there, she put her hand in and began to feel around.

"Anything?" Libby called up.

"Not yet," Bernie said. By now, her arm was all the way into the knothole. A moment later, she felt something with the tips of her fingers. She leaned in as far as she could and pulled it toward her.

"Got something," she announced a minute later, as she looked at the gallon plastic freezer bag containing a manila envelope.

Libby sneezed. "It just goes to show . . . You think you know someone . . ."

"Yeah," Bernie agreed as she carefully climbed down the ladder, the rungs made slippery by the rain. "I would have put her down as a safe-deposit box in a bank type of person, but then I wouldn't have figured her for the cars, either."

"I guess she wanted to keep whatever is in the envelope close by."

"Fat lot of good it did her," Bernie said, thinking of how Margo had ended up.

A moment later it stopped raining, and the sun came out.

"Told you we should have waited," Libby said to her sister as she wrung out the front of her T-shirt. Water dripped onto her feet.

Bernie didn't reply. She was too busy looking at what was in the manila envelope.

Chapter 17

The members of the Longely Mystery Book Club stared at what was on the dining room table.

Betsy was the first to speak. "I don't believe it," she said. Her voice was flat, devoid of emotion. "I refuse to believe it."

Her husband, Tom, picked up the passport, read it, reread it, then thumbed through it again, taking note of the dates, before putting it back on the table. He shook his head. "Is this some kind of joke?" he demanded.

"Afraid not," Libby replied.

"It has to be," Gilda said. "People like us, regular people, don't have fake passports. Where would you go to get something like that made?"

"A forger," Bernie replied.

"Do you know one?" Gilda asked.

"Doesn't everyone?" Bernie cracked.

"Seriously?" Gilda replied.

"Not seriously," Libby said, answering for Bernie. What she didn't say was that her father knew someone who did and that he had promised to contact Eckleburger after he called the Longely PD and spoke to his friend Clyde.

Lydia twisted a strand of her hair around her finger. "I saw this coming. I warned Margo this would end badly."

"Stop it, Lydia," Toni Musclow snapped. "This is not the time for your nonsense."

Lydia drew herself up. "It's not nonsense," Lydia protested. "I have a gift."

Toni snorted and touched the cameo she'd pinned to her sundress. "Is that what you're calling it these days?"

Libby interrupted before Lydia could reply. "What do you mean, Lydia?" she asked her. "What would end badly?"

"What I saw," Lydia replied, looking around the table defiantly, daring anyone to interrupt. No one did, although Bernie could see it was taking a great deal of restraint on their part not to. "I saw Margo, and she was traveling to all these places, but there was a black shadow following her. It was tall and dark."

"And handsome?" Irene couldn't help herself from asking.

"I'm serious," Lydia cried.

"That's it, Lydia?" Toni asked, her voice full of suppressed emotion. "That's your great dream?"

Toni's husband, Brad, put out a restraining arm. "Easy, doll. You're upset. Everyone's in shock," he explained to Libby and Bernie.

"Of that I have no doubt," Bernie said. She and her sister certainly had been when they'd looked in the envelope. Or maybe *surprised* was a better word.

"We're usually a lot nicer than this," Brad said.

"I'm sure you are," Bernie replied.

After she and her sister had opened the manila envelope, they'd gone home and shown their dad. While he spoke to his friend Clyde, Bernie and Libby had called an emergency meeting of the LMBC.

It was late, a little after nine, by the time everyone arrived at Steve and Irene Offenbach's house. The house was located at the end of a cul-de-sac that backed up onto the Thruway; the hum of traffic was noticeable, even though the Thruway was hidden by a large concrete retaining wall that New York State had installed years ago.

The Offenbachs' house was on the smaller side—more of a cottage, really—with ivy growing on the front wall and fairy lights flanking the path to the porch. Tonight, everyone was huddled around the oversized dining room table that, along with the chairs, took up most of the room. It had cooled off, the storm having ushered in a cold front, and a pleasant breeze was blowing through the open mullioned windows.

"We copied them from a cottage we stayed at in Suffolk—Suffolk, England—when Irene and I were there on sabbatical," Steve explained when he saw Bernie studying the windows. "They cost a fortune, but it was worth it. We had to wait for over a year to get them. The guy that made them got sick, and then after he recovered, one of his machines broke."

"We're not here for an architectural treatise," Lydia told Steve before he could embark on a lecture of the history of glass windows in homes, which he could do at length since he'd written his PhD thesis on that subject.

"You're right. We're not," Steve agreed. "I'm sorry." He pursued his lips, then picked up a cookie, put it on his plate, broke a piece off, and ate it. "I suppose that, like everyone else, I'm having trouble believing what I'm seeing. I'm not sure what to say or do."

"You can say that again," Gilda said as she readjusted the fringed yellow shawl with bright red flowers she was wearing over her black dress, a shawl that reminded Bernie of something that Frida Kahlo would have worn.

Steve leaned over, picked up the passport, and leafed through it, before putting it back on the table. "France. Germany. The Emirates. Interesting."

"Maybe Margo was working for the CIA," Toni suggested.

Gilda snorted. "Yeah," she said. "She was going to sneak into North Korea, like in that spy story we read where the wife is smuggled in there in a lifeboat so she could rescue her husband."

"Because once she got there, Margo would have no problem passing as Korean," Tom said.

"No need to get sarcastic," Gilda's husband, Harry, told Tom.

Tom shrugged. "I was just trying to introduce a note of reality into the proceedings."

Brad buttoned a button on his polo shirt that had come undone. "I still can't believe this. She lied, and we believed her. We didn't have a clue."

"Why shouldn't we have believed Margo when she said she was going to Vermont to visit an old school friend?" Harry countered. "How could we have known she was going off to Paris . . ."

"Berlin," Tom corrected.

"Okay, Berlin," Harry said. He took a sip of his iced tea and continued. "Not that it makes any difference. The principle is the same." He leaned forward in his chair. "In truth, we had no reason not to believe her. Trust is the foundation of friendship, and Margo was our friend."

"I thought she was," Betsy replied. "I really did." And she made a fist and lightly hit the dining room table with it. Everyone looked at her.

She shook her head. "I don't know. All the mysteries we read. You'd think we'd be better at detecting discrepancies. Better at seeing things. But this happens, and no one knows anything. No one sees anything. It's disturbing."

"People see what they expect to see, even if it's not there," Harry pointed out. "That's a well-known fact. It's what makes witness identification so difficult. Just because we read mysteries doesn't make us exempt; it doesn't make us detectives."

"Speak for yourself," Toni said. "I think my powers of observation are excellent."

"Is that why you missed the guy who was casing our car?" her husband asked.

"He wasn't casing anything," Toni retorted. "You were just being paranoid."

Tom looked around the table, his complexion grayish in the pale yellowish light cast by the ceiling light fixture. "Or maybe someone here knew something and decided not to say anything."

"What are you implying, Tom?" Brad demanded, his jowls shaking slightly.

"I'm not implying anything," Tom replied. "I'm just making an observation. After all, you know what they say what detectives and journalists should do. Check everything twice, and then check it again, even if it was your mother who told you."

"Since we're neither, I don't understand your point," Brad told him.

"Forget it," Tom told him.

Steve's wife, Irene, took Margo's passport and looked through it again. "Why did she choose the name Martha Goodrich?" she mused.

"For Martha Grimes?" Toni suggested.

"Doubtful," Irene said. "She wasn't in love with the Brits."

"My aunt was named Martha," Toni observed. "Not

many women are named Martha these days," Toni continued. "Does the name mean anything to anyone?"

Everyone shook their heads.

"Maybe whoever Margo went to to get her passport
suggested it," Bernie said.

"Could be," Brad replied. "Or maybe they already had
a set of documents attached to the name." He took a bite
of a cookie. "Getting back to what Tom was saying: you
know, it happens all the time in the books we read. Some-
body knows something and, for whatever reason, keeps it
a secret, and as a result someone dies."

"Like Margo did," Betsy said.

"Only this is real," Tom said "This isn't fiction. This
happened to a friend of ours."

Irene studied her hands for a moment, then looked back
up. "Was she a friend?" she asked the table.

"Of course, she was," Brad answered immediately.

"She lied to us," Irene said. "Friends don't lie."

"What planet are you on? You mean you've never lied
to us?" Toni asked.

"Of course I have," Irene replied, thinking of the time
she'd told everyone she had the stomach flu when she'd
just wanted to stay home and binge watch *Stranger Things*.
"But not like Margo did. Everyone tells white lies, but
Margo had a whole different identity. She always seemed
to be so quiet. Someone who didn't like to take chances.
You know, she had her routine, and she stuck with it."

"You don't question people like that," Toni reflected.
"You just assume they're going about their day doing what
they usually do."

"Good point," Libby said.

She and Bernie studied the faces of everyone there. If
anyone did know something germane, they weren't revealing it. Everyone seemed to be in one of various stages of

shock. Libby and Bernie had brought an assortment of cookies, and Steve and Irene had supplied the iced tea, but no one was eating or drinking much. Just a bite here and a sip there. They were all too nonplussed.

Bernie pointed to the passport on the table, the passport with Margo's picture and the name Martha Goodrich, the passport claiming that Martha had been born in Westport, Connecticut. "Did Margo ever mention a Martha Goodrich?"

"Not to me," Toni said.

Everyone agreed with her.

"How about the money?" Libby asked, referring to the $100,000 in hundred-dollar bills they'd found in the envelope.

"What about it?" Brad inquired.

"Did you ever hear her say she was getting an inheritance or coming into money?" Libby asked.

Everyone shook their heads.

"Quite the contrary," Brad said. "In fact, Margo was always complaining about how little money she had."

"And then there are those cars," Gilda said. "Margo was always talking about how stupid it was to spend money on an automobile. I bought an Infinity a couple of years ago, and she never let me forget it, and now you're telling me she spent God knows how much money on cars? That's just nuts."

Everyone nodded.

"How much are they worth, do you reckon?" Steve asked Bernie.

"Honestly, I don't know," Bernie replied. She didn't know much about cars, especially fancy ones. "It depends on the models, but I'd guess a fair chunk of change."

"Where did all the money come from?" Betsy asked.

"That is the question, isn't it?" Brad said. "Certainly

not from Margo's work. She got paid well, but not that well. Unless she was doing work on the side we didn't know about."

"Which is looking more likely," Irene noted.

"Did she have investments?" Libby asked.

Toni smiled ruefully. "Before today, I would have told you she was totally risk-averse."

"Not that I know of," Brad answered.

A moment later, everyone in the group echoed Toni and Brad's sentiments.

"What about that guy Margo stored the cars with?" Betsy said, changing the subject.

"You mean Chung?" Bernie asked.

Betsy nodded.

"He's a really good mechanic," Steve volunteered. "My ex used to take her Porsche to him."

"That's hardly the point," Betsy retorted. She turned back to Bernie. "Do you think he had anything to do with Margo's death? Like maybe he found some stuff in one of her cars, maybe money or something like that, and decided to see if there was more where that came from. So he kidnaps Margo, and when she won't tell him anything, he kills her and makes it look like an accident. Then a couple of days later, he ransacks her house, hoping to find more money."

"He could have killed her by accident," Irene pointed out. "Maybe he didn't mean to."

"What difference does that make?" Tom said. "Dead is dead."

"The law takes motive into account," Harry pointed out.

Gilda held up her hand. "The Case of the Missing Art Restorer."

"That sounds like an Erle Stanley Gardner title," Tom said.

"What's wrong with that?" Gilda asked.

"Nothing," Tom said. "Just making an observation." He indicated Bernie and Libby with a nod of his chin. "Let's hear what these two have to say. After all, that's what we're paying them for."

"Say about what?" Libby asked.

"The scenario Betsy suggested," Tom replied. "Do you think that's likely."

Bernie carefully picked her words. "I think you need more facts before jumping to conclusions," she said. "A lot more facts. You don't want to narrow down the field too quickly," she added. "That's how you miss things."

"Did you tell your dad?" Tom asked.

Both Bernie and Libby nodded. Their dad had been the chief of the Longely Police Department.

"What did he say?" Betsy asked.

"He said the whole thing was interesting," Libby replied.

"Does he think Margo was killed?" Steve asked.

"He's tending toward that conclusion," Bernie answered.

There was another moment of silence. Then Irene said, "I still can't believe it. It's like something out of one of the books we read."

"Only this is real," Tom said.

"So you keep saying," Gilda replied. "But it doesn't feel that way to me. It feels surreal. I keep waiting for Margo to pop up wearing that sweater she always wore with the two missing buttons . . ."

"And those sneakers with the glitter," Toni said.

Betsy laughed. "They were so Miami Beach. Very ironic. Meme-worthy, really. And her car . . . It was always such a mess. It's like she lived in it."

Toni pointed to what was on the table. "I still can't believe that."

"Frankly, neither can I," her husband, Brad, said.

"None of us can," Harry added.

Brad took a sip of his tea and put it down. "This kind of thing doesn't happen to people like us."

"And what kind of people are people like us?" Libby asked.

"You know, middle-class people, professionals," Brad explained.

"People in the arts," Betsy added.

"I don't know why, but I'm thinking about that author who wrote a book about how to kill her husband and then followed the method she'd written about," Toni said. She laughed. "Talk about unclear on the concept."

Harry shook his head. "We should read it."

"What I want to know," Tom said, "is did she write the book before or after she killed him?"

"Before, obviously," Betsy said as Lydia buried her face in her hands and started to weep.

"This is all my fault," Lydia got out between sobs.

"Oh, God, not again," Harry said. "Talk about a one-note wonder."

Libby leaned forward. "How's that, Lydia?"

Lydia raised her head and wiped her tears away with the backs of her hands. "Because I should have insisted. I should have been more forceful. If only I'd made Margo listen, she'd be here today."

Betsy got up, walked over to Lydia, and began to massage her shoulders. "There, there," she murmured. "This isn't your fault."

"Then why do I feel as if it is?" Lydia asked her.

Gilda opened her mouth and closed it again.

"What were you going to say?" Lydia demanded.

"Nothing," Gilda replied.

"No. You were going to say something. Tell me," Lydia insisted. "I really want to know."

Bernie spoke before Gilda could answer. "We'll find out what happened," Bernie assured Lydia, putting more confidence into her voice than she felt.

"You can bet on it," Libby added.

Chapter 18

Sean's friend Clyde came to see Sean, Bernie, and Libby at eight the next evening. Cindy the cat stopped batting a stuffed mouse up and down the steps and accompanied him up into the Simmons' flat.

"You brought the rain," Sean noted, listening to the droplets that had begun tapping on the windowpanes as Cindy jumped up on his lap and butted her head against his stomach.

"Me?" Clyde pointed to himself. "Miss Mary Sunshine?"

Sean laughed. Around the station, Clyde was known as the Grim Reaper for his unbridled optimism.

"Interesting," Clyde said as he took his place on the sofa and stretched his legs out.

"What we found?" Libby asked, nodding at the passport and money spread out on the coffee table.

"That too, but I was talking about this," and Clyde pointed to the cake Libby had just brought upstairs from the kitchen moments before he had arrived. "I thought you were going to bake me a strawberry shortcake."

"I did," Libby told him.

"It doesn't look like one to me," Clyde protested.

"The elements are the same," Bernie explained.

"But they're arranged in a different order," Libby added.

"So you're using me as a guinea pig?" Clyde demanded, trying to sound angry and failing. Past experience had taught him that anything Bernie and Libby made was bound to be good. No, not good. Great.

"It's a deconstructed version," Bernie told him.

Clyde laughed. "What does that even mean?"

"It means means it's another take on an old classic," Bernie answered. "Instead of biscuits, we used a short pastry crust."

"So it's like a big cookie?"

"Kinda," Libby said. "But not really. For one thing, there's no baking powder, and the ingredient proportions are different."

"You'll like it," Sean reassured his old friend.

"Have you tried it?" Clyde asked him.

Sean allowed as how he hadn't. "But I'm sure it's terrific," he added, out of loyalty to his daughters.

A terrible thought occurred to Clyde. "It's not made with sprouted whatever, fake butter, and coconut oil, is it?" he asked anxiously. His wife had him on an anti-inflammatory diet, and he had been looking forward to Libby and Bernie's strawberry shortcake all day.

Libby laughed. "No. Just good old butter, sugar, and flour. And if you don't like it, I'll bring you a piece of the strawberry shortcake from downstairs," she told him.

Clyde grinned. "Well, in that case," he said, rubbing his hands as he contemplated the mass of whipped cream, glistening strawberries coated with melted raspberry jam, and golden pastry, "I'll have to make the sacrifice."

Libby cut Clyde a generous slice, placed the slice on a plate, handed it to him, and watched him take a bite.

"Not bad," he said, a big smile crossing his face. "Not bad at all." He tapped the crust with his fork. "This literally melts in your mouth."

"It's the butter," Bernie informed him. "Lots of good butter from Guernsey cows. Their milk has a higher butterfat content."

"Nothing beats it," Clyde said as he took a second bite, sighing with pleasure as he did. "Listen," he said after he swallowed, "if you see my wife . . ."

"We won't say anything," Bernie promised.

"She'd be upset. I mean she's just trying to do what's good for me."

Sean nodded. "We know. Very admirable." Fortunately, his wife hadn't been afflicted with any such need, but he didn't say that to his old friend and ex-partner. There was no point rubbing things in.

"So what do you think about the money and the passport?" Sean asked Clyde instead after Clyde had finished his second piece of strawberry shortcake or whatever his daughters were calling what they'd baked.

Clyde put down his fork. He'd been contemplating a third piece but decided that might be taking things too far. "I called Winslow."

Sean raised an eyebrow. Winslow was Clyde's brother-in-law; more importantly, he had worked for the FBI before he'd retired last year.

"I just wanted to make sure I'd covered all the bases."

"And what made you think there were bases to cover?" Sean asked as he placed a dab of whipped cream on one of his fingers and held it up for Cindy. She licked it off, the sound of her purring filling the room.

"Because the Fibbies came around four years ago, give or take, asking questions about art stuff. At least, that's what I heard."

"From who?" Sean asked.

"Whom," Bernie automatically corrected.

Clyde ignored the interruption and answered his friend's question. "Rendazzo."

Sean's forehead wrinkled as he frowned. "Who's that?"

"He came on right after you left."

"Ah." It was a time Sean preferred not to dwell on. When he did, he just got angry all over again. "So what were they looking for?"

Clyde shrugged. "Who knows. They're not going to confide in a local Leo, you know that."

Sean did indeed. Usually the feds swept in, did what they did, and left again without local law enforcement being any the wiser. *Above your pay grade* was the phrase most frequently thrown around by the feds.

"Anyway, I heard fraud."

"From?" Sean prompted.

"Rendazzo, but he's not the most reliable source. There were no wants, and no warrants were issued."

Cindy meowed, and Sean fed her another dab of whipped cream from his plate. "You think there was anything there, or were the Fibbies just fishing?"

"There might have been," Clyde answered.

"How so?" Sean wanted to know.

Instead of answering immediately, Clyde took a sip of his iced coffee. He was one of those people who could drink coffee right before he went to bed and fall asleep immediately, an ability Sean envied because he'd never had it.

Clyde put his glass down. "Winslow called one of his friends who's still at the Bureau."

"And?" Sean asked.

"He told Winslow the feds have a file on Margo."

Sean raised two eyebrows. Bernie and Libby leaned forward.

"And the Glassbergs," Clyde continued. "The husband

and the wife. They have a file on them, too, as well as the Westovers."

"You're kidding," Bernie said.

Clyde shook his head. "No, I am not."

"Are the files open?" Sean asked his friend.

"I'm not sure," Clyde said. "Winston said he'd check."

Sean picked up a strawberry that was on his plate, dipped it in the vanilla-flavored whipped cream, and popped it in his mouth. "But no prosecutions?" he asked after he'd swallowed.

"Nope," Clyde responded. "None."

Sean fed Cindy another dab of whipped cream. "Just because the feds have a file on them doesn't mean much," Sean commented. "Especially these days."

"I never said it did," Clyde pointed out. "However, given the circumstances . . ." And he let the sentence lapse.

"Talk about not having a clue," Libby commented, thinking about her and her sister's conversation with the LMBC last night. "Anyone else from the group attract the FBI's attention?" Libby asked.

"Not that Winslow mentioned," Clyde answered.

"What did the files say?" Sean asked.

Clyde crossed his arms over his chest and sighed. "Winslow couldn't say."

"Couldn't say or wouldn't say?" Sean asked.

"Don't know, and I didn't want to push it, but it amounts to the same thing anyway, especially since no charges were filed."

"I suppose," Sean said, although he wasn't sure he agreed with Clyde's assessment of the situation in this particular case.

"Did Winslow give you a hint?" Libby asked.

"No. But more to the point, as I just said, no one was ever charged."

"So that means that Margo, the Glassbergs, and the Westovers didn't do anything?" Bernie asked, trying to get an accurate read on the situation.

"Not necessarily," Clyde said. "It just means the Fibbies didn't choose to proceed with the case. There could be hundreds of reasons why they didn't. Or, on the other hand, they could be putting together a much larger case in which your friends are bit players. It's hard to know. I've seen the feds take ten years to file indictments."

The room was silent as the two Simmons sisters digested this new piece of information.

"What about on our end?" Sean asked Clyde. "Any of the LMBC crew get themselves in trouble around here?"

"No. Except for Gilda Westover, who racked up a thousand dollars' worth of parking tickets, and Brad Musclow, who dumped a bag of dog poop on his neighbor's front steps in retaliation for said neighbor's dog pooping on his lawn. The neighbor called the police, but the incident was peacefully resolved."

"Ah," Sean said. "The exciting life of the local constabulary. Just thinking about it gets my blood pumping."

Clyde laughed.

"Anything else?" Bernie asked.

Clyde shook his head. "A couple of parking tickets, some noise complaints, that's about it," he replied. "And, believe me, I looked."

"Disappointing," Sean noted as he watched a bolt of lightning illuminate the street. Then another bolt cleaved the sky, turning night into day. It looked as if the storm the weather forecaster had predicted earlier in the day had arrived in all its fury.

Chapter 19

Raindrops rat-tat-tated on the windows, while the lights in the Simmonses' flat flickered on and off. Libby crossed her fingers as she thought about all the food they had stored downstairs in the coolers and the fridge. *Please don't hit a transformer*, she silently prayed to the gods of thunder and lightning.

"It'll be fine," Bernie said to Libby as the lights flickered again. Another clap of thunder sounded as if it was right above them.

"God, that was loud," Clyde observed after a moment had gone by.

"These storms are getting worse," Sean noted as he watched the tree limbs thrashing around in the wind and thought about how glad he was that he hadn't parked his new old car under a tree. "We need to get a generator. Just in case."

Bernie and Libby both nodded.

"We do," Bernie said. "The kind that attaches to our electrical system and you can turn on with the flick of a switch." They were expensive, but it was still cheaper than losing all their perishables.

Conversation ceased as everyone watched the storm. Ten minutes later, it had moved on, and conversation resumed. Bernie could feel the tension flow out of her body. She took another bite of the strawberry shortcake. It was excellent, if she had to say so herself.

"What about Chung?" Bernie asked, getting back to what they'd been talking about previously.

"What about him?" Clyde asked.

Bernie rested her fork on her plate. "Did your friend . . ."

"My brother-in-law's friend."

"Fine. Did your brother-in-law's friend find anything on Chung in the files?"

"I didn't ask him." Clyde sat back and thought about that third piece of strawberry shortcake. He knew he shouldn't. Then he thought of his wife's spinach bread, which tasted as bad as it sounded, and decided he should.

Libby looked disappointed. "How come?"

"I didn't want to push it," Clyde explained after he asked for another piece. "I owe him big as it is, and, believe me, he's going to collect. Winslow never forgets anything." Clyde grimaced. He wouldn't care if he liked his brother-in-law, but he didn't. "Anyway, we know Chung didn't kill Margo," he said as Libby put a third slice on his plate. "He's not a person of interest in Margo's death."

"You sound pretty sure," Bernie noted.

"I am," Clyde said as he took a bite of the strawberry shortcake. *Worth every calorie,* he decided.

"How can you be so sure?" Libby wanted to know as she sat back down.

Clyde answered, "I can be so sure because around the time of Margo's death, Chung was in our jail, waiting to be processed for a DWI. I was there when Feldman brought him in."

"You said Margo's death," Bernie said to Clyde.

"That I did."

"So you don't think her death was a homicide, either?"

This time, Clyde considered for a moment before answering. "I'm not sure," he finally allowed. "But let's say I'm tilting strongly in the direction of believing that it was. If I wasn't, I wouldn't have called Winslow."

Bernie nodded. She guessed that would have to do. She turned to her dad. "He hates you, you know."

"Chung?"

"Yes."

"No big news there. I already told you that when you asked me to talk to him."

"Why does he feel that way?" Libby asked.

"Because I arrested him."

"But, Dad, you've arrested lots of other people," Bernie observed.

"Some people hold grudges," Sean said, "and Chung is evidently one of those people. Maybe because Chung's wife left him after I arrested him on a drunk and disorderly." Sean pictured the scene in his mind. "I forgot about that one. He was banging Pete Anderson's head against the wall when I walked into The Dive." The Dive was just what it sounded like—a dive bar. "He was lucky I got there when I did. Otherwise, he might have been serving time for manslaughter."

"His wife leaving him wasn't your fault," Libby protested. "He can't blame you!"

"He did then, and he does now—never mind that I heard he slapped his wife around some."

"You did him a favor," Libby protested.

"Yes, I did," Sean answered. He rubbed the tips of Cindy's ears. She responded with a loud purr. "I didn't even charge him for the swing he took at me, but Chung doesn't see it that way. I suppose it's easier for him to do that than do what he needs to do to stay sober. At least Chung only goes on a bender every two months instead of once a week," Sean reflected. He knew this from Brandon, Bernie's boyfriend. "And he usually takes an Uber when he does, so that's progress."

"Some progress," Clyde scoffed.

"Well, he isn't getting worse," Sean pointed out.

"What would you call this time?" Clyde demanded. "That sure wasn't maintaining. Any more alcohol in his system, and we'd have had to cart him off to the hospital."

"I wonder what happened," Bernie mused. "I wonder why he went off the rails."

"Who cares?" Clyde said. "It could be anything. Once a drunk, always a drunk, I say."

"Not true," Libby answered, thinking of a few of her friends who had gotten sober and remained so.

Sean read the expression on Bernie's face. "What are you thinking?" he asked.

Bernie shook her head. "Nothing." She had an idea, but she didn't want to share it just yet. Instead, she asked Clyde if he thought Chung could have hired someone to kill Margo.

"I suppose he could have," Clyde said, "but I just don't see him for it. Anyway, he's too cheap. If he were going to do something like that, he'd do it himself. And he's more of a spur-of-the-moment instead of a planning-it-out kinda guy. No," Clyde concluded, "if he's going to hurt anyone, he's going to do it himself."

"I'll go with that," Sean said. "Chung may not be the pleasantest person in the world, but that doesn't make him a murderer." Sean broke off a piece of crust and popped it in his mouth. He couldn't decide which he liked better, this version or the traditional one, before he finished his thought. "I've known some very nice people, at least on the surface, who have killed their nearest and dearest, and I'm not talking about crimes of passion, either. I'm talking about extensive pre-planning."

"But what about that building he owns?" Bernie inquired, pushing.

"You mean the one behind the pizza shop?" Clyde asked.

"Yes, that one," Bernie replied.

"What about it?" Clyde asked.

"It just seems so suspicious," Bernie said.

Clyde laughed. "There's nothing suspicious about it. It's just a place for people to store their vehicles."

"It's not what I would call convenient," Bernie replied. "And when you add in the security . . . well."

"That's because Chung can be a little paranoid," Clyde agreed. "Well, a lot paranoid, and security stuff is cheap now, so why not? Lots of people are into that sort of thing."

"I don't know. To me, it looks as if he's hiding something in there," Libby noted.

"The building does look that way," Sean agreed. "But then it always has."

"Why buy something like that?" Bernie asked.

Sean answered again. "Well, Chung's partner convinced him to buy the place. I believe they planned to store spare auto parts there and sell them to other garages. But when Howard left, Chung lost interest. After a little while, some of his customers started asking him if they could store their spare vehicles there."

"Like Margo," Libby said.

Sean nodded. "Exactly so."

Clyde took over the narrative. "Word got around, as it does in a small town like ours, and Chung saw a niche, as they like to say these days, and he filled it. It's an extra revenue stream for him, especially since he only accepts cash."

"So no taxes," Bernie said.

"Exactly," Clyde replied.

Libby frowned. "But why would anyone store their vehicles there in the first place? Especially people with fancy vehicles," she countered. "It's not exactly convenient. Not even from its main entrance." She and her sister had scouted it out.

"That being said, there isn't a lot of storage space for vehicles in this area," Clyde pointed out. "Aside from the McMansions in Bradford Hills, most houses in this area come with two-car garages."

Libby crossed her arms over her chest. "And two cars are usually what most people have."

"Not necessarily," Sean said. "People have campers and RVs that, due to local codes, they can't park in their driveways, or they collect cars and they don't want to leave them outside in the winter, or maybe they bought a new vehicle and they don't want their wife . . ."

"Or husband," Clyde put in. "Can't be sexist here."

". . . to know about it," Sean said, finishing his sentence.

"I still think Chung had something to do with Margo's death," Libby persisted.

Clyde cleared his throat. "Sometimes the obvious person is the obvious person, and sometimes it's not," he pontificated.

"What's that supposed to mean?" Bernie demanded.

"Nothing," Clyde told her. "Just trying to be inscrutable."

"This is what comes from watching too many old Charlie Chan movies," Sean told him.

"I can't help it if they relax me and help me sleep," Clyde protested.

"So if you were me and you were investigating this? Where would you start?" Bernie asked him.

"I wouldn't," Clyde said. "I'd leave it to the professionals. Of course, if you did that, I wouldn't be eating this." And he nodded toward the strawberry shortcake.

"Anyway, we are professionals," Bernie told him.

"Professional cooks," Clyde replied.

"And semi-professional detectives," Bernie said. "We are," she insisted, whipping out her phone and googling the word *professional*. "See," she said, passing the phone to Clyde. "It says here that a professional is an individual who gets paid for their services. That's Bernie and me."

Clyde looked at Sean for support, but Sean just shrugged. He'd stopped arguing with his daughters a while ago. It took too much energy. And then there was the fact that, even when he won, he lost.

Chapter 20

Clyde had left, and Libby and Bernie were getting ready to go to bed when Brandon called.

"You should get down here," were the first words out of his mouth when Bernie answered her cell.

"No 'Hi, sweetie'? No 'I miss you'?" Bernie responded.

"Fine. Hi, sweetie. I miss you. Now get your ass down here."

"Okay, why?"

"Remember when we were talking about Chung?"

"Of course, I remember. And do you remember I told you that I did talk to him and things did not go well."

"I think you might find that things will go differently this time."

"How so?"

"Well, he's here now, and he's very drunk. Sloppy drunk."

"So?"

"He's very chatty."

"That's nice. And what exactly does that have to do with me?"

"He's talking about Margo."

"Ah." Bernie paused for a moment while she turned the lamp on her nightstand on. "Are you sure?"

"Of course, I am." Brandon had to raise his voice to be heard over the chatter of customers sitting at the bar. "He's pretty incoherent, but he keeps muttering her name, and I'm fairly certain I heard him say 'I'm so sorry' a number of times. I figured you'd be interested."

"I am," Bernie said, shifting her phone to her left hand as she grabbed with her right hand the eyelet skirt she'd thrown on the chair. "Very." So maybe she'd been right, after all. Maybe her hunch about why Tommy Chung had upped his drinking wasn't so far-fetched.

"I figure you might like to come down and hold his hand and make sympathetic noises," Brandon told her.

Bernie paused, remembering her and Libby's last meeting with Chung. "I will, but odds are he'll get up and leave when he sees Libby and me. He hates my dad, and Libby and me by extension."

"Never underestimate the power of booze, Bernie, and who should know better than me?"

"True," Bernie allowed.

"Plus, your dad isn't charming. You are. Most of the time, anyway. So be charming."

"You're right. I am charming, aren't I," Bernie said, a smile in her voice. "Okay. I'll be right there."

"Excellent," Brandon said.

"And if Chung orders another drink before I arrive, tell him it's on me," she instructed Brandon before she hung up. *Now let's see if I'm charming enough to get Chung to talk to me*, Bernie thought as she reached for a bright pink shell and slipped it over her head. She hadn't done so well the last time, but then Chung hadn't been drunk, either.

"What's up?" Libby asked as Bernie came into her room.

"Put something on. We gotta go," she told her sister.

"Go where?" Libby asked, a tinge of panic evident in her voice. She was in her PJs and was just about to climb into bed. "What happened? Is anyone hurt?"

"No. It's Chung."

"What about him?"

"I'll explain on the way to RJ's." And Bernie went to Libby's dresser, opened the middle drawer, took out a pair of Bermuda shorts and a black T-shirt, and threw them at her. "Here. Put these on," she ordered.

"Is this really necessary?" Libby asked.

"Yes," her sister replied. "It is. This might be our one and only shot to get him talking."

Libby sighed. "What the hell," she groused. "Who needs sleep anyway?"

"That's what I say too," Bernie replied.

"Be careful," Sean warned his daughters when they stepped out into the living room. He'd overhead Bernie's conversation with Libby.

"Always," Bernie replied as she bent down and kissed his forehead.

"Ha," her father retorted. "That'll be the day!"

Libby gave him a peck on the cheek. "It'll be fine," she assured him.

"It always is until it isn't," Sean said, thinking of some of his past calls, the ones he'd considered a slam dunk that weren't. "Just remember, drunks are unpredictable."

But Bernie and Libby didn't hear their father's last words because they were halfway down the stairs by then.

The street was glistening, the streetlights reflecting off the wet surfaces, when the Simmons sisters stepped outside. Bernie sniffed as she closed the door behind her. The air smelled of worms and damp grass.

"I guess we don't have to wash Mathilda after all," Libby remarked as she contemplated the van's shiny exterior. "So what exactly is going on?" Libby asked as she and Bernie climbed into the van.

Bernie told her after she'd started Mathilda.

"Talk about a fool's errand," Libby said.

"Maybe he'll say something. Who knows? Maybe my innate charm will bring him to his knees."

Libby rolled her eyes. "Talk about unbridled optimism."

Bernie threw her a look. "You have a better suggestion?"

Libby allowed as how she didn't.

"Exactly," Bernie said after Libby was done talking.

They got to RJ's ten minutes later. The parking lot was uncharacteristically full due to a bowling competition that was in town, so they parked toward the rear of the lot and made their way to the entrance, careful to avoid the pools of standing water filling the potholes. When they walked inside, Brandon stopped wiping down the bar and pointed in the direction of the back room, a space that was mostly used around Christmas for private parties. "He's in there," Brandon told them. "He said he wanted to be alone."

"How Greta Garbo," Libby cracked. She'd been watching old movies with her dad.

"Did you give him another drink?" Bernie asked.

Brandon shook his head. "He hasn't asked."

"Then give me one for him and one each for Libby and myself. We'll have what he's having."

"Right," Brandon said. "Three seven and sevens coming up."

Libby wrinkled her nose. "I hate seven and sevens."

"Drink it anyway," Bernie told her. She'd read somewhere that mirroring someone's behavior encouraged bonding.

"I'll take a sip," Libby said as they carried the drinks to the back room. "But that's all."

"Hi, Tommy," Bernie said when they walked in.

Tommy Chung's head whipped around. Bernie could see that his eyes were red and he was sporting a heavy five o'clock shadow. He'd been watching a golf tournament replay on the giant TV hanging on the wall when the Simmons sisters walked in, and he looked annoyed at being interrupted.

"What the hell are you doing here?" he demanded belligerently.

Bernie noted that Chung's speech was slurred, and he seemed to be putting a lot of effort into forming his words. She lifted the seven and seven. "I brought you another drink."

"Out," Chung said, but Libby decided he didn't sound as if he meant it. They'd heard him when he had.

Bernie and Libby ignored the comment, advanced into the room, and sat down on either side of Chung. Bernie pushed the seven and seven toward him. "I believe this is your poison of the moment."

"Who says?" Chung asked.

"Brandon," Bernie replied.

Chung belched. Alcohol fumes filled the air. Bernie wanted to move back to avoid the smell, but managed not to. "You know Brandon?" Chung asked.

"He's my boyfriend." Bernie pushed the seven and seven closer to Chung with the tips of the fingers of her right hand.

Chung stared at them. "Your nails are blue. Why are they blue?"

Bernie shrugged. "To change things up."

"Weird," Chung said, shaking his head from side to side. "People shouldn't go around with blue nails."

"Why is that?" Libby asked.

"Because dead people have blue nails," Chung replied.

Bernie and Libby exchanged a look.

"Brandon told me you were upset about Margo," Bernie began.

"Not upset," Chung said before he bowed his head, but in that split second, Bernie could see tears welling up in his eyes.

Libby had seen them, too. "She was a nice lady," Libby observed.

"I told her," Libby thought Chung said, but she couldn't be sure because his head was down and he was mumbling to the table.

"What did you tell her?" Bernie asked.

Chung didn't say anything.

"I'm sure it was important," Bernie said.

There was no response from Chung.

"Tell me," Bernie coaxed. She leaned in closer. "I really want to know."

"That I'm sorry and to be careful," Chung muttered. "Always be careful. You never know, you know that?"

"That's what my dad says," Bernie responded.

Chung jerked his head up, started to say something, and stopped.

"What should we be careful of?" Libby asked.

Chung grinned, a sly expression on his face. "Wouldn't you like to know?" He reached for his old drink and finished it off in one long swallow. Bernie pushed the drink she'd bought for him closer and took a sip of hers.

"Not bad," she said for Chung's benefit.

He nodded.

"Tommy," she began.

He blinked. "My mom used to call me that."

"It's a nice name," Libby observed.

"Did you like Margo, Tommy?" Bernie asked softly as the noise in the bar rose and fell. Someone had won at darts.

Chung's head went up and down in a staccato burst. He rubbed his chin. "She was my friend." He hiccupped. "I told her . . ."

"To be careful of what?" Libby asked again.

"Her friends." Chung reached over and took a big gulp of the seven and seven Bernie had given him. "You can't promise something and go back on your word."

"You mean friends like Betsy and Tom Glassberg and Lydia?" Bernie asked.

"All of them. Margo thought they liked her."

"But they didn't?" Libby persisted.

Chung didn't answer. He hiccupped again, leaned over, put his arms on the table, laid his head on them, and went to sleep.

"I guess that last drink tipped the scales," Bernie noted as Chung began snoring.

"I think that's safe to say," Libby commented. She still hadn't taken a sip of hers.

Chapter 21

Brandon helped Bernie and Libby walk Chung outside—well, not walk really, more like drag—and load him into Brandon's old Volvo station wagon. It was lower and had more space than Mathilda did, not to mention a back seat.

"Just don't let him puke in it," Brandon pleaded.

"Wouldn't dream of it," Bernie replied.

"I don't know how you're going to get him out of the Volvo and into his house," Brandon said. "It's taken the three of us to get him this far."

"I don't know, either, but we'll manage," Bernie said.

"You could call an Uber," Brandon suggested. He was having second, third, and fourth thoughts about loaning out his car. It was a classic. Well, not really. But he loved it. The seats were leather. Just contemplating what Chung could do inside the Volvo made Brandon shudder. But using Mathilda was out of the question. Chung was out cold. And he was a big guy. Maybe two hundred and twenty pounds. They'd never get him in there.

"The driver probably wouldn't take him in this condition," Bernie replied, interrupting Brandon's thoughts. "I know I wouldn't."

Brandon had to admit he wouldn't, either.

"Do you know where Chung lives?" Bernie asked.

Brandon told her. It was about five minutes from RJ's. Not far at all.

"And, besides, it's good to be neighborly," Bernie concluded.

"Is that what you're calling this?" Brandon said to Bernie as he watched her go through Chung's pockets.

"In a manner of speaking," Bernie replied.

Brandon nodded toward RJ's. "I have to get back in there. Shorty can't handle things by himself. What are you looking for, anyway?"

"These," she said, holding up Chung's keys. There were a lot of them on his key chain.

"What are you thinking?" Brandon asked as Bernie studied them.

"You don't want to know," she told him as she stowed them away in her bag.

"You're right, I don't," Brandon said, although he had a pretty good idea what Bernie was contemplating.

"Why doesn't he want to know?" Libby asked Bernie.

"It's called plausible deniability," Brandon told her, answering for Bernie.

It took a few minutes, but the three of them managed to load Chung into the Volvo's front seat. Brandon watched as they set off in his car. Bernie was driving, and Libby was sitting in the back.

"Good luck," he called out to them. "They're going to need it," he said to himself, opening the door to RJ's. A wave of noise hit him when he stepped inside. He hurried toward the bar. He could see from the doorway that Shorty was in the weeds.

As it turned out, Brandon was wrong. The drive to

Chung's house took fifteen minutes, not five, because they had to stop on the side of the road so Chung could throw up. They drove the rest of the way with all the windows open.

Bernie turned onto Edgewater Road. Chung's house was on the outskirts of Scottholm, a development comprised of cookie-cutter ranch houses and capes built in the fifties and sixties. The houses were set back from the road, each isolated in their own quarter acre of grass, not connected by sidewalks, or illuminated by streetlights, or threaded together by front porches. Most people in the neighborhood had turned off their lights and gone to bed by the time Bernie and Libby arrived. It was so quiet Bernie could hear the slight huff the Volvo's engine was making as she pulled into Chung's driveway.

His house turned out to be the most modest house on his block. Libby was surprised. She'd expected something grander, but 80 Avalon Drive was anything but grand. Chung's home—Libby estimated it was probably around fifteen hundred square feet—was all white, the plantings along the front and sides sparse, the greenery that was there planted in pea gravel. She reflected that the house might look better in the daylight, but she doubted it.

"I think we can say that Chung isn't exactly house proud," Bernie observed as she killed the Volvo's engine.

Then she and Libby got out. Bernie walked up to the house and, after finally finding the right key on Chung's keychain, opened the door. The air inside the house smelled stale as Bernie propped open the screen door and walked back to Brandon's Volvo. She opened the passenger-side door and spoke to Chung.

"Come on," she said.

There was no response.

She shook him.

Chung groaned, opened his eyes, and closed them again.

Libby leaned into the Volvo. "You have to get up," she told Chung, trying not to breathe in the smell of rye and vomit coming off of him.

Chung didn't say anything. Libby and Bernie looked at each other.

"This is going to be fun," Bernie said as she and her sister each took hold of one of Chung's arms and pulled. Chung's eyes opened.

"What?" he cried, his voice thick with sleep.

"You're home," Bernie explained. "Can you walk?"

Chung didn't answer. He'd closed his eyes again.

Bernie leaned in and shook him harder. "Come on," she told him. "You have to get up."

Chung startled awake, his arms flailing. Libby and Bernie stepped back to avoid being hit. He started to get out of the Volvo, but lost his balance and fell back into the seat. "Don't touch me, Blue Nails," he snarled as Bernie reached out a helping hand.

"Fine," she said, pulling her hand back.

She watched Chung drag himself out of the Volvo. He stood, swaying as he did. Then he began stumbling toward the house. Bernie and Libby followed behind, holding their breaths. It was like watching a tree about to fall. Chung tripped over the front step to his house, but he righted himself and kept on going. When he got to the living room, he collapsed on the sofa and closed his eyes again.

Bernie leaned over him. "Tommy," she said.

Chung didn't answer. He was out.

Bernie straightened up and looked around. "Let's see what we can find," she said to her sister.

Libby nodded. After all, that's what they were there for. They didn't find much. Chung's phone was password-protected, as was his laptop, and after wasting a few minutes trying to figure out the passwords, Bernie started in on Chung's office, while Libby looked through the living room, dining room, kitchen, and two bedrooms.

There wasn't a lot in those spaces, just laundry that needed to be washed, stacks of old magazines, and empty fast-food containers, beer bottles, dirty glasses, and a collection of empty rye-whiskey bottles.

"Nothing," Libby said as she joined Bernie in Chung's office. "Anything here?"

"Definitely," Bernie said, and she handed her sister a card she'd found on top of a stack of old newspapers on Chung's desk.

The card was to Margo, but it had never been sent. It was one of those cute ones you can get in any drugstore. A large dog sat on the cover, with his paws up in the air. The inscription underneath the animal read, *I'm sorry.* Libby opened the card. The inscription inside read, *I really am.*

Libby put the card back down. "I wonder what Chung was sorry about?"

"Good question," Bernie said. "It looks as if they had something going on."

"I never would have put those two together," Libby reflected.

"Me either," Bernie agreed as she thought of her and Brandon and Libby and Marvin. No one would have put them together, either. You just never know, she decided, as she pointed to the monitor on the desk. "I was hoping I could get into Chung's phone and disable the video cams around the storage unit, but since I can't, that's not going to happen."

"Then let's go home," Libby said. She checked her

watch. It was almost one o'clock in the morning. "We need to get up early tomorrow."

"We always need to get up early," Bernie countered. "This might be our only chance to get into the storage space."

"At least let's use the other road."

"We could," Bernie agreed, "but it'll take us three-quarters of an hour to get there, and it has security cameras too." Bernie drummed her fingers against her thigh while she thought about a solution. Then she had it. "I know what we're going to do."

"Rappel in from the roof?" Libby asked. "Use a battering ram?"

"I like the battering ram. No. We're going to wear hoodies and hats and keep our heads down. It's dark. Chung won't be able to see anything."

"*If* we had hoodies, Bernie." They did have baseball hats in the van.

Bernie answered, "They have them at CVS. I saw them when I ran in to pick up some cottage cheese last week. Even better, CVS is open twenty-four/seven."

"Fantastic."

Bernie grinned. "It is, isn't it? So let's go. We can stop on the way, swap out vehicles with Brandon, and get our baseball hats."

"Remember what Dad said about being careful. This is what he was talking about," Libby told Bernie as they walked out of Chung's house.

"You worry too much," Bernie answered, locking the door behind them. She slipped Chung's keys into her bag, figuring she'd return them on their way back, and headed for Brandon's Volvo.

"And you don't worry enough," Libby told her sister.

Bernie didn't answer. What could she say? It was true.

Chapter 22

Bernie and Libby slipped and slid their way down the slope that led to Chung's storage facility, the rain having turned the path into a mudslide.

"Good thing we didn't try to drive down," Libby noted as she grabbed a branch to steady herself. Her sister had parked their van behind the pizza shop.

"Yes, it is," Bernie agreed as she concentrated on keeping her footing in the muck.

She'd changed out her heels for an old pair of sneakers she kept in the van for emergencies and put on a pair of ripped cargo pants and an old stained T-shirt she'd fished out of the fabric-recycling bag she kept meaning to donate to Goodwill.

In addition, she and her sister were both wearing the hoodies they'd purchased at CVS fifteen minutes ago and the baseball hats they'd collected from the back of their van. Bernie had left her bag in the van and stowed her phone and the keys she'd gotten off of Chung in her pants pockets.

"I'll tell you one thing—it's definitely not hoodie weather," Libby whined. "If I get heat stroke, will you take me to the hospital?"

"What do you think?" Bernie retorted. Then she and Libby stopped talking. It was taking every ounce of concentration on both of their parts to keep from falling. For a brief moment, Bernie considered sliding down on her butt, but she decided against it. She didn't want that captured on video. Even if Chung was the only one to see it and didn't know who they were. Too undignified.

Ten minutes, two falls, and one slightly twisted ankle later, Libby and Bernie were in front of the storage facility door. It was a normal-sized door made out of metal, flanked on each side by a security camera. Bernie hit it with the flat of her hand. It was solid, the kind of door people installed in panic rooms.

"Interesting," Libby said, careful not to look up.

"Isn't it, though?" Bernie agreed. She eyed the door for another minute before she spoke. "So now we know for sure," she said, indicating it with a nod of her head. "No vehicle is getting in through there."

"A clown car could."

"Not even that." Bernie took out her phone, turned on the flashlight, and swept the ground with the beam. At first, she didn't see anything except mud, but then she noticed small slabs of slate partially covered in the mud. They were arranged one after the other.

"I believe that's a path, Watson," Bernie said, pointing to the pavers.

"By Jove, I believe you're correct," Libby replied.

Bernie played the light farther ahead of them. The path continued along the side of the building.

"Shall we?" Bernie asked.

Libby extended her hand. "After you."

"By all means," Bernie answered as she kept the flashlight trained on the ground, while she and Libby stepped from slate slab to slate slab, trying to avoid the mud. The slate led around the corner to two garage doors. A keypad on the right-hand corner granted access to the place.

"I guess the key I've got is for the other door," Bernie observed.

Libby nodded as she studied the area in front of her. There was a small, black-topped area where cars were presumably parked. That, in turn, connected to a dirt road that snaked through a copse of trees about twenty feet away. The road was flat, and Libby could see that it was deeply rutted, the tire tracks filled with water, indicating it had been used frequently. She and her sister headed back the way they'd come.

"What if the door is alarmed?" Libby said when they were standing in front of the back door.

"Then we'll need a lawyer," Bernie said as she put the key in the lock. She was about to turn it when she realized the light from her cell was growing fainter. She glanced down at her phone. "Damn." She had about a minute left before her phone went dead. She'd charge it when they got back to the van.

Libby had noticed the waning beam of light as well. "We should have taken the flashlight."

"Agreed," Bernie said. "Maybe you should get it, Libby."

"Maybe you should, Bernie."

"I'm not climbing back up there."

"Well, neither am I," Libby told her sister.

"Okay, then." And with that Bernie turned the key. She waited for a moment. Nothing happened, not that that meant anything, she knew, as she pictured an alarm ringing in a security office somewhere. She gave the door a hefty push. A large rectangle of blackness yawned in front of her. "Here we go," she said, stepping inside.

Libby followed, stumbling over something in the doorway. Whatever it was clattered as the door closed behind her with a thud. She straightened up.

"I can't see anything," Libby complained. "It's pitch black in here."

"Tell me about it," Bernie replied. She literally couldn't see her hands in front of her face. She stood there for a minute, listening to the hum of the air conditioner. "At least it's cold in here."

"It's not cold, it's freezing," Libby said.

"Let's not exaggerate."

"I'm not exaggerating. I have goose bumps on my arms."

"Actually, I think I do too," Bernie admitted as she began feeling around the wall for the light switch. "It has to be here somewhere," she muttered.

"The light switch?"

"No, the coffeemaker."

Libby thought about the flashlight they had left in the van. It was one of those good ones, the kind that could light up a room, the kind the cops used. Her dad had insisted they carry it because, as he said, "You never know."

"No kidding," Bernie rejoined, thinking of her dad's words as well. He would not be pleased. Of course, he wouldn't be pleased if he knew what she and her sister were doing.

"Hopefully not," Libby said, thinking of the climb back up the slope. She had a feeling it would be worse than the climb down.

A moment later, Bernie's fingers encountered something.

"Found it," she cried triumphantly. She was just about to turn on the light when a voice came out of the darkness.

"Don't move," it said. "I have a gun."

Bernie froze.

Chapter 23

Definitely a man's voice, Bernie decided, as she stood there.

"I mean it," the voice said.

"We're not moving," Libby reassured him.

"Good, because I'll know if you do."

Bernie wanted to say, *How will you know? Do you have X-ray vision?* but thought better of it. "Never antagonize the person with a gun" was her motto, so instead she said, "What do you want?"

"What do I want? Ha. That's a good one. What do *you* want?" the man said, his voice rising as it emphasized the word *you*.

He sounds nervous, and that makes him dangerous, Bernie thought. And he also sounded young, she decided. Which made him inexperienced, and that didn't help the situation. If, indeed and in fact, he had a gun. Which he might not have, even though he said he did. On the other hand, he could have a knife or a baseball bat, and those, as her dad would say, were nothing to sneeze at either.

"Well," the voice demanded impatiently.

"Well, what?" Bernie asked, stalling for time while she tried to come up with a plan.

Libby was trying to come up with a plan as well, when she realized the voice sounded familiar. Who was it? She knew she'd heard it recently, but where? She couldn't remember, and then, all of a sudden, she did.

"Hey, Jason, is that you?" she asked.

Libby could hear a sharp intake of breath off to her left, then a moment of silence, and then Jason asked in a more subdued tone, "Who are you? How do you know my name?"

"We met at the garage. Then we talked at Starbucks. It's Libby and Bernie," Libby told him.

"How do I know you're telling the truth?" Jason challenged. Libby could hear a slight quaver in his voice.

"Why would I lie?" Libby asked him.

"Let me turn on the light, and you can see we're who we say we are," Bernie urged.

"I don't know," Jason told her.

"Of course, we could be vampires, Jason," Bernie added.

"Then you wouldn't want me to turn on the light," Jason replied.

"True," Bernie conceded. "Would you believe zombies?"

"You're not funny," Jason told her.

"So I've been told," Bernie conceded.

"Please, Jason," Libby begged. "What have you got to lose?"

There was a moment of silence, then Jason said, "Okay. Do it."

Bernie flicked the switch. Suddenly, the room was bathed in a harsh, bright-white fluorescent light. Libby blinked as colors danced in front of her eyes. When the colors subsided, she realized the three of them were standing in an office.

The office was a good-sized room. Jason was positioned in front of a large metal desk a couple of feet away from Bernie and Libby. Two gray metal file cabinets with an old coffeemaker sitting on top of the left-hand one, three bookshelves filled with auto-parts catalogs, and a couple of rickety-looking chairs comprised the rest of the room's scanty furnishings. The walls were a dirty white, and the floor was covered with scratched black-and-white lino-leum tiles that had definitely seen better days. The only decoration in the place was a four-year-old calendar, with a picture of a basset hound on it, hanging above the desk.

Bernie nodded toward the metal pipe Jason was grip-ping with both hands. "I like your gun," she told him. "What kind of ammo does it take?"

Jason blushed. "Hey, excuse me, but you scared the crap out of me," he said, the relief in his voice palpable as he lowered the pipe he was holding. Jason's cowlick was standing straight up, and his eyes were crusted with sleep. He was wearing flannel pajama bottoms, a hoodie, finger-less black wool gloves, and a pair of wool ski socks.

"Sorry about that, but I could say the same about you," Libby replied, letting out the breath she didn't know she'd been holding while her heart rate dropped back to normal.

"What the hell are you doing here, anyway?" Jason de-manded. "How the hell did you get in?"

Bernie held up the keys and explained.

Jason gave her an incredulous look. "You stole Chung's keys? He's going to be really pissed when he finds out."

Bernie corrected him. "I believe *borrow* is the correct term, and I might ask what you're doing here as well."

Jason pointed to a blow-up bed in the far corner of the room. It had one of those good-to-twenty-degrees-below-zero mummy sleeping bags on it.

"I was sleeping when you came in. You woke me up."

He rubbed his eyes. "Talk about making a lot of noise. Aren't robbers supposed to be quiet or something?"

"You sleep here?" Libby asked him.

Jason laughed. "Just the last couple of days. It's not great, but at least it's quiet." He went on to explain. "My roommate's family is staying at our place for the week, so I decided to move out and give them a little more space. It's pretty tight in there—seven people in a two-bedroom flat."

"I can imagine. Does Chung know you're here?" Libby asked.

Jason snorted. "Of course, he knows I'm here. He was the one who suggested it." Then he changed the subject. "You really don't give up, do you?"

Bernie grinned. "Nope. We're like a dog with a bone, a cat with a mouse, a squirrel with . . ."

Jason held his hand. "Enough."

Bernie shrugged. "Fine. If you feel that way."

"I do," Jason assured her.

Libby took a step forward. "More importantly, are you going to tell Chung we were here?"

"And if I said I was?" Jason asked.

"Obviously, we'd have to kill you," Bernie said.

Jason chuckled. "Obviously."

"Seriously, please don't," Libby told him, thinking of what she imagined Chung's reaction would be. "We just want to check out Margo's cars."

Jason laid the pipe down on a chair over by the door Libby and Bernie had come through. It was, Libby reflected, a large pipe, capable of cracking skulls if swung with a modicum of force, so she was glad to see Jason laying it down.

"There's nothing in them," Jason told them.

"How do you know?" Bernie challenged.

"Because when Tommy . . ."

"It's Tommy now?" Bernie asked, interrupting.

"He's not as bad as he seems," Jason confided.

"If you say so," Bernie replied.

"I do," Jason answered.

"Go on," Bernie instructed.

Jason did. "Anyway," he continued, "when Tommy heard about what happened to Margo, he went over her vehicles with a fine-tooth comb."

"Why?" Bernie asked.

Jason shrugged. "The same reason you want to, I assume. He was hoping to find some sort of clue that would tell him what happened to Margo."

"And I take it he didn't?" Libby asked.

"Nope," Jason told her. "And, believe me, we looked."

"When did he search her cars?" Bernie asked Jason as she took another look around the office they were standing in. The place was about as bare-bones as you could get.

"We went through Margo's vehicles right after I came back from talking to you at Starbucks," Jason replied. "That's why he told me to get my ass back to the shop. His sister had just walked in, so he put her in charge, and he and I came here and spent a couple of hours going through Margo's vehicles. We tore them apart."

Libby stifled a sneeze. "And?"

Jason made a circle with his thumb and middle finger. "Like I said, zero, nada, nothing."

"I get the idea." Bernie rubbed her arms—it really was freezing in the storage space—and changed the subject. "So he and Margo were close?"

"You could say that."

"And what would you say?"

"I'd say I heard them on the phone. They were talking about moving in together, and then something happened. I'm not sure what."

Bernie thought of the card they'd found in Margo's house. "Did they have a fight recently?"

Jason laughed. "They were always fighting. Well, not really fighting. You know . . . like picking at each other."

"You mean bickering?"

"Yeah. That's exactly what I mean," Jason replied. "That's what they did all the time. But this one was serious."

"Do you have any idea what happened?" Bernie asked.

Jason shook his head. "I didn't ask either. None of my business."

"Do you think your boss had anything to do with Margo's death? You know, like they had a lover's quarrel and he snapped. That kind of thing?" Libby asked even though her dad had told her about Chung's alibi.

Jason snorted. "If you're asking me if he killed her, the answer is no. They loved each other. Don't ask me why, but they did. I suppose the whole 'opposites attract' thing."

"People who love each other sometimes kill each other," Libby observed.

"Not in this case," Jason responded firmly.

"Did you?" Libby asked just because she thought she should.

Jason wrinkled his forehead. "Do what?"

"Kill her," Libby replied.

No," Jason cried, taking a step back, a look of shock on his face. "What kind of question is that?" he squawked.

"A pertinent one," Libby replied.

"Are you nuts? Why the hell would I do that?"

Libby shrugged. "I don't know. You tell me."

"I didn't even know her."

"That's not what you said, Jason," Libby reminded him.

Jason squared his shoulders. "I told you I met her, that's all. It isn't like she was my friend or anything." He shook a finger at Libby. "I watch TV. I know what you're trying to do," he told her.

"What's that?" Libby asked him.

"You're trying to get me to confess."

"Are you guilty?"

"Screw you. Maybe it's time for you and your sister to leave," Jason told her stiffly.

Libby apologized. "Sorry," she said. "I had to ask."

Before Jason could reply, Bernie stepped into the conversation. "So, Jason, does Chung have any idea what happened to Margo?" she inquired, curious to see if what Jason said would match up with what Chung had told her and Libby at RJ's.

Jason cleared his throat. "Yeah, he does. He thinks one of her friends killed her. At least that's what he told me."

Libby zipped up her hoodie and jammed her hands into its pockets. "Which friends?"

"The ones in that book club of hers."

Libby and Bernie exchanged glances.

"The Longely Mystery Book Club?" Bernie asked, just to make sure they were all on the same page.

"Yeah, that one."

"Why does he think that?" Libby wanted to know. Frankly, she still couldn't think of a less likely group of people to murder someone, but then she reminded herself that she never would have believed Margo had a fake passport and lots of spare cash, either.

Jason shrugged. "You'll have to ask him."

"I'm asking you," Bernie said.

"I don't know. He just said all those people were crooked and that Margo was doing bad stuff for them, and he was trying to get her to stop."

"How bad?" Libby asked.

"Getting arrested bad." Jason shifted his weight from

his left to his right foot. "He was worried she was gonna take the fall for what they were doing. At least, that's what he told me."

"Anything else?" Libby asked.

Jason shook his head. "And I don't think he would have told me that if he hadn't had a couple of shots for lunch."

Like Libby, Bernie's mind went to the passport and the money they'd found hidden in the tree in back of Margo's house. "He wasn't more specific?"

"Nope."

"And you didn't ask him?"

"No, I didn't. Every time he started talking about it, he got really upset."

"Yeah. I can believe that," Libby said, thinking back to Chung's behavior at RJ's.

Jason ran his hand through his hair. "Listen, it's late, and I gotta get up early in the morning."

"So do we," Bernie said. "So if you don't mind, we'll just take a look at Margo's cars and be on our way."

"What if I do mind?" Jason asked.

"Do you?" Libby asked.

"No. But then why did you say that?"

Bernie could see from the expression on Jason's face that he was honestly puzzled. "I was trying to be polite." She wondered if he was on the spectrum. "We'll make it fast," she promised.

Which they did, because Jason was correct. There was nothing in the three vehicles. Nothing in the front seats, nothing in the back seats, nothing underneath the seats, nothing in the glove compartments, and nothing in the trunks.

"Did Chung take anything out of Margo's vehicles?" Libby asked Jason when they walked back into the office.

Jason opened his eyes. He'd fallen back asleep sitting in

the chair behind the desk, waiting for Bernie and Libby to leave. He shook his head. "Not that I saw. If you're so curious, why don't you ask him?"

"We intend to," Bernie replied.

"Have fun." Jason stifled a yawn, hoisted himself up, and made his way over to the blow-up mattress. "Turn the light off on the way out," he told the sisters as he slipped into his sleeping bag and zipped it up.

"Will do," Libby promised.

"Nighty, night, sleep tight, and don't let the bedbugs bite," Bernie sang out as she flicked the switch and the room was once again bathed in darkness. As Bernie closed the door behind her and Libby, she thought she heard Jason say, "Go to hell," but she couldn't be sure.

Chapter 24

It was a little after two o'clock in the morning by the time Libby and Bernie returned to Chung's house. The air was heavy with rain, and a slight drizzle was falling on Bernie and Libby's heads. The moon kept appearing and disappearing behind the slowly drifting clouds, the occasional rays cutting through the patches of fog obscuring the road, while a low-flying plane's lights twinkled in the sky. The smell of a skunk lingered in the air.

When Bernie and Libby walked inside Chung's house, they could hear him snoring from the entryway. He was sprawled out on the sofa, in the same spot they had left him in when they'd gone to check out the storage facility. The sisters tiptoed by him, and Bernie put Chung's keys on the dining room table. Then she and her sister turned to leave. They'd almost cleared the living room when Bernie's hip connected with a small occasional table she hadn't seen.

"Damn," Bernie cursed as the package that had been sitting on it fell onto the wood floor, landing with a thud.

The package didn't make a lot of noise, but it made enough, because Chung's eyes opened as Bernie crouched to pick it up. Their eyes met, but Chung started to cough before he could say anything. For a moment, Bernie was afraid he was going to throw up.

"What are you doing here?" he cried when he was able to speak.

"Returning your keys," Bernie said, standing up.

Chung started to sit up, wobbled, and sank back down into the sofa cushions. He rubbed his forehead. "Why do you have my keys?" he croaked.

"We brought you home," Bernie explained. Which was true. They had. She believed in never lying if you didn't have to. Which she wasn't. She was just omitting certain facts. Not the same thing at all.

Chung swallowed. "Why would you do that?"

Bernie told him. "Because you were drunk, and my boyfriend asked us to."

"Your boyfriend?" Chung repeated. He shook his head, trying to pierce through the fog that was curled around his brain. "Who's that?"

"Brandon," Bernie said. "He works at RJ's. He's the bartender. Remember? I told you last night."

"The big red-headed guy?"

"Yeah. That's the one."

"I must have blacked out." Chung rubbed his forehead again, trying to make the dull ache in it go away. "I feel like crap."

"I can't imagine why," Libby told him. "You could hardly walk, let alone stand. It took three of us to get you out of the bar and into Brandon's Volvo."

Chung looked at her with bleary eyes. "Brandon's Volvo?"

"He lent it to us, because we couldn't get you in our van," Libby explained. "You should thank him."

"I need a drink," Chung declared.

"I would think that would be the last thing you'd need," Libby observed.

Chung glared at her. "I didn't ask you, did I?"

"I'll get you one," Bernie volunteered. "Where do you keep your booze?"

Chung pointed to the kitchen. "In the top cabinet, on the bottom shelf to the right of the sink. A couple of shots of rye with a little bit of ginger ale and a couple of ice cubes."

Bernie came back with his drink a couple of minutes later. "Here," she said, handing him the glass plus two Benadryl she'd found in the kitchen cabinet.

"What are these for?" Chung asked, staring at the pills suspiciously.

"Trust me. It'll help with the hangover," Bernie told him.

Chung shrugged and put them in his mouth, washing them down with a slug of rye. He shuddered and wiped his mouth with the back of his hand, took another gulp of his drink, put it on the end table, leaned back on the sofa, and closed his eyes.

Bernie shook him. "Wake up," she told him. "We have to talk."

Chung's arm flew out, and Bernie jumped back to avoid getting hit in the face. He opened his eyes.

"Go away," he croaked, his voice thick with phlegm.

"I can't," Bernie said. "Not until we have a chat."

Chung just stared at her, a mulish expression on his face.

"It seems as if Margo's death hit you hard," Bernie observed, trying to coax him to talk.

A minute went by before Chung spoke. "That's none of your business," he finally told Bernie, closing his eyes again.

"Do you think she'd want you to be drinking like this?" Bernie asked him.

Chung raised his head and opened his eyes for the third time. "I don't need a lecture from you." He reached for his drink, his hand shaking. "I have my sister for that."

Libby and Bernie watched as Chung spilled a little of his drink on his pants before he managed to get the glass to his mouth and take another swallow. Then he plonked the glass down on the coffee table.

"Maybe you do," Libby told him. "But what you're doing isn't helping Margo."

"Nothing is going to help Margo," Chung replied. "Remember, she's dead." And with that he reached over, picked up his glass, and finished the rest of his drink.

"But you could help us find out what happened to her," Bernie gently suggested.

Chung let out a bark of a laugh. "That's funny coming from you."

"How so?" Libby asked.

"You know," Chung said, accusingly.

"No, I really don't," Libby replied.

Chung reached for his glass, saw it was empty, and turned to Bernie. "I need another drink," he told her.

Bernie went and got it for him.

"What? No lecture?" Chung asked as he took it from her.

"No," Bernie said quietly. "It's not your fault, you know."

Chung didn't say anything. He just took a hefty swallow of his rye and ginger ale and put the glass back on the coffee table. Bernie noted that the table was stained with ring marks.

"It's not," Bernie went on, pretty sure she'd found the right track.

Chung turned his head away. "You don't know anything," he replied in a strangled voice.

"Then tell us what you think happened," Bernie urged,

moving closer and squatting down beside him after he'd composed himself. "Maybe we can help."

"You can't," Chung told Bernie.

"Sure we can," Libby said.

"It's too late. Way, way too late." And Chung started to shake his head, thought better of it, and stopped.

"You want to tell me why you're saying that?" Libby asked.

Chung rubbed his forehead again. "Ask Lydia." Bernie noted that his speech was becoming increasingly slurred.

"We're asking you," Bernie said. She patted Chung's hand. "Please help us."

"You wouldn't believe me if I told you," Chung mumbled.

"Try us," Libby urged.

But instead of answering the question, Chung told Libby to tell her dad he was sorry. "I was an asshole."

"He'll be glad to know that," Bernie informed him. "Now what about Lydia?"

But Chung didn't answer. Instead, he closed his eyes and started snoring again.

"I guess she's our next victim," Bernie observed, once she'd levered herself up. Those last two drinks had done it for Chung. "He did say Lydia, didn't he?" she asked her sister.

"That's what I heard," Libby replied.

"Me too." Bernie rubbed her thighs. Her quads and calves ached from squatting. Pathetic. She really had to go back to the gym. She just didn't know when she could fit it into her day.

"You should have made those drinks weaker," Libby pointed out.

"They were weak," Bernie replied as she studied Chung. He was sprawled out on the sofa, arms akimbo, head tilted back, mouth opened. He looked the way he had when they'd come in.

"Lydia." Libby shook her head, remembering their last conversation with the LMBC members. "I can hardly wait."

"I'm not exactly looking forward to it, either," Bernie said as she glanced at her phone. It was definitely time to go to bed. "At least Dad will be happy to hear Chung's apology."

"He'll say, 'Better late than never,'" Libby predicted, and she was correct. That's exactly what Sean did say.

Chapter 25

Four Days Later

Bernie drummed her fingers on Mathilda's steering wheel. Driving across the Tappan Zee on a Friday in the summer was not her idea of a good time, yet here they were, because Lydia had insisted on meeting them outside of Longely, across the bridge, in a small restaurant in Nyack. She guessed that's why she and her sister got the big bucks.

"Talk about cloak and dagger," Libby groused as she studied at the traffic in front of them. Even though it was early—a little after three o'clock in the afternoon, to be precise—the bridge was already clogged with people heading out to their summer homes.

"At least Nyack is a nice little town," said Bernie, trying to be positive.

"So is Longely," Libby noted.

"Maybe Lydia really has a reason for setting up the meeting at Le Café," Bernie countered as they crawled along. At this rate, it would take them an hour to get across the bridge.

"Other than she's nuts?" Libby replied, thinking of all the work they had to do for the weekend, especially the French macarons they'd agreed to make. Why had they agreed? Those things took forever, and you couldn't rush them. She'd rushed this morning, and look what had happened. She'd had to spend half an hour fishing eggshell bits out of the egg whites. She was obsessing about the eggshells, hoping she'd gotten all the pieces out of the meringue, when Bernie spoke.

"Even crazy people . . ."

". . . are right some of the time," Libby said, finishing her sister's sentence for her. "I know. I know." It was one of their dad's favorite sayings.

"We can't afford to not meet Lydia," Bernie pointed out. "Maybe she does know something. Maybe Chung is right."

"He was drunk," Libby objected. "He was barely coherent."

"Nevertheless, we need to talk to her."

"This is going to be a massive waste of time," Libby predicted. "I don't see any useful information coming out of her."

"We won't know until we try," Bernie countered.

"Fine, but she sure didn't sound as if she knew anything the last time we talked to her," Libby noted, remembering everyone's reactions.

"Maybe she'll do better on her own," Bernie suggested. "And what if Lydia really is psychic, Libby? What if she's the real deal?"

Libby snorted. "What if I could run a marathon?"

"What's one thing got to do with the other?" Bernie asked as she opened her window all the way to catch any errant breeze.

"They're both impossible."

"No, they're not. One is highly unlikely, while the other is possible. You could run a marathon if you wanted to. All you have to do is train."

"Right." Libby took a sip of her cucumber and strawberry flavored water before replying. "I don't want to train. I hate running."

"Exactly my point." Bernie honked at a BMW cutting her off. The guy gave her the finger, and she returned the favor. "You could, but you won't. Which is why your sentence makes no sense. It's a non sequitur."

Libby crossed her arms over her chest. "It's not to me," she declared, a mulish expression on her face. Even if her sister was right, she was damned if she was going to admit it.

Bernie decided it was time to change the subject to a more neutral topic. There was no point in continuing when her sister got like this. "At least they did a nice job on the bridge," she observed, searching for a neutral topic. This was the first time she'd been across the Tappan Zee since they'd rebuilt it. "It kinda reminds me of the East Bay Bridge."

"If you say so," Libby replied absent-mindedly. She wasn't really listening to Bernie. She was too busy outlining the weekend battle plan in her head. She was still thinking about how she and Bernie were going to get everything that they needed to do done, when she and Bernie arrived at Le Café.

Lydia was sitting outside, underneath the green-and-white-striped canvas awning, alternately fanning herself with a magazine she'd brought to read and sipping her iced coffee. When she saw the sisters, she put the magazine down and called out to them.

"Sorry we're late," Bernie said, taking a seat across from her. "The traffic was terrible."

Lydia waved away Bernie's apology. "Don't worry about it." Then she picked up her fork and pointed to the strip of peach tart she was eating. "This is really good."

"It looks it," Bernie told her as she studied the gleaming piece of pastry while a waitress hurried over, dropped a couple of menus on the table, and then departed to wait on a two-top.

The fruit strip looked perfect. It reminded Bernie of her first trip to Paris, when she'd spent hours dawdling in cafés, people watching and trying everything on the menus. Like the fruit tarts she'd eaten back then, the puff pastry was a light golden brown, the edges carefully crimped with the tines of a fork; the peaches were sliced thin and gleamed with what Bernie assumed was an apricot jam glaze, and the top was graced with a sprinkle of finely chopped pistachios. At least, Bernie decided, even if they didn't get anything worthwhile out of Lydia, they'd have had something good to eat. That was always a plus in her mind.

Libby was thinking the same thing as her sister as she studied the scene in front of her. The place was full, people sitting under the awning, taking in the summer day while having a coffee and a pastry or relaxing with a glass of wine and an open-faced sandwich.

Looking around, it occurred to Libby that she and Bernie should reapply for a permit for outside seating for A Little Taste of Heaven. *Maximizing one's resources* was the phrase that came to mind. Actually, it would be easier and cheaper than getting a grill, and she suspected that when everything was added up, they'd be making as much money from the outdoor seating as they would from the grill. If they submitted their application now, they could get everything up and running by next spring at the latest.

She and Bernie had tried for a permit five years ago and

been rejected by the zoning board, which had ruled that the table and chairs would constitute an impediment to pedestrian traffic, but the people on the board had changed in the intervening time, and a couple of the ones now serving had been friends with her mom. It couldn't hurt to try again. Never underestimate the personal connection. Libby was thinking about whom on the zoning board she should talk to first when Lydia asked her what she thought of the café.

"It's nice," Libby said, glancing inside. "Very nice." She could see that the owner had furnished the place like a bistro in Paris, or at least what a bistro looked like in the movies. It had the classic chairs and tables, the walls decorated with French posters advertising various aperitifs, and the black-and-white-checked floor.

"I like it," Lydia said. "I'm glad you do too."

She'd lost weight since she'd seen her last, Libby noted. She looked tired and stressed, but there could be a lot of reasons for that, Libby decided, as the waitress came by to take their order. Bernie considered for a moment and ended up ordering a coffee éclair and a cappuccino while Libby decided to try a napoleon and an iced coffee.

"I thought it would be better if we met here," Lydia said once the waitress had collected the menus and left.

"And why is that?" Bernie asked, curious to hear what Lydia had to say.

"Because I don't want to be seen talking to you and your sister," Lydia said, giving Bernie the obvious answer.

"I figured. But you haven't told us why you feel that way," Libby said.

Lydia took another bite of her pastry, then laid down her fork. "Isn't it apparent?"

"You had a dream and Margo warned you not to be seen with us," Libby couldn't keep herself from saying, the words tumbling out of her mouth before she could stop them. "Sorry," she quickly apologized. "That was uncalled for. I'm just tired," she explained. Which was true. She still hadn't fully recovered from getting only three hours of sleep the other night. Unlike her sister, she needed at least seven hours a night or she wasn't the nicest person to be around. "My sister can testify to that."

Bernie nodded her head. "Definitely true."

"I know you guys don't take my dreams seriously," Lydia said. "It's okay. No one does." Lydia looked from Bernie to Libby and back again. "But I saw what I saw, and no one can make me say different."

"Chung takes them seriously," Bernie lied.

Lydia smiled. "Not really. But he knows Margo and I used to talk. I imagine that's why he told you to get in contact with me."

"He seems to be taking her death pretty hard," Bernie noted.

"It's very sad," Lydia agreed. "We all are upset."

"So did they have a thing?" Libby asked, double-checking.

Lydia nodded.

Bernie leaned back in her chair. "Were they having problems?" she asked, thinking of the card she'd found in Chung's house.

"Doesn't everyone?" Lydia replied.

"And no one else in the book club knew about them?" Bernie inquired.

Lydia shook her head. "Margo said not to tell anyone, so I didn't." She blinked back tears. "I just wish she'd listened to me. If only she'd listened, she'd still be here. I know I keep saying that, but it's true. She was so stubborn." Lydia's tone was fierce. "Whenever I said anything to Margo, she just laughed and told me everything was going to be fine."

"What did she mean by that?" Bernie inquired as she reached into her bag, took out her sunglasses, and put them on. The sun was in her eyes. "What was going to be fine?"

Lydia shook her head. "I don't know. She didn't say."

Libby put on her sunglasses as well. "So you didn't know about the passport and the money?" she asked Lydia.

Lydia shook her head again. "I was just as shocked as everyone else."

"Do you think Chung knew about them?" Bernie inquired.

"I doubt it," Lydia answered, falling silent as the waitress came back with Bernie and Libby's order.

"Why do you say that?" Bernie asked.

"Because it doesn't sound as if she wanted anyone to know." She pointed to the pastries. "Taste them," she said. "I'm curious to hear what you think."

"Excellent," Bernie said after a couple of bites. The pate a choux was the proper texture; the custard melted in her mouth, and both the filling and the icing were the perfect coffee flavor. She turned to Libby. "How's yours?"

Libby nodded. "Very good. Excellent, in fact."

"We should make these again," Bernie observed after she'd taken another bite of her éclair and put her fork down.

"And the napoleons as well," Libby added. They'd stopped making them because they weren't selling well, but maybe their time had come again. Libby was thinking that there were fashions in pastry, like in everything else, as she turned to Lydia. "So," she said, changing the subject, "as much as I appreciate finding a new place to eat, do you want to tell me why we're in Nyack instead of Longely."

"I already did," Lydia said.

"A few more details might be helpful," Bernie pointed out.

"You're the detective. You tell me," Lydia said.

"Hmm." Bernie stroked her chin, pretending to think. "Hmm. Let me see. Could it be that you're scared someone will see us together and bad things will happen to you?" Bernie inquired.

"If by bad you mean dead, then yes," Lydia answered. "Of course, I'm scared," Lydia went on. "Someone killed Margo. How could I not be?"

Bernie took a sip of her cappuccino and put her cup down. "So I assume this means you think whoever killed Margo might want to kill you too?"

"How the hell should I know?" Lydia snapped. "But if it's all the same to you, I'd rather not take that chance."

"Do you think whoever killed Margo thinks you know something—something that could lead him or her to harm you?"

"But I don't know anything," Lydia exclaimed.

"Then why are you scared?" Bernie asked.

Lydia bit her lip.

"There must be a reason," Libby said.

Instead of answering, Lydia studied the table.

Bernie took a sip of her cappuccino, put the cup down, and considered the woman in front of her. She knew something. But what? "Look, Lydia, you dragged us all the way over here to tell us something. What is it?"

"I just don't like speaking ill of the dead," Lydia mumbled.

We're losing her, Bernie thought as Libby rolled her eyes and said, "It's a little late for that, isn't it?"

Bernie wanted to kick her sister. Sarcasm was the last thing they needed right now.

"Margo was a nice person," Lydia insisted.

"I'm sure she was, which is why you should tell us whatever it is you dragged us across the bridge for," Bernie said. Then she added, "You know you want to."

Lydia began fingering the scarab on the necklace she was wearing. "The other people . . ."

"The members of the Longely Mystery Book Club?" Libby clarified.

Lydia nodded. "They are my friends, too. I don't know what to do," she admitted, choking back a sob.

Bernie leaned forward, took off her sunglasses, and looked into Lydia's eyes. "I think you do. That's why you brought us here. There's something you want to tell us."

"Maybe I'm wrong. I could be," Lydia said.

Neither Bernie nor Libby replied. They just sat and waited.

After a couple of minutes of silence went by, Bernie said, "Don't you want Margo's murderer to be caught?"

Lydia nodded.

"Well," Bernie continued, "we can't do that without your help."

"What if one of the people who is paying you is the one that's responsible for her death?" Lydia countered. She leaned back in her chair. "What then?" she demanded.

"Then we'd go to the police," Libby assured her.

Lydia shook her head.

"We wouldn't?" Bernie asked. "Is that what you think?"

"I don't know what to think," Lydia confessed.

"We would. Pinky swear," Bernie told her.

Lydia smiled in spite of herself as Bernie finished off her éclair.

"If you really believed that about us, you wouldn't be here right now," Bernie continued after she'd swallowed. "You wouldn't have agreed to meet us."

"I guess that's true," Lydia allowed after a moment's hesitation.

"You know it is," Libby replied.

"Please," Bernie said. "Pretty please with a cherry on top."

This time Lydia laughed. "When you put it that way." Her voice trailed off as she studied two sparrows perched on the wrought-iron railing, watching for crumbs. "There's someone you need to talk to."

After another minute, Lydia gave Libby and Bernie the name.

Chapter 26

Rebecca Bell's art gallery was ten blocks away from Le Café. It was located off the main drag, atop Venner Hill, on a block that consisted of private homes. Bernie had just made a left onto Skidmore, the street the Peterson Gallery was on, when Libby nudged her sister.

"Look," she said, pointing down the street.

"At what?" Bernie asked. "I don't see anything."

"There," Libby replied. "Isn't that Gilda Westover coming out of the Peterson Gallery?"

Bernie squinted into the sunlight. "By Jove, I believe you're right, Sherlock," she said, doing her best Watson impersonation, which even she had to admit wasn't very good.

"What are you doing?" Libby asked as Bernie parked Mathilda in the space in front of a fire hydrant.

"Seeing what we can see, Libby," Bernie replied as she watched Gilda put an elaborately framed painting into the back of her Saab, adjust it, then go back into the Peterson Galley. She came out a minute later with another painting, which she carefully placed in the back seat as well. Then she got in the Saab, pulled out onto Skidmore Street, almost hitting a car passing by in the process, and sped away while the driver of the Corolla screamed at her.

"She seems like she's in a bit of a hurry," Libby noted.

"Probably needs to be back at her gallery," Bernie guessed as she pulled out of the space she was in and headed toward the parking space Gilda had vacated. "So much for Lydia dragging us out here so no one from the LMBC would see us meeting," she observed as she concentrated on shoehorning the van into the empty space. It was going to be a tight fit, Bernie decided, but she was fairly confident she could make it.

"I wonder if those paintings Gilda was loading into her car are the missing Eakins the Glassbergs are going on about?" Libby mused.

Bernie paused, turning the steering wheel, and gave her sister a sharp glance. "That's so random. What makes you say that?"

Libby shrugged. "Just a wild guess. We have two people saying that someone in the Longely Mystery Book Club is responsible for Margo's death, and when you add in the missing pictures . . ."

"We don't know that they're related," Bernie interrupted.

"And we don't know that they're not," Libby countered. "They could be."

"*Could* being the operative word here," Bernie said.

"True," Libby admitted as her sister gave Mathilda's wheel one last turn.

"Did it!" Bernie crowed, an unmistakable tone of satisfaction in her voice. She turned off Mathilda and took the key out of the ignition while she studied the building the gallery was housed in. "It reminds me of our place," Bernie noted of the light blue, clapboard, two-story house that had clearly been someone's home at one time. "Except for the gingerbread and the gables, that is."

"And the dress shop on the second floor," Libby added. "Did you know, Mom wanted to move to a house and stop living over A Little Taste of Heaven?"

Bernie shook her head. This was the first she'd heard of it. "No, I didn't. What happened? Why didn't they move?"

"Mom said Dad didn't want to."

"Why not?" Bernie asked.

"He said he wouldn't see as much of Mom and us if they did."

"That's so sweet."

"It is, isn't it?" And Libby changed the subject. She pointed to two large freestanding flower boxes on either side of the entrance that were filled with perennials. "Those are nice."

"Yes, they are," Bernie agreed, noting the riot of colors. "We should change ours out," Bernie said.

"We should," Libby agreed. "But we won't." They'd had this conversation multiple times over the years, and somehow they never got around to it.

"Maybe we should hire someone to do it for us," Bernie suggested.

"That's probably the only way it'll happen," Libby said. She pointed down the hill. "I'm glad we drove."

"Yeah," Bernie agreed. "Me too. That hill is worse than Chung's. It's almost San Francisco steep," she said, remembering their trek up from Chung's place. "But it is a nice view." They could see the Hudson from where they were. "So how do you want to play this?" she asked her sister. "Straight? Or do you want to pretend to be in the market for a painting?"

"Let's start off pretending . . ."

"And if that doesn't work, we can do good cop, bad cop."

"Except we're not cops," Libby pointed out.

"You're always so literal, Libby. I was using 'good cop, bad cop' as a metaphor."

"Oh, is that what you were doing?" Libby said after she'd gotten out of Mathilda and closed the van door.

"Yes," Bernie replied, walking toward the gallery. "It was," she said as she opened the door. The bells on the door jingled as she and Libby stepped inside.

Chapter 27

"I'll be there in a minute," a pleasant-sounding woman's voice called out as Bernie and Libby looked around.

"No rush," Bernie replied, enjoying the cool air. *Air-conditioning*, she thought. *One of the greater inventions of the twentieth century.*

The gallery was small, probably no more than eight-hundred square feet, Bernie estimated. The cream-colored plaster walls were hung with oils, while the maple floor was polished to a high shine. Off to the left side was an old oaken rolltop desk and an equally antique office chair. A vase full of yellow roses stood on top of the desk.

"Now, what can I help you with?" a woman asked as she emerged from the back of the shop.

"Rebecca Bell?" Libby asked, not that she needed to. She fit Lydia's description perfectly: early forties, bright orange hair cut into a pageboy, long fake eyelashes, short, thin, dressed in a vintage sundress, tattoo of a dragon on the front of her right calf.

The woman smiled and nodded. "That's me."

"Lydia sent us," Libby said. "She told us you might be able to help us."

"I'd be delighted to, if I can," Rebecca said. "How's she doing? She was in rough shape the last time I talked to her."

"Okay, considering," Libby replied.

"That's good to hear," Rebecca said. "These things take time."

"Yes, they do," Libby replied, assuming that Rebecca was talking about Margo's death.

"And speaking of time," Bernie said, changing the subject, "I love your dress," she told Rebecca. "It's so fifties." The fabric, a polished cotton with large, bright yellow sunflowers splashed over a pale blue background, had been made into a sundress with a fitted bodice, spaghetti straps, and a full skirt.

Rebecca's grin grew larger. "It's vintage."

"Where'd you find it?"

"Stella's."

Bernie nodded. She knew the store. It dealt in second-hand clothing. "I love that place," she told Rebecca.

"Me too," Rebecca agreed. "You never know."

Bernie laughed. That was the store motto. It was painted over the entrance door.

"Now, what are you interested in?" Rebecca asked, changing the conversation back to why she assumed Bernie and Libby had walked into the place. She gestured to the walls with a sweep of her hand. "At the moment, we have an exhibition of some of the lesser-known artists of the Hudson River School, as well as a nice selection of local artists hanging in the back room."

"Actually, we're interested in Eakins, or perhaps a Childe Hassam," Bernie said.

Rebecca laughed. "Why not a Sargent? Fifty years ago, no one wanted those guys, and now . . . Well, I'm afraid those are a little above our price range," Rebecca said.

"You need to go to New York if you're interested in something like that." And she named two galleries that carried the painters Rebecca had named.

"Oh." Libby acted disappointed. "That's what Gilda said, but Lydia said you might be able to help us locate them."

Rebecca cocked her head. "You know Gilda, Gilda Westover?"

Bernie and Libby both nodded.

"You just missed her!" Rebecca exclaimed.

"I know," Libby said. "We saw her leaving as we turned onto the block. Tell me, was she loading the Eakins into her car?" she asked, following up on her hunch.

Rebecca gave her an odd look. "Why do you say that?"

Libby did nonchalance. "She was talking about them last week, and when I saw the frames, I thought they might be them."

"Well, they weren't," Rebecca informed Libby in a voice grown less cordial. "How do you and your sister know Gilda and Lydia anyway?"

"We're from Longely," Libby explained.

"From the book club," Bernie added.

Rebecca frowned. "I thought I knew everyone in it," she said. "Evidently, I was wrong."

"We just joined," Bernie responded.

"Ah. I see." Rebecca resumed, smiling. "So what do you collect?" she asked.

"A little of this and a little of that," Libby answered.

Rebecca wrinkled her brow. "That's rather a wide range, isn't it?"

"We're just starting out," Bernie confessed, jumping into the conversation. "But I guess that's pretty obvious. Margo was helping us," she added. "And now that she's gone, I have to admit we're at a little bit of a loss for guidance."

Rebecca shuddered and hugged herself. "Poor Margo. Dying all alone like that. I can't even imagine."

"Did you know her well?" Bernie asked.

"As well as anyone, I expect," Rebecca replied. "Not that that's saying much. Margo did a little work for me from time to time," Rebecca went on, "and once in a while, we'd go out and have martinis."

"Martinis?" Bernie said, surprised. "I have to say, I wouldn't have thought that was her drink of choice."

Rebecca laughed. "That's exactly what I thought the first time she ordered one. Margo." Rebecca shook her head. "She was a real character, but I have to say, she was very good at what she did. She had a very good eye."

"She always wanted to be a painter," Bernie said. After all, it could be true. "I guess what she did was the next best thing."

"She was very good at copying and fixing, but there's a big difference between doing that and having an original vision," Rebecca pointed out.

"Did she copy things for you?" Libby asked.

"Not for me, but when I had a client who wanted a copy of one of their paintings, I referred them to Margo."

"Did that happen a lot?" Libby asked.

"Not a lot," Rebecca told her. "I'd say once in a while."

"Why would someone do that?" Bernie asked. She was genuinely puzzled.

Rebecca explained. "Sometimes when people own expensive works of art, they store the original in a vault for safekeeping and hang a copy of the work on their walls. Most people can't tell the difference."

"I don't get it," Libby said. "Why have it in the first place if you're not going to display it?" she asked.

"Ego. Investment. Having young children," Rebecca explained, mentioning a client of hers whose child had used a magic marker on a Sargent. Her phone rang. She looked down at it. "Excuse me, I have to get this," she said, and walked into the back room.

Bernie and Libby looked at each other. Then, unable to resist, they both headed over to the rolltop desk. Bernie glanced at the laptop's screen, which contained a review of the gallery's current show, while Libby started to go through the papers piled on the desk. They seemed to con-sist of receipts, reviews, invitations, and scribbled notes on pieces of pink notepaper. Libby was studying an invitation to a lecture given by Steve Offenbach on the hidden mean-ing of Michel Zest's art when she heard a cough.

"Find anything interesting?" Rebecca asked as Libby and Bernie whirled around.

Chapter 28

Rebecca was standing in the doorway, arms crossed over her chest, tapping her foot on the floor. She did not look amused.

Bernie held her hands up and said the first thing that came into her mind. "Okay, sorry about this. We were looking for a catalog. We probably should have asked."

"You think?" Rebecca said, her eyes narrowing.

"Are you going to Steve Offenbach's lecture?" Libby ad-libbed. "It sounds fascinating."

"What the hell are you two up to?" Rebecca demanded, ignoring Libby's question, as she walked toward Bernie and Libby.

"We told you," the sisters answered in unison.

"Try another story," Rebecca instructed.

"Would you believe we were looking for your business card?" Bernie chirped.

Rebecca's face flushed. "At least put some effort into your lies, because from where I was standing, it appeared as if you two were looking through my desk."

"That's absurd," Bernie said, trying for outrage and failing. "Why would my sister and I do something like that?"

"Why, indeed? You tell me," Rebecca replied.

Bernie put her hand to her heart. "Are you saying we're lying?"

Rebecca made a gun with the fingers of her right hand and pointed it at the sisters. "Bingo. You and your sister aren't collectors, are you?"

"Whatever gave you that idea?" Libby protested.

Rebecca snorted. "Maybe because it's obvious that you and your sister have no idea what you're talking about."

"I wouldn't say that," Libby said.

"I would," Rebecca snapped.

"Any other reason?" Bernie inquired.

"Besides your looking through my desk?" Rebecca asked. "My customers usually don't do that type of thing."

"Yes, besides looking through your desk," Bernie said.

Rebecca pointed to the van, which was visible out the gallery's window.

"And then there's that."

"You mean Mathilda?" Bernie replied, insulted.

Rebecca nodded. "If that's what you're calling the vehicle."

"What's wrong with Mathilda?" Bernie protested.

Rebecca frowned. "Let's just say that the people who collect what I sell usually don't arrive in something like that. Even the lesser-known artists of the Hudson River School are commanding a hefty price these days."

"That seems a bit . . ."

"Snobbish? Snotty?" Rebecca said, supplying the words.

"I was going to say short-sighted. We could be . . . humble," Bernie said. "You know, the kind of people who don't flaunt their wealth."

Rebecca snorted and pushed her bangs out of her eyes. Bernie reflected that they needed to be trimmed.

"Listen," Rebecca told her, "I have paperwork to do, so either tell me why you're really here or leave. I mean, do you even know Lydia and Gilda? Did Lydia even send you?"

"We do know them, and Lydia did suggest we talk to you," Libby assured Rebecca. "And as for why we're here—we're investigating Margo's death."

Rebecca looked from Libby to Bernie and back again. "I'm afraid I don't understand," she said, sounding puzzled. "I heard she died in an accident."

"Maybe not," Libby replied.

Rebecca cocked her head. "What do you mean? Explain." Then she listened attentively while Bernie and Libby did just that. "Even if that's the case, what's that got to do with me?" Rebecca inquired when the sisters were done talking.

"As I just said, we're looking into Margo's death," Bernie explained. "Lydia thought you might be able to help us."

"How?" Rebecca asked.

"She didn't say," Libby responded.

Rebecca wrinkled her forehead. "You're detectives? You don't look like detectives to me."

"We are. Kinda," Bernie said.

"Kinda?" Rebecca repeated. "What does that mean?"

Bernie told her.

Rebecca raised an eyebrow. "Like Miss Marple type detectives?"

"Yeah, except we're a lot younger and much better dressed," Bernie replied. "Or at least one of us is."

"Excuse me," Libby said, turning to her sister.

"Am I lying?" Bernie shot back.

Rebecca interrupted. "So you're unlicensed? You have no legal status?"

"How about moral authority?" Bernie countered. "We have that."

"Not good enough. Tell me why I should talk to you."

"Because Margo was a nice lady, and you might want to help us find out what happened to her," Libby answered.

"She wasn't a nice lady," Rebecca countered.

Now it was Bernie's turn to raise an eyebrow. "That's not what I heard. That's not what you said earlier."

"No, I didn't," Rebecca argued.

"You said her death was sad," Libby pointed out.

"And it was, but that's far from saying she was a nice person," Rebecca answered. "I mean, it's amazing how everyone becomes a saint after they're dead."

"I don't think that word is going to apply to Margo," Libby observed.

"You want to tell me why you didn't like her?" Bernie asked Rebecca.

Rebecca checked the time on her phone, then spoke. "Okay, I misspoke. It's not that she wasn't nice; it's just that she was difficult to work with. Extremely picky. She wasn't one for small talk, and she took offense easily. Very thin-skinned." Rebecca raised her hands. "On second thought, let's just say she had lots of issues, and lately she'd become more . . . irritable. Something was bothering her."

"Did you ask her what it was?" Bernie inquired.

Rebecca shook her head. "No. We didn't have that type of relationship."

"Why did Lydia tell us to talk to you then?" Bernie asked Rebecca.

Rebecca shrugged. "Frankly, I have no idea."

"I think you do," Libby said.

"Maybe you should call Lydia and ask her," Rebecca told Libby.

"Don't worry, you won't get in trouble," Bernie assured Rebecca, although she had no idea why Rebecca should get in trouble. It just seemed like a good thing to say.

"Why would I get into trouble?" Rebecca demanded.

Instead of answering Rebecca's question, Bernie said, "We need to know what you know," Bernie said.

"About the Hudson School painters?" asked Rebecca, purposely misunderstanding what Bernie had said.

"Ha ha. About Margo," Libby clarified.

"Margo was killed for a reason," Bernie added.

"So you told me, but frankly I find that difficult to believe," Rebecca replied. "I think all the mysteries Margo's friends read have gone to their heads. Otherwise, they'd go with what the police are saying."

"Margo's house was ransacked," Bernie told her. "Did you know that?"

Rebecca leaned forward. "No, I didn't know."

"Well, it was," Libby replied. "And then my sister found one hundred thousand dollars in hundred-dollar bills and a fake passport hidden in a tree . . ."

"You're kidding," Rebecca cried, visibly shocked.

"Do I look as if I am?" Bernie asked.

"How do you know the passport and the money were Margo's?" Rebecca demanded. "You said you found them in a tree in Margo's backyard?"

Bernie nodded.

"Anyone could have come along and put them there," Rebecca argued.

"I suppose they could have," Libby said, "except the passport had Margo's picture on it. Does the name Martha Goodrich mean anything to you?"

Rebecca shook her head. "Was that the name on the passport?"

"Yes," Libby replied.

"I don't know what to say," Rebecca told her. "I don't often say this, but I'm really shocked."

"I think everyone feels that way," Bernie said. "Where did the money come from?"

Rebecca didn't say anything. Instead, she looked out the

window, studying the flowers in the planters outside the gallery. "Margo, leading a double life," she murmured after a minute had gone by. "Who would have thought?" Then she said, "But I still don't understand what you want from me."

"Margo moved in your world," Bernie said.

Rebecca nodded. "That's true."

"We were hoping you could point us in the right direction. Tell us a little more about her friends."

"You mean the people in the Longely Mystery Book Club?" Rebecca asked.

"Those and anyone you can think of."

Rachel's eyes got even bigger as she connected the unspoken dots. "You think someone there killed her? Is that what you're saying?"

"No, no, no," Libby quickly replied. The last thing she wanted was word getting back to the group. "Let me rephrase that. My sister and I are just interested in learning more about Margo's world. What was she doing that would make her that kind of money?"

Rebecca readjusted the shoulder strap on her sundress again before replying. "Offhand, the only thing that comes to mind at the moment is copying works of art."

"So you're saying she was scamming people, selling the copies as original paintings?" Bernie asked.

Rachel nodded. "Possibly. Or she could have been working for someone who was selling them and Margo was just the worker bee, so to speak."

"Do you know anyone who does that kind of thing?" Libby asked.

"Doesn't everyone? I was being sarcastic," Rebecca explained, seeing the expressions on Libby and Bernie's faces. "No. Of course, I don't."

"Have you heard any gossip?" Bernie persisted.

"About that kind of thing happening?" Rebecca asked. Bernie nodded.

"As a matter of fact, I have," Rebecca told her, "but bear in mind that this kind of gossip is pretty common."

Bernie nodded encouragingly. "Go on."

"I would say you should talk to Jane."

"The Jane who owns Stella's?" Bernie guessed.

Rebecca nodded. "But she's out in New Zealand taking care of her mum right now. Poor lady slipped and smashed up her hip. Anyway, Jane bought what she thought was a Prendergast watercolor a couple of years ago, and she found out it was a copy when she went to sell it."

"Who did she buy it from?" asked Libby.

Rebecca didn't answer. Instead, she adjusted the strap on her dress.

"Was it from the Westovers' gallery?" Bernie persisted. "Or did she buy it at auction from the Glassbergs?"

"They refunded her money when she went to them," Rebecca replied.

"The Glassbergs?" Libby inquired.

Rebecca nodded. "They apologized and said they didn't know."

"But you think they did know?" Bernie questioned.

Rebecca rubbed her hands together. "I didn't at the time, but now . . ." She lifted her hands and let them drop, leaving the rest of her sentence unsaid. "On the other hand, there are always authentication issues in this business."

"Do you think Margo did the copy?" Libby asked.

Rebecca shrugged. "Your guess is as good as mine. I'd like to think that wasn't the case, but I could see it happening." She paused. "After all, we are talking about a lot of money."

"How much?" Libby asked.

"A lot," Rebecca replied as two well-dressed women in their fifties walked into the gallery. Bernie watched Rebecca put on her game face. "How can I help you?" she asked them, the relief in her voice palpable.

Bernie nodded to Libby. It was time to go. They'd gotten all they were going to get. Which wasn't much.

"Still," Bernie said when they were outside, "every crumb counts."

"Let's hope so," Libby replied. "You think she was telling us everything she knows?"

"No," Bernie said. "I don't at all."

"Me either," Libby said.

Chapter 29

While Bernie and Libby were driving back from Nyack, Sean was sitting in a back booth at Taylor's Steakhouse, waiting for one of his former colleagues to join him. He was leafing through the local paper, sipping a beer, and eating a sliced-steak sandwich when Eckleburger and another man came through the door. As Sean waved Eckleburger over, he automatically assessed Eckleburger's companion. It was an old habit of his—like the way he always sat facing the door—left over from his cop days.

The guy had a sour face. One thing was for sure. He definitely didn't want to be here, Sean decided, as he looked him over. He was a little under six feet tall and on the skinny side. He had brown hair and brown eyes, was in his late twenties to early thirties, and sported a buzz cut and two diamond studs in each ear. There was nothing much to distinguish him except his gait. He walked with a pronounced limp.

"Glad you finally made it. I was beginning to worry," Sean told Eckleburger as Eckleburger and his friend slid into the booth.

"Traffic," Eckleburger explained. "Where's Clyde? I thought he was supposed to be here."

"He was, but he got tied up," Sean told him.

"Is he working on the Digby killing?" Eckleburger asked.

Sean nodded. Stephen Digby, an accountant for a painter's union, had been killed on the steps of the Longely Courthouse just as he was going in to testify about a wide-ranging kickback scheme. Even though it was midday, no one had seen or heard anything.

"It looks like a professional hit," Sean added. "So he'll be here when he can. If he can."

"Understandable," Eckleburger said.

"Clyde's getting a lot of pressure," Sean said. Then he nodded toward the man standing next to Eckleburger. "And who is this gentleman? I don't think I've had the pleasure of his acquaintance."

"Pleasure of his acquaintance," Eckleburger repeated. "How Victorian of you. This is Rodney. I think you'll be interested in what he has to say."

The corners of Rodney's mouth twitched in a pretend smile. Then he mumbled a hello, slumped down in his seat, and began picking at his cuticles. Sean could see that they were bleeding.

"The place still looks the same," Eckleburger observed, glancing around Taylor's. It had been a couple of years since he'd been here.

"It's looked the same for the last thirty years," Sean noted, referring to the gold-flocked wallpaper, the red leather booths, and the dark wood floor.

"That's why they call it a classic," Eckleburger replied.

A moment later, their waitress came over. A middle-aged woman, she projected an air of someone who had been on the job for too long. She was wearing her hair in a messy bun on top of her head and carrying an extra thirty pounds around her middle. Her earrings, large gold hoops that came halfway down her neck, bounced up and down every time she moved.

"What happened to Martha?" Eckleburger asked her.

"She retired and moved down to Florida last year."

Eckleburger shook his head sadly. "At this rate, there won't be anyone left up north."

"So what can I get you?" the waitress asked, her pencil beating an impatient tattoo on her ordering pad, even though there was no one else in the place. Business wouldn't get into high gear for a couple more hours.

Eckleburger pointed to what Sean was eating. "I'll have what he's having."

The waitress nodded and turned to Rodney. "And you?"

"Can I look at a menu?" Rodney asked her.

"You don't need one," Eckleburger told him. "Have the rib eye." Then he nodded toward Sean. "He's paying," Eckleburger told the waitress. "In fact, put everything on my friend's tab. He's a very generous man."

"I am?" Sean said. "That's news to me."

"You're not? Listen," Eckleburger said, leaning forward, "don't cheap out on me now."

Sean sighed. "Okay," he told the waitress. "Give the man whatever he wants."

"In that case," Rodney said, "I'll have the rib eye, medium rare, with a baked potato with sour cream and butter, and roasted asparagus, if you have them."

"We do. Twelve or sixteen ounces for the steak?"

"Sixteen ounces."

"And to drink?"

"Whatever you have on tap," Rodney answered.

"Double the drink order," Eckleburger said.

The waitress nodded and moved away.

"This better be worth it," Sean groused as he estimated the meal was probably going to set him back three hundred bucks, maybe more if everyone had another round or two of drinks, coffee, and dessert.

"When have I ever steered you wrong?" Eckleburger demanded.

"Do you really want me to answer that?" Sean asked.

Eckleburger frowned. "The Kruntz case wasn't my fault. Okay, maybe a little bit," Eckleburger conceded when Sean snorted. "But this is different," Eckleburger told him as the waitress came back with two beers. "You're going to thank me for this. And I'm not even charging you."

"What do you call my paying for dinner?" Sean asked him.

"A nice gesture," Eckleburger replied.

Sean threw up his hands. "You win," he told Eckleburger as he turned toward Rodney. "So what do you do for a living?" Sean asked him, even though, given the fact that Eckleburger was a handwriting expert who specialized in forged documents, he had a pretty good idea what Rodney's answer was going to be.

"Oh, a little of this and a little of that," Rodney replied, keeping it vague.

"Rodney's just being modest," Eckleburger informed Sean. "He copies things, don't you, Rodney?"

Rodney sat up straighter. "Well, it's a little bit more than that," he said, coming alive for the first time since he'd walked into Taylor's. "I create things."

"He is very good at what he does," Eckleburger said. "Really, almost genius level."

"What kind of things do you create, Rodney? Inquiring minds would love to know," Sean said.

"All kinds of things," Rodney told him, slumping back down in his seat again, his burst of energy gone.

Sean watched as Eckleburger leaned over and gave Rodney a solid whack on the back of his head with the flat of his hand.

"Tell the man," Eckleburger ordered.

Rodney rubbed the spot where Eckleburger had hit him. "That hurt," he whined. "You could have given me a concussion."

"If I wanted to give you a concussion, I would have. I'm being nice," Eckleburger told him.

"It's true," Sean said to Rodney. "He is. You should see him when he isn't."

"There's no reason to use physical force," Rodney complained.

Eckleburger laughed.

"What's so funny?" Rodney asked.

"Obviously, you have no idea what physical force is," Sean said.

"Such a delicate soul," Eckleburger said as he leaned back. "Rodney, I thought you and I had a deal."

Rodney didn't answer.

"Well, don't we?" Eckleburger demanded, his voice louder this time. "I mean, if you've changed your mind, if don't want to talk to my friend here, that's okay. I'll be happy to exercise the other option we discussed earlier."

"No, no," Rodney said quickly. "No need for that."

"Then tell my friend what you know," Eckleburger instructed.

"Give me a minute." And Rodney took a swallow of his beer and put the glass back down on the table.

Sean took another bite of his sandwich while he waited. You could say what you wanted about the décor in here, Sean reflected, but, God, were their steaks good, probably because they aged them in a temperature-controlled room in the back of the restaurant.

"Did you know Margo?" Sean asked in the face of Rodney's continuing silence.

Rodney nodded.

"Did she come to you?" Sean asked.

Rodney nodded again.

"How did she find you?"

Rodney looked puzzled. "What do you mean?"

"Well, you're not in the yellow pages, are you?"

Rodney wrinkled his forehead. "What's the yellow pages?" he asked.

Sean threw up his hands in disgust. Talk about feeling old. "Never mind, Rodney. What I mean is that you don't exactly advertise your services, do you?"

"Not exactly," Rodney conceded.

"So how did she know to come to you?"

"Someone gave her my name," Rodney finally conceded.

Sean leaned forward. "And who would that be?"

Rodney turned to Eckleburger. "Do I have to tell him?"

"You most certainly do," Eckleburger answered.

Rodney fidgeted with his glass. "That's like violating a confidentiality agreement."

"Last I looked, forgers don't have confidentiality agreements," Sean pointed out.

"Tell him," Eckleburger ordered.

"Fine." And Rodney did.

Sean raised both eyebrows. "Are you sure?"

Rodney looked offended. "Of course, I'm sure."

"Interesting," Sean said, and he took another sip of his beer and thought about what Rodney had just told him. "So what did you charge her?" he asked.

"Margo?"

"No, the King of Siam."

"Forty thousand."

"For one passport?"

"Yup."

Sean whistled.

"Obviously, we've been in the wrong business for all these years," Eckleburger commented.

"Obviously," Sean responded before he turned back to Rodney. "I assume she paid in cash."

Rodney barked out a laugh. "Well, it's not like I'm going to take a check, am I?"

"No. I suppose not," Sean conceded. "Did Margo say anything?" he asked Rodney.

"She told me what she wanted, and I told her the price, and that was that."

"Aside from that."

"Like what?"

"Like did she say why she wanted it?" Sean asked.

"Yeah. To hang on her wall."

"A little less sarcasm and a little more substance, if you don't mind," Sean remonstrated.

"Sorry," Rodney muttered, although Sean reflected that he didn't look sorry; he looked resentful. "To answer your question, no, she didn't say why she wanted it, and I didn't ask."

"I suppose the less you know, the better," Sean observed.

"You could say that," Rodney replied.

Sean finished off his sandwich. He hadn't realized how hungry he was. "So what about the name on the passport?" he asked after he'd swallowed his last bite and picked up an onion ring. He loved French fries, but he loved onion rings even more.

Rodney looked up from tracing the outline of his beer stein on the table. "What about it?"

"Did the name have any significance to her?" Sean asked.

"Why would it?" Rodney replied. "It's not like she got to choose. That was the document I had. I just her put her picture in it and laminated it."

"So no chitchat?" Sean asked as the waitress came back with Rodney and Eckleburger's steaks.

Rodney cut into his steak and nodded his okay to the waitress, as did Eckleburger.

"We talked about the Yankees. She's a fan," Rodney told Sean after he'd taken his first bite.

"Seriously?"

"Yes, seriously."

Sean ate another onion ring and thought about what else to ask. "Did Margo get anything else from you?"

"You mean like a social security card? Driver's license? That sort of thing?"

Sean nodded.

"No, just the passport."

"And she picked it up?" Sean asked.

"We met at the Panera's on South Street."

"Why there?"

Rodney didn't answer. Instead, he took another bite of his steak. "God, this is good," he announced.

"Why there?" Sean prodded after Rodney swallowed.

Rodney shrugged. "They're busy. No one pays attention to anyone."

"How did you get started with this anyway?" Sean asked out of curiosity.

"Art school," Rodney said.

Sean's eyebrows shot up again. Now, there was an answer he hadn't expected. "You're kidding."

Rodney grinned ruefully. "Nope. I was going to be a great artist. Change the world with my vision."

"So what happened?"

"The usual," Rodney said. "I got a couple of exhibitions in a gallery on the Lower East Side, but I never sold anything. And then I met a former classmate at a coffee house on Orchard Street."

"Margo?" Sean guessed.

Rodney shook his head. "We didn't go to the same school."

Sean apologized for interrupting. "Go on."

"Hal asked me if I wanted to do a little side job for him, something that paid well. So I said sure. At that point, I was working as a waiter at Red Robin. Turns out, I have a talent for this kind of thing. Actually, like Eckleburger said, I'm really, really good at it." He shook his head. "Who would have thought?"

Bernie and Libby are going to love this, Sean thought, as he watched Rodney demolish his steak.

"I told you you'd like this," Eckleburger said to Sean a little later while they were waiting for Rodney to come back from the men's room.

"And you were right," Sean replied. "How you'd meet Rodney anyway?"

Eckleburger put his hand on his heart. "I can't reveal my sources."

"Cut the crap," Sean told him.

"Remember Orestes Zagreb?"

"How could I forget that name?"

"Well, he just got out of jail a couple of years ago, and now he's working for me."

"He gave you Rodney?"

Eckleburger nodded.

"So now you have felons working for you?"

"White-collar felons."

Sean snorted.

"What's that supposed to mean?" Eckleburger asked. "We used CIs when you and I were on the force."

"It's not the same thing," Sean told him.

"Actually, it's better," Eckleburger told him. Then he added, "I didn't realize you'd gotten so sensitive in your old age. If you feel that way, don't call next time you want some information."

"Look who's being sensitive now," Sean rapped out as he watched Rodney cross the floor.

"I think the words you're looking for are 'thank you,'" Eckleburger told him.

Sean glared at him.

"I'm waiting," Eckleburger said.

"Fine. Okay. Thank you," Sean said grudgingly after another minute had gone by. "Satisfied?"

Eckleburger grinned. "Getting you to apologize? You betcha. And you know something? Your daughters are going to be satisfied, too."

"Of that," Sean replied, "I have no doubt." On his way home, he called Clyde to fill him in on what he'd learned. Then he called Bernie and Libby.

Chapter 30

Libby stopped walking. "The Glassbergs?" she asked her dad in a shocked tone of voice. "Are you sure?"

"That's what this guy Rodney told me," Sean replied. "He said they gave Margo his name."

Bernie moved off the path onto the grass to let a pair of joggers decked out in reflective gear go by. "How do you know he isn't lying?" she asked, remembering the shocked reactions of everyone when she'd shown them the money and the passport they'd found hidden in the tree.

"Besides the fact that Eckleburger vouched for him and Rodney has no reason to lie?" Sean asked.

"Yes, besides that," Libby answered.

"How about because my gut says he's telling the truth?" Sean responded. Then he made his way over to a nearby empty bench facing the river and sat down. His knee had started bothering him on the walk over to the park. He just hoped his MS wasn't flaring up again and that he would have to start using his cane.

"And your gut is always right," Libby said.

"About ninety percent of the time," Sean answered

equably, patting the bench with the palm of his hand to indicate that he wanted his daughters to join him. "And then there's the fact that Rodney has no reason to lie, not to mention what Chung and Lydia said. Or at least what you said they said. Let's not forget that."

Bernie responded as she sat. "You mean about one of the book club members being responsible for Margo's death?"

"That's not exactly what they said," Libby said, correcting her sister. "They said that some people in the LMBC did not wish Margo well. There's a difference between not wishing someone well and murdering them."

"A degree of difference," Bernie said.

"More than a degree," Libby said.

Sean interrupted. "Let's review what we know."

"Which is?" Bernie asked.

"Let's assume for the moment that Rodney was telling the truth," Sean said.

"Which would mean that the Glassbergs' reaction was totally bogus when we showed them the passport," Bernie said.

Sean smiled. "Exactly."

Libby rubbed her chin, remembering the scene. "They certainly seemed shocked when we told them."

"As did everyone else," Bernie said.

"If that's the case, they're really good actors," Libby reflected. "Oscar-caliber actors."

"We've met people like that before," Bernie reminded Libby.

"Yes, we have," Libby agreed. "Still . . ."

"Still what, Libby?"

"I don't know."

"What don't you know?" her dad asked Libby as she took her place on the bench next to her sister.

Bernie answered before her sister could. "Ah-ha," she crowed, "you finally admit it."

"I was talking about this case," Libby snapped.

"That's not what you said, Libby."

"You're always so literal, Bernie."

"Me?" Bernie pointed to herself. "What about you?"

Sean shook his head as Libby answered her sister. Nothing ever changed. His girls had been bickering since they could talk. Sean checked his watch, letting his daughters' words roll over him. It was eight forty-five. The shop had closed at eight, and he and his daughters had decided to stroll down to the river to watch the sun set before night closed in.

He loved this time. The in-between time. The magic time. The heat of the day had dissipated, and a gentle breeze was blowing off the water. He studied the lights of a large yacht making its way downstream and wondered what it was like when Henry Hudson arrived here. What he must have thought.

"It would be fun taking a boat down the Hudson to New York City," Bernie reflected wistfully, echoing her father's thoughts. It was something she'd always wanted to do.

"It would be nice," Sean agreed. "In the meantime, you could always take the Circle Line cruise up to Bear Mountain," Sean suggested.

"Not the same thing," Bernie protested as she admired the red and purple streaks in the sky as the day drew to a close.

"Well, it's the closest you or I are going to get for the moment," Sean observed.

"I suppose," Bernie allowed as she watched the lights from the apartments on the opposite shore ripple in the water. She turned to her father. "I have a question for you," she said.

"Only one?" Sean asked. He laughed. "Okay, what is it?"

"The Glassbergs seemed to be the ones pushing the investigation into Margo's death."

"And?" Sean prompted, his attention momentarily diverted by a couple rollerblading. He hadn't seen that in a while.

"But why do that if they were involved in Margo's . . ."

"Activities," Sean said, supplying the word.

"I was going to say death," Bernie said.

"Maybe one thing has nothing to do with the other," Sean suggested, thinking about what Clyde had told him about the FBI opening a file into the goings-on of the Glassbergs and the Westovers. That could mean nothing, or it might be relevant to the matter at hand. There was no way to tell without seeing the file, and unless a miracle occurred, that wasn't happening anytime soon. "Maybe Margo and the Glassbergs were involved in a forgery ring, and someone objected to their activities."

Libby jumped into the conversation. "Or maybe Margo stole the Eakins, and the Glassbergs found out and killed her."

"They could have," Bernie said. "That's true. Here's the thing, though: Why supply Margo with the means to get out of town if you want to kill her? I would think you'd want her to stay put. And for that matter, why pay for an investigation to find out who killed Margo if you're the ones that did it? Especially since her death has already been ruled accidental? Why not let that stand?" Bernie asked. "They were home free."

"Because Lydia made such a fuss," Libby suggested, "and this was a way of shutting her up."

"That's one answer," Bernie allowed.

"And another would be?" Libby inquired.

"Deflection," Bernie answered. "Sending us down the wrong path."

"That seems pretty far-fetched," Libby noted. "Not to mention expensive."

"Agreed on both counts, but I'm just listing the possibilities." Bernie turned to her dad. "What do you think?"

"I think there are a lot of options on the table," Sean observed. "I think it's time for you and the Glassbergs to have a little chat. It'll be interesting to hear what they have to say."

"That's what I was thinking, too," Bernie said. She took her cell out of her skirt pocket and checked the time. It was nine-thirty. "I guess there's no time like the present."

"What if Tom and Betsy are getting ready to go to bed?" Libby asked.

"Then they'll go to sleep a little later," Sean told his daughter. "Plus, it's always better to catch someone off guard."

"Who goes to bed this early anyway?" Bernie asked Libby.

"You would if you were smart," Sean observed.

"It was a rhetorical question, Dad."

"I know it was, Bernie."

Libby was just about to add her two cents to the conversation when Mike Crenshaw strolled by them.

"Fancy meeting you here," he said, smiling as he stopped. "Nice night for a walk."

"Indeed, it is," Bernie replied, happy that the heat of the day was gone.

Sean wrinkled his forehead as he studied the man in front of him. The guy looked familiar, but he couldn't put a name to his face, which was annoying because he prided himself on his facial-recognition skills.

"Do I know you from somewhere?" Sean asked Mike. "I feel as if I should."

"That's because he's a steady customer, Dad," Bernie informed Sean.

"On the seven-fifteen Metro North," Mike said proudly.

Sean smiled. "Ah, a commuter."

Mike patted his stomach. "I couldn't live without your daughters' cinnamon rolls and coffee in the morning. They make the ride bearable. Worth every pound I've gained, although I think my girlfriend would disagree with that."

Libby smiled. "You're exaggerating."

"Only a little," Mike said, and he laughed. "I used to walk my dog here," he continued, "but now he's too old." Mike blinked. "Poor thing. Now I walk him up and down the length of our driveway, but then I come down here for a stroll when I can. I miss the river. It's so peaceful this time of night. Habit's a funny thing. Monty and I had a routine, and now that he can't do it, I still feel as if I should."

"Tell me about it," Sean said as he levered himself up and took an experimental step. Good, his knee was feeling better. It was probably nothing that a couple of aspirin and an ice pack couldn't fix, he told himself.

As he and his daughters said good-bye to Mike and started on their walk back home, Sean had an uncomfortable feeling. *There's something I'm missing in regards to Margo's death*, he thought. *Something about the river? No, that isn't it. Damn.* It was on the tip of his tongue.

Then Bernie started talking about her upcoming meeting with the zoning board, and the thought went clean out of Sean's head. He sighed. Hopefully, the thought would come back later. Probably when he was thinking about something else. That was usually the way things like that worked.

Chapter 31

Libby and Bernie arrived at the Glassbergs' house at ten-fifteen. "Looks as if they're still up," Bernie said as she turned off Mathilda and pocketed the key. "The lights are still on."

"All I know is that I'd be pissed if someone came to my door at this time of night," Libby noted as she and her sister walked up the driveway.

"I would too," Bernie agreed.

"Then why are we here now?" Libby asked as a white Lexus drove by them, took a sharp right, and disappeared into the night.

"Because hopefully we'll catch them off balance. At least, that's the theory," Bernie said as she rang the doorbell. She could hear it echoing inside as she watched a large moth circling around the porch light.

It occurred to Bernie that this was the first moth she'd seen this summer. There used to be swirls of them fluttering around the lights at night. Where had they all gone? For that matter, what had happened to all the lightning bugs and the praying mantises? Bernie realized she hadn't seen any in years as she rang the doorbell again.

Still no response. She was about to tell Libby it looked as if it were a no go, when she heard footsteps and Tom Glassberg yelled, "Hold on. I'm coming." A moment later, the door swung open, and Tom was standing there in a pair of khaki shorts, a paint-stained T-shirt, and flip-flops.

"What's going on?" he asked, running his hand through his hair. "Is everything alright?"

"It's fine," Bernie replied.

"Then why are you here?" he asked, looking from Bernie to Libby and back again. "I know," he said, answering his own question. "You're here because you found out who killed Margo, right?"

"Perhaps," Libby said as she and her sister stepped inside the Glassbergs' house.

"Perhaps?" Tom repeated as his wife joined him.

"Perhaps what?" Betsy asked. "Is there something wrong?"

"We have some new information about Margo that we thought you'd find interesting," Libby explained.

"Go on," Betsy said. She was barefoot, and the batik print caftan she was wearing had seen better days.

Watching her, Bernie reflected that Betsy looked ten years older without her makeup. She wondered if the same held true for herself.

"We found out where Margo got the passport," Bernie told her.

"Really," Tom said as the sisters watched him exchange a quick glance with his wife. "That's good, right?"

"Very good," Bernie said. "It gives us a lead."

Betsy nodded toward the kitchen. "I was just making myself and Tom a cup of tea. Perhaps you two would like to join us?"

"Certainly," Bernie said. "We'd love to."

"So this is very exciting news," Betsy observed once Libby and Bernie were seated at the kitchen table, although Libby decided she didn't sound very excited. Quite the opposite, in fact.

"I suppose that depends on your point of view," Libby replied.

"I don't understand," Betsy said brightly as she turned on the electric kettle.

"I think you do," Libby replied.

Bernie leaned forward and gave Betsy her biggest smile. "Rodney says hello. He told me to thank you."

Betsy blinked.

"Now, I'm totally confused. Who is Rodney?" Tom asked.

"And why is he thanking us?" Betsy added, having recovered from her initial surprise.

"Because you referred Margo to him," Libby said. "Forty thousand dollars for a passport. That's not chump change. And he doesn't even have to pay taxes on it. No wonder he's grateful. I would be, too, if I were him. How did you meet him, anyway?" Libby inquired of Tom and Betsy.

Bernie watched Tom and Betsy exchange another glance.

Betsy wrinkled her forehead. "This Rodney fellow?"

Bernie nodded. "That's who I'm talking about."

"I don't know where you got your information," Tom said stiffly, "but they're mistaken."

"No. I don't think so," Bernie replied. "My source is pretty reliable."

"Not in this case," Tom replied.

"Does this Rodney person have a last name?" Betsy asked as she got four mugs out of the cupboard.

"I'm sure he does, but I don't know what it is," Libby replied.

"Maybe, if you describe him," Tom said, "that would jog my memory. After all, Bets and I meet lots of people in the course of the day."

"Indeed, we do," Betsy added. "We're in and out of people's houses all the time. It's hard to keep everyone straight."

"It must be," Bernie said, and she told the Glassbergs what Rodney looked like.

Tom shook his head. "Nope. I'm sorry, but your description doesn't ring a bell." He turned to his wife. "Does this person sound familiar to you?"

"No," Betsy replied. "Absolutely not, and I would remember because I have an excellent memory for faces."

"She does," Tom assured Bernie and Libby. "Thank God, because I don't remember anyone."

Betsy nodded vigorously. "I don't know who this Rodney person is, and I don't know why he's saying what he's saying about us, but there isn't one word of truth in it."

"So this is a case of mistaken identity on his part?" Bernie inquired.

"Absolutely," Betsy said quickly.

"Maybe he has something against you," Libby suggested.

"How could he when he doesn't know us?" Betsy declaimed before changing the subject. "Do you mind herbal tea? That's what Tom and I were going to have."

"That'll be lovely," Bernie said.

"Ginger or mint?" Betsy asked.

"Mint, please," Bernie and Libby said at the same time.

They watched as Betsy nodded, opened a canister, and took out four tea bags. Both sisters noticed that her hands were shaking ever so slightly.

"You can't be giving credence to this accusation," Tom said.

"Yeah," Bernie told him, "I think my sister and I are."

Tom opened his mouth and closed it again, stifling the comment he was about to make.

He looks pale, Libby decided, as she asked him if he categorically denied what Rodney had said.

"Of course he does," Betsy replied, answering for her husband. "He just told you that."

"Absolutely," Tom replied, looking annoyed that Betsy had answered for him.

Bernie turned toward her sister. "That's too bad."

"Yes, it is," Libby said. "And I thought we were on the right track."

Tom beat a silent tattoo on the table with his fingers. "Track? What in heaven's name are you talking about?"

"Finding Margo's killer, of course," Libby answered. "I don't understand why you're saying you don't know Rodney, especially since it would let you off the hook," Libby added.

"What hook is that?" Betsy demanded as she took the four tea bags out of their envelopes and placed them in the mugs. "I'm not following you at all."

"Suspicion of murder," Bernie replied.

"You're crazy," Betsy snapped. "We loved Margo. We're devastated by her loss. She was our friend. Our good friend."

"How could you even think something like that?" Tom added. "That's appalling."

"We hired you to find out who killed Margo. Why would we do that if we had killed her ourselves?" Betsy asked. "That makes no sense."

"That's what I told my sister," Libby told Betsy, "but she isn't convinced."

Bernie shrugged. "Sometimes people do strange things." She pointed to the electric teakettle. "The water is boiling."

"Oh," Betsy said, and she lifted the kettle up and began to pour the water into the mugs, spilling some on the counter.

"You really are nuts," Tom told Bernie as he watched his wife reach for the sponge on the kitchen sink. "See, Bets," Tom told his wife, "I told you. This is what comes of hiring amateurs."

"I wouldn't call us amateurs," Libby objected.

"I wouldn't call you professionals, either," Tom said to Libby.

"You want to blame someone, blame Gilda," Betsy told her husband, as she cleaned up the spill. "She was the one who suggested these two."

Libby drew herself up. "These two? That's pretty rude."

"And you agreed," Tom told his wife, ignoring Libby. "You could have said no."

"So could you," Betsy shot back.

Bernie slammed her hand down on the kitchen table. Everyone turned to look at her. "If I may interrupt here."

"Yes?" Betsy said.

"We need to know why Margo needed the passport," Bernie said, taking control of the conversation. "If Margo really was your friend, and you want us to find out who murdered her, you'll tell us."

"We don't care what you do business-wise. Or have done," Libby said. "But we need to know where Margo was getting her money from. We need to know why she needed the passport. Otherwise, we can't help you. Or maybe you don't want us to. Maybe you just want to send us off on a wild goose chase."

"Maybe you should leave," Betsy said. "We're not paying you to insult us in our own house."

"Would it help if it were someone else's house?" Bernie asked.

Tom lifted his hand and pointed toward the door. "Out. I've had quite enough. Bets and I have a busy day tomorrow, and this is the last thing we need at this hour of the night."

"We'll go if you want," Bernie told him, "but before we do, have you considered the power of social media?" she asked, a new thought having just occurred to her as she studied her nails. She really needed to get a manicure.

"What the hell are you talking about now?" Tom asked.

Bernie looked up. "Allow me to explain."

"Make it fast," Tom said.

"I'll try," Bernie told him.

"Well," Tom said after a moment had passed, "we're waiting."

Bernie apologized. "Sorry. Just trying to organize my thoughts," she told him. "What I'm thinking is that you and your wife hired Margo to copy some of the works that you sell."

Betsy glared at her. "How dare you?"

"Easy," Bernie said. She held up her hand. "Let me finish."

"Go ahead and finish," Tom said, a grim expression on his face. "Then I want you gone."

Bernie nodded and took up where she'd left off. "So you auctioned them off, and either you and Margo split the money or you paid her a flat fee."

"You can't prove that," Tom said.

"So you're saying you did it," Libby asked.

"He's not saying anything like that," Betsy snapped.

Bernie continued as if she hadn't been interrupted. "Here's the problem with social media. If I post what I just said, and it goes viral, well . . ." Bernie's voice faded out. She snapped her fingers. "There goes your business. Even if it's not true. Sad to say, truth doesn't matter these days. Many times, the accusation is enough. Actually, more than enough."

"That's blackmail," Betsy cried.

"Yes, it is," Bernie agreed in an equable tone.

"You wouldn't," Tom said.

Bernie smiled. "Maybe we will, and maybe we won't."

"We could sue you," Betsy said.

"You could," Bernie agreed, "but by then the damage might be done."

Libby stepped in. "Listen, my sister isn't serious . . ."

"I certainly am," Bernie said.

"She really isn't," Libby assured the Glassbergs.

Tom looked from Libby to Bernie and back again and laughed. "I get it now. You two are you playing good cop, bad cop, aren't you?"

"No," Libby replied. "We're just trying to do what you hired us to do: get to the bottom of Margo's death."

"You sure have a funny way of going about it," Tom observed.

Bernie shrugged. "One works with what one has."

"Listen," Libby added, "we don't care what you've done. Or are going to do. We don't care if you've copied the *Mona Lisa* and sold it to head of the Sinaloa Cartel for . . . I can't even guess. We're just trying to figure out what Margo was doing, that's all. Hopefully, that will lead us in the right direction, so anything you can tell us—anything at all—would be helpful."

"After all," Bernie pointed out to Tom and Betsy, "we are doing this on your dime."

"We haven't forgotten," Tom said. Then he and Betsy

exchanged another glance. "If you'll excuse us for a moment," Tom said to Bernie and Libby, "my wife and I need to talk."

"By all means," Bernie said as the Glassbergs got up and left the room, at which point Bernie went over, picked up the mugs on the counter, and handed one to Libby. "Might as well have some tea while we wait," she observed.

"Not bad," Libby allowed after taking a sip. Normally, she wasn't a big fan of herbal tea.

"Alright," Tom said when he and his wife came back five minutes later. "Hypothetically speaking, what if what you said is true?"

"About the *Mona Lisa*?" Bernie cracked.

Betsy laughed. "Ha ha. I wish."

"Go on. We're listening," Bernie said, encouragingly.

"And once in a while, we did hire Margo to copy some works for us."

"Like the Eakins?" Libby asked.

"Hypothetically?" Betsy replied.

"Yes, hypothetically," Bernie said.

"Then, yes," Betsy said.

"Are they really worth that much money?" Bernie asked.

Tom shook his head. "Maybe a hundred thousand, which, in the scheme of things these days, isn't that much."

"So where did Margo get all her money from?" Libby asked.

Tom shook his head. "Not from us, that's for sure. She was doing something else. Something big."

"She wouldn't tell us what it was," Betsy said. "But she seemed excited in the beginning. A few months after telling us that she'd gotten the job, whatever it was, and that we should be happy for her, she came to us and asked us about the passport."

"She wouldn't tell us why she needed it," Tom said. "She just told us she'd made a big mistake."

Betsy frowned. "We asked her what was going on repeatedly, right, Tom?"

Tom nodded. "But she wouldn't let us in on it."

"We could see she was scared," Betsy added. "I tried to get Margo to open up about what was going on, but she told me I was better off not knowing." Betsy bit her lip. "I should have made more of an effort."

"You could say the same for me," Tom said. He blinked several times. "I thought I did a good thing giving her Rodney's name. I thought maybe she'd done something for someone, and that something went south, and she needed to, you know, disappear for a while."

"Here's a question," Bernie said. "How did Margo know to ask you?"

"I don't understand," Betsy said.

"Well, it's not as if everyone knows who to go to for a fake passport," Libby pointed out. "I certainly wouldn't."

Tom blushed. "I may have mentioned Rodney."

"May have?" Betsy said. "Ha. We were reading a spy novel by this English writer, and there was a chapter about someone needing a fake passport, and we started discussing how one would go about getting one, and my husband here bragged he knew someone who did that," Betsy explained.

"I should never have had three piña coladas," Tom said.

"I told you you'd be sorry," Betsy said.

"And I was," Tom said. "The next morning was hell. I crawled out of bed."

"Literally," Betsy clarified.

Bernie laughed. She'd had a few of those herself. "Where did you meet him?" Bernie asked Tom.

"Rodney?"

Bernie nodded.

"At an art opening at the Peterson Gallery."

"The one in Nyack?"

Tom nodded again. "We got to talking, and it turned out we'd gone to the same art school. Then we had a few drinks, and, well . . ."

"Confidences were exchanged," Libby guessed.

"Yes," Tom replied.

Betsy reached over and grabbed Bernie's wrist. "We didn't kill her," Betsy said. "You have to believe us."

"I'm beginning to," Bernie replied, which was more or less the truth.

Libby took a sip of her tea and put her mug down. "Where did she get her money? Do you know?"

"Not exactly, but I can guess," Betsy replied. "She told us she'd worked on some big stuff over the past four years."

"By big stuff you mean art stuff?"

Betsy nodded. "That's what I assumed. After all, besides reading mysteries, that's what Margo did."

"Can you be more specific?" Libby asked.

"Not really," Betsy said.

"Also she was very frugal," Tom said. "She never spent money if she didn't have to."

"Actually the word is *cheap*," Betsy said. "Almost pathologically so. She bought all of her clothes at garage sales, for example. You know how people say that so and so had the first penny she earned. Well, Margo was like that."

"And yet she paid to get her house painted," Bernie commented.

"Not really," Betsy said. "Those were kids from the

local vocational school. They did it for class credit, and she got the paint from a store that was going out of business."

"What about the vehicles she was storing?" Bernie asked.

"I'd be willing to bet she looked on those as an investment," Tom said.

"And her relationship with Chung?" Libby asked.

Betsy shook her head. "I gotta tell you that was news to me."

"Anyone else you can think of who would know anything about Margo's other line of work?" Libby asked Betsy and Tom. "Anyone at all?"

Tom and Betsy exchanged another glance.

"You mean someone in our book group?" Betsy asked.

"In or out of it," Bernie clarified. "We're not picky."

Betsy turned her hands palms up. "I don't know what to say."

"Say whatever comes into your head," Libby suggested.

"What if nothing does?" Betsy asked.

"I'm sure something will," Bernie told her. "You get around, you hear things."

Tom spoke first. "Well, the Offenbachs travel a lot. They give lectures all over the place and know a ton of people in the art world. But I can't believe they would be involved in this kind of thing. On the other hand, I guess you really never know what people do, do you?"

"What about the Musclows?" Bernie said.

"You know what I think?" Betsy said, answering a question with a question.

"No, what?" Libby replied.

"I think maybe Margo was working for the CIA. Maybe she was a spy. Maybe that's why she was killed."

Bernie snorted.

"Why the snort?" Betsy demanded.

"I thought we were sticking to reality," Bernie replied.

"I am," Betsy told her. "Stuff like this happens all the time."

"Not quite all the time," Libby observed dryly. "In books, maybe; in real life, not so much."

"Or Margo could have double-crossed someone," Tom suggested. "You know, like she was hired to copy something, but she gave the people who hired her the copy and sold the original, and the people found out, and she needed the passport to get out of town."

"That sounds more plausible," Libby said.

"Or," Tom continued, encouraged, "maybe Margo was collateral damage. Maybe the person who hired her is a sheikh or a Russian oligarch or an American billionaire. You know, someone who stole the work of art and has it stored in their vault, and Margo's copy is hanging in the Louvre or the Met, and they killed Margo to make sure she didn't talk. I could see that happening."

"The art world isn't so nice," Betsy noted. "People think it is, but it isn't."

"Especially when big money is involved," Tom added. "But then that's true in any field, isn't it?"

Bernie allowed as how it was.

"So what do you think?" Bernie asked Libby as they made their way back to the van.

Libby stifled a yawn. "I think I need to go to sleep."

"Besides that," Bernie said as she looked for the van keys, which were buried at the bottom of her Louie.

"Besides that, I think that the more I hear, the more confused I get," her sister responded.

Bernie yawned as well. "Make that two of us. Business or personal?"

Libby brushed a mosquito away. "Margo's homicide?"
Bernie nodded.

"If I had to say, at this point in the game, I'd pick business. You?"

"The same," Bernie replied as she climbed into Mathilda and started her up. It was time to go home and fall into bed.

Chapter 32

The Next Morning

Libby took a taste of the feta and turned to Bernie. "Try this," she told her.

Bernie looked up from her cell phone. "Why?"

"Just try it."

Bernie did and made a face. "It's turning."

"That's what I thought."

"But we just got it yesterday!"

"I know. I'm going to call Sal now." Libby looked at the clock on the wall. It was ten-thirty. People would start coming in for lunch in another hour, and they still had two more salads to make. This is what she got for sleeping in. "But what do we use in the meantime for the watermelon and feta salad?"

Bernie tapped the fingers of her right hand on her thigh while she thought. "Parmesan?"

Libby shook her head. "Too expensive, and the texture is wrong. Too grainy. What about farmer cheese or mozzarella?"

"The mozzarella could work," Bernie said, thinking of

feta's flavor profile. "Although it is very bland. Maybe if we added something salty?"

Libby thought about what they had in the pantry. "We have pepitas. Those might work."

"Or pistachios?" Bernie suggested, thinking of the pop of bright green the pistachios would add.

"Better," Libby allowed. "And maybe shred some fresh basil and toss it in."

"Or," Bernie said, "I can run over to Tom's place and get some feta right now."

"What about Mrs. Schmidt's salade Niçoise? You haven't started on that yet."

"This is true," Bernie said as she stopped checking her email and put her phone down on the prep table. "It would be cutting it close. So I guess we'll stick with the mozzarella."

"We just have to remember to change it on the menu," Libby said as she went back to cubing the watermelon.

Bernie put her phone on her charger. "Maybe we should start getting Greek sheep's milk feta instead of the French cow's milk stuff."

"The French feta is smoother."

"Agreed, but it goes bad faster. This is the second time this has happened in a month."

"I think we need to get it in the brine instead of crumbled. I think that may be a factor."

Bernie was just about to tell her sister she might be right when the Offenbachs burst through the prep room door with counter girl Amber in hot pursuit right behind them.

"I told them they couldn't come in here," Amber said. Her face was flushed, which, Bernie reflected, clashed with her bright purple hair. "I told them I'd ask you if you could talk to them, but they pushed right by me. Didn't even say I'm sorry or excuse me. Do you want me to call the police?"

"The police?" Irene echoed. "Why would you do something like that?"

"It's okay, Amber," Bernie reassured her.

"Are you sure?" Amber asked.

Bernie nodded. "Positive. You can go back to work now."

"Okay, then," she answered. "But I'm right on the other side of the door if you need me."

"We appreciate that," Libby told her.

Amber turned to go and then turned back. "Oh, and by the way, we're going to need more quarters soon. I'm almost out."

"She's a little overreactive, isn't she?" Steve observed after Amber left.

"She's protective," Bernie explained. "Very protective."

Steve looked around. "For God's sake, why? This isn't some dive bar at two in the morning, not that I would know much about places like that," he added.

Bernie answered. "Let's just say we've had a few bad actors show up here from time to time."

"Ow, bad actors." Irene shivered in delight. "That must have been so exciting."

"Not really," Libby replied, thinking of Mike Williams waving a gun in her face. "Now, what's this about? Why are you two here? I'm figuring it isn't just because you want coffee."

"We're here to defend our good name," Irene answered.

"Such as it is," Steve put in.

Bernie raised an eyebrow. "How so?"

"I understand you think we had something to do with Margo's death," Irene informed her.

"Did you?" Bernie asked.

"Ha ha. Funny lady," Steve said.

"I try." And Bernie gave him her best modest smile.

"To answer your sister's question," Steve replied, "since we were passing by on our way to give a lecture at Rutgers, we decided to beat you to the punch, metaphorically speaking."

"That's considerate of you," Libby remarked.

Irene leaned in. "At first, when I heard about your conversation with the Glassbergs, I was really upset," she confided. "After all, we hired you to find Margo's killer, and to suspect us . . ." She shook her head at the absurdity of the idea. "I thought you should be concentrating your efforts elsewhere, to engage in a more fruitful line of inquiry."

"We were quite angry," Steve said, repeating what his wife had just said.

"We were just shocked that you'd think that any of us had anything to do with Margo's death," Irene said. "We were friends."

"Sometimes friends kill friends," Bernie pointed out.

"Not in this case," Steve assured her.

"But then Steve and I started talking, and I realized that in the police procedurals that we read, private detectives always suspect the people that hire them," Irene said, "so I calmed down."

Steve sniffed the air. "It smells wonderful in here," he noted, changing the subject.

"It's the chocolate-chip bars that just came out of the oven," Libby replied.

Steve's face lit up.

"Would you like one?" Libby asked.

"Please. If you don't mind," Steve said. "We haven't had breakfast yet."

"Too busy going over our notes and answering our emails," Irene added.

"My pleasure," Libby said, and she escorted the Offenbachs into the office while Bernie went to get the bars and something to drink.

A moment later, everyone was settled down with glasses of iced coffee and a plate of chocolate-chip bars.

"It gets cozy in here," Bernie noted as she managed to fit another chair into the space so she could sit down.

"This place is even smaller than my office at the college," Steve noted as he bit into one of the chocolate-chip bars. "And that used to be a broom closet—literally."

"He's not kidding," Irene said.

"I believe you," Bernie said, thinking of her old college adviser's office.

Steve took another bite. "Delicious," he pronounced.

"What makes them so good?" Irene asked as she nibbled on her first one.

Libby answered. "They're thicker than usual, and there's a lot of good chocolate in there."

"And cinnamon," Bernie added, and she finished her bar, even though she'd told herself she was just going to eat half. "Don't forget the cinnamon. It balances the sweet with a little heat. Plus we added ground almonds. It's a loose take on Mexican chocolate."

"Well, they are excellent, whatever they're paying homage to," Steve commented as he finished his first bar and reached for a second.

"So what do you want to know?" Irene asked after a few moments went by.

"Well, you two do a lot of traveling overseas," Bernie began, thinking as she did that this line of questioning was a waste of time. On the other hand, one never knew until one tried.

"Yes, we do," Steve agreed.

"And so did Margo," Libby said.

"So we were wondering if you two were ever in the same place at the same time?" Bernie asked.

"I'm sure we have been over the years. I don't get where this is leading," Steve said.

"Well, we were thinking that perhaps you could shed some light on some of the people Margo met with on her travels," Libby said.

Steve and Irene exchanged looks.

"Any particular people you had in mind?" Steve asked.

"I think you have to narrow your parameters," Irene informed Libby. "Are you talking about waiters? Bellhops? Taxi drivers?"

Steve turned his wife, "Darling, let's not be so persnickety."

"You're right," Irene said. "My apologies, but can you be a little more specific?"

"By all means," Libby replied. "Well, we understand that sometimes Margo was involved in some . . . work . . . that might have not been strictly legit."

"Is that what Tom said?" Irene asked.

Bernie nodded.

Irene flushed. "And he implied that we would know who those people she worked for were?"

"In so many words, yes, he did," Libby said.

"That's funny," Steve said, "considering that, business-wise, Tom and Bets are not always on the up . . ."

"And up," Bernie said, finishing his sentence for him.

"You said it, I didn't," Steve answered. "Tom's statement is absurd. We're academics; we don't deal with forgeries. Isn't that right, darling?"

Irene nodded. "That is correct. Now, cribbed papers are another matter." She sighed. "There is a tawdry underbelly to the art world."

"That's what Betsy told us," Bernie noted.

"Well, she should know." Irene put her hand to her mouth. "I didn't mean for that to sound the way it did," she said, even though Bernie was pretty positive that she had.

"We used to do authentications for insurance companies," Steve told Bernie. "Millions of dollars on the line on our say-so. It was very stressful."

Irene shuddered. "Steve, remember that awful thing with the Degas."

"How could I forget, darling," her husband replied. "Irene and I couldn't sleep for weeks," he confided to Libby and Bernie. "We were vindicated in the end. The work was a forgery—a good forgery, but a forgery nevertheless.

Irene leaned forward. "It was horrible getting to that point. I honestly thought I was going to have a nervous breakdown."

"That's too bad." Bernie took a sip of her iced coffee and began her spiel. "This may sound as if it's coming out of left field, but we were wondering if either one of you introduced Margo to someone who could have given her a job . . ."

"You mean a job that didn't turn out so well for her, a job that could have gotten her killed?" Steve asked, finishing Bernie's question for her.

"Exactly," Bernie replied.

"Hardly," Irene said. "For that matter, I don't remember encountering Margo when we were overseas? Do you, Steve?"

Steve shook his head.

"What about introducing her to someone here?" Bernie asked, continuing her questioning.

Irene frowned, "Here. There. It's the same thing. My husband just said we don't know people like that," she snapped.

Bernie raised an eyebrow. "Anyone like that?"

"That's right, anyone," Steve responded angrily.

"You must lead a sheltered life," Bernie remarked, deciding to lean on Steve a little and see what happened.

"No. Far from it," Steve shot back.

Bernie took another sip of her iced coffee. "There's a statement—I forget who said it—about how everyone has a private life, a public life, and a secret life. What's your secret life?"

"What's yours?" Steve countered.

Bernie waggled her eyebrows. "I'll tell you mine, if you'll tell me yours."

Irene reached over and squeezed her husband's arm before he could reply. "Slow down," she told Bernie. "First of all, Marquez said that, and second of all, it certainly doesn't apply to my husband or me. If you want to talk about shady, you should talk to Tom and Betsy and the Westovers about those Eakinses."

"Now, Irene," her husband remonstrated, while Libby thought about the pictures that she and her sister had watched Gilda put in her vehicle and the reaction of the Peterson Gallery's owner when she'd asked about them.

Irene turned toward her husband. "It's true, Steve. I don't see why we can't say anything after they pointed the finger at us."

"They didn't point a finger at us . . ."

"No, Steve, they implied, which is worse. What nonsense." Irene snorted. "From what you two say, Tom and Betsy made it sound as if all of us used the same travel agent—metaphorically speaking. We don't . . . didn't live in each other's pockets. We were friends. Or, at least, I thought we were. We met once a month at book club. Occasionally, we took in a movie or had a bite to eat." Irene glared at Bernie. "And even if we happened to be in, let's say, Paris or Munich or Dubai at the same time, so what? That's what's called a coincidence."

"Is that what it's called?" Bernie asked.

"Yes, it is," Irene answered. "Consult the OED, if you need a definition."

"The point my wife is trying to make," Steve clarified, "is that even if we were all at the same places at the same times—which we weren't—it doesn't mean anything."

"If you say so," Libby said.

"We do," Irene declared. "But I'll tell you who met Gilda in Paris last year . . ."

"That was to see the Leonardo exhibition . . ."

"So Margo said, Steve. But how do we know?"

"That's true, considering everything that's gone on," Steve allowed, after mulling his answer over for a moment.

"Do you happen to know where Margo's passport is?" Bernie asked, trying a different path. "We didn't see it in the house, and it might be handy to look through." Of course, they hadn't exactly looked for it, either, but Bernie was curious to hear what the Offenbachs had to say.

"You mean her legit one?" Irene asked.

"Yes, that one," Libby said.

"I believe it was stolen a couple of months ago," Irene replied. "At least, that's what Margo told me. She left it in her hotel room down in the city, and when she came back, it was gone."

"Convenient," Bernie murmured. It might mean something, or it might mean nothing at all.

"Not for her," Irene shot back. She looked at her watch and declared it was time to go.

"One last thing," Bernie said. "Is there anything you can think of that would help us. Anything at all, no matter how silly it seems."

Irene thought for a moment and then said, "I ran into Margo about a week before she disappeared, and she came over and gave me a great big hug," Irene replied. She took a sip of her iced coffee.

"And," Libby prompted.

"And that's it," Irene replied.

"I don't get why you're telling us that," Libby said.

"I'm telling you that," Irene explained, "because Margo never hugged anyone."

Steve nodded. "At least, I never saw her do it."

"It sounds as if Margo could have been saying good-bye," Libby observed.

Irene nodded. "That's what I think now."

"And then?" Libby asked.

"Frankly, I didn't think too much about it. I had other things on my mind."

"Anything else?" Bernie asked.

Irene got up. "Not that I can think of. You, Steve?"

Steve shook his head. "Nothing comes to mind."

"So what do you think?" Libby asked Bernie after Steve and Irene left.

"I think the Offenbachs were very well rehearsed."

"Yes, they were, not to mention quick to throw their friends under the bus."

"That too," Bernie agreed. "I wonder what else they are?"

Chapter 33

Bernie laid her cell phone on the corner of the prep table and turned to her sister. "Evidently," she told her, "the Westovers' gallery is only open by appointment, except for Tuesday and Wednesday afternoons. At least, that's what the recording says."

Libby looked up from the cucumber, blueberry, radish, and tomato salad she was dressing. Featured on the menu along with fried chicken, it was the last thing she had to make before the dinner rush. "That must be nice," she commented. Then she said, "Maybe they're home."

"No time like the present to find out, I always say," Bernie replied.

Libby looked at the clock on the wall. It was a little after one-thirty, the quiet time between A Little Taste of Heaven's lunch and dinner onslaught. "Agreed," she said. "And on the way to the Westovers, we can stop at the bank and get some quarters since we are now officially all out. And feta. We need the feta for tomorrow."

Bernie nodded. They definitely did. The feta and watermelon salad was one of their summer staples, and the mozzarella they'd substituted didn't work nearly as well.

On the way out of the shop, the sisters stopped and made sure Amber and Googie had everything under control. Then they climbed the stairs to say good-bye to their dad.

"Are you sure that's him, Clyde?" they heard Sean say as they stepped inside the living room.

"Who's him?" Bernie asked, interrupting her dad's conversation.

Sean startled. "Sorry. I didn't hear you come up."

"What are you two talking about?" Libby asked.

"Nothing you need to be concerned about for the moment," Sean replied. "You two look like you're going somewhere."

"We are," Bernie said, and she told him where.

"Be careful out there," he warned.

"We know, Dad," Libby said. It's what her father always said, even when they were going out to get milk.

"I'm serious," Sean told them. Then he went back to speaking to Clyde.

"I wonder if anything new has come to light," Libby said as she and Bernie descended the stairs.

"Why are you saying that?" Bernie asked.

"Dad's tone of voice," Libby replied as she opened the door to the outside.

"I'm sure Dad will tell us, if there is," Bernie said, stepping outside.

According to the weather report, it was ninety degrees, but it felt hotter to Bernie.

"I'm glad I'm wearing my sundress," Bernie noted as she opened the van's door and the hot air from Mathilda rushed out and slapped her in the face.

"What I wouldn't give for air-conditioning that actually worked in here," Libby observed as she got in. The seat burned the underside of her knees, making her wish she'd worn long pants instead of her gingham skirt.

"Remind me to park Mathilda in the shade next time, Libby," Bernie told her sister as she took her hand off the steering wheel. It was too hot to the touch.

"Good idea," Libby replied as she tried not to touch the leather seats with her thighs.

They looked at each other and, without saying anything, got out of Mathilda and waited for the van to cool off. A few minutes later it had, and they were under way. Main Street was quiet in the heat, the sunbaked street deserted.

Bernie knew that people would come out in the early evening when it cooled off, but for now, everyone was inside. Even the pigeons that normally perched on the rooftops were snoozing in their nests. There was no traffic on the surface roads either, and Bernie and Libby made good time, even with stopping at the bank. The cheese store they used was half a block away, but they didn't stop, deciding they'd pick up the feta on the return trip, because they couldn't leave it in the van.

"No car in the driveway," Bernie noted as she pulled into it. She hadn't called because she'd wanted to surprise them.

"Maybe it's in the garage," Libby suggested. She got out and looked through the garage window once Bernie parked the van. "It's here," she called out. In fact, it was the same vehicle that she and her sister had seen in front of the Peterson Gallery the other day. "I guess they're home," she concluded as she followed her sister up the path to the door.

But the Westovers weren't home, or least no one came to the door when Bernie rang the doorbell. After waiting a minute, Bernie rang the bell again. She could hear the chime inside the house, but no footsteps. She tried once more. Nothing.

"They must be out in the Range Rover," Libby observed, which made sense. Most people in Longely had two cars; they had to, considering how poor mass transportation was in the area. As Libby started back to the van, she realized that Bernie wasn't following her. "Where are you going?" she asked her sister, who was now headed in the opposite direction.

"Just taking a look around," Bernie threw over her shoulder as she started toward the back of the house.

"Yeah, right."

Bernie halted and turned around. "What are you saying, Libby?"

"I'm saying, it would be nice if you stopped there."

"You know what they say about if the opportunity presents itself . . ."

". . . you'd be a fool not to take advantage of it," Libby said, finishing the sentence for her sister. "Yeah, I know. It's the motto you live by."

"Let's not exaggerate," Bernie said, before turning and continuing on. "But since the house isn't alarmed, and there isn't a dog . . ."

"You don't know that," Libby told her.

Bernie corrected herself. "A dog that doesn't bark, I see this as one of those opportunities . . ."

"To get arrested?"

"No. To solve the case. You do want to do that, don't you?"

"Of course, I do."

Bernie threw out her arms. "Well, then."

Libby didn't reply. Why bother? When her sister got like this, there was no point in arguing. She'd just go ahead and do what she wanted anyway. Instead, Libby just sighed and followed her sister.

A moment later, they reached the Westovers' backyard.

It was surrounded by a six-foot wooden fence. Bernie opened the latch on the gate, and she and Libby slipped inside. The yard was on the smaller side, but large enough for a brick patio containing an expensive gas grill, a picnic table, and four chairs. The grass was strewn with wildflowers; the small vegetable garden, containing tomato plants, was doing well, and the dwarf apple tree in the corner looked as if it would produce a good crop this year.

"Pleasant," Bernie noted after she'd taken a look around.

"A far cry from Margo's backyard," Libby replied, remembering what they'd seen there.

"True," Bernie said as she studied the house. This must be the weather side, she decided. The paint on this side was beginning to bubble up on the second floor by the chimney, and some of the windowsills needed to be repainted.

More importantly, from where she was standing, she could see that the Westovers had left the window to the kitchen open a couple of inches. She assumed it was for ventilation, since they didn't have central air-conditioning. She went over and tried to push the window up. It didn't move. It was stuck. She tried again. Still nothing. It was probably the humidity, Bernie thought, as she pushed harder. Humidity would make the wood swell.

"Let's go," Libby said as Bernie straightened up.

"Give me another minute," Bernie told her.

"What are you doing?" Libby protested as she watched Bernie look around.

"What does it look like I'm doing? Obviously, I'm looking for something I can use to pry open the window," Bernie said as she spotted a small garden shed in the corner and walked over to it. Maybe there was something in the shed she could use. She tried the door handle. She was in luck. It wasn't locked. She pushed the door open and studied the shed's contents. It was filled with the usual jumble of stuff.

There were rakes, a lawn mower, a couple of shovels, a stack of used paint cans, a couple of recycling bins, and two large garbage cans. Three shelves ran along one side of the shed. They were filled with a mixture of plastic bags, wrenches, small wooden boards that looked as if they'd once belonged to a cabinet, and piles of old newspapers. Nothing helpful here, Bernie thought. She was just about to call it a day and leave when she spied a hammer and chisel sitting off to the left.

"This should do it," she said, taking out the hammer and showing it to her sister.

"You're going to smash the window?" Libby asked. "Isn't that a little excessive?"

"No, I'm going to see if I can bang the window open."

"And then?"

"What do you think?"

"We're going to leave."

Bernie snorted. "Seriously?"

"You're going to go in and look around."

Bernie clapped. "Give the girl a gold star."

"And if the Westovers come back while you're inside?" Libby asked.

"That's why you're going to sit in the van and call me if you see them coming," Bernie replied. "You do have your phone, don't you, Libby?"

Libby allowed as how she did.

Bernie smiled. "Okay, then."

"That probably won't work," Libby said as she watched Bernie advance on the window, hammer in hand.

"Well, it worked in Brandon's cabin," Bernie retorted. "I guess we'll find out whether it will work here as well."

And, with that, she tapped on the underside of the window sash and then on the opposite spot. "See," she said to Libby as the window moved up a quarter of an inch. "A piece of cake."

"Wonderful," Libby muttered as she turned and started back to the van.

"I'll get this window open in a jiffy," Bernie called after her sister before turning back to what she was doing.

"I'm not holding my breath," Libby said loudly enough for Bernie to hear.

But as it turned out, Libby was wrong. Five minutes later, Bernie had managed to jimmy the window open wide enough so she could wiggle through it.

Chapter 34

Once Bernie was inside the Westovers' house, she paused to pick a sliver of wood out of her thigh, straighten her dress, and put on her sandal, which had somehow slipped off her foot. Then she looked around the kitchen. There were dishes piled in the sink, last night's dinner dishes on the table, and a frying pan that needed to be washed sitting on the stove. Bernie was surprised. It certainly hadn't been like this the last time she and Libby had been here.

She took a quick look around, opening and closing cabinet drawers, and peering in the pantry and the broom closet. She didn't expect to find anything in those places, and she was correct. She didn't. Next, she moved on to the living and dining rooms.

In contrast to the kitchen, they looked the same as they had last time. Neat, furnished in good taste, dominated by the pictures hanging on the walls. Once again, Bernie paused to study them, drawn in by their power. How wonderful to live with something like this, Bernie decided.

Odd that the house wasn't alarmed, Bernie thought, as

she moved on to the office, but, then again, it would take a special kind of thief to steal these paintings. It wasn't as if you could hock them at the local pawn shop. In contrast to the kitchen, the office was spotless. "A place for everything and everything in its place" was the phrase that sprung into Bernie's head.

An expensive oriental rug graced the floor, while three walls were covered with made-to-order, floor-to-ceiling oak bookshelves, all filled with art books. A large poster that featured a picture of the Westovers' gallery hung on the fourth wall above the desk.

Bernie plunked herself down in the chair in front of the desk and studied the laptop sitting on top of it. *It reminds me of a Cyclops with the screen as the giant eye*, she thought as she tried the MacBook Air, but it was password-protected, which she had expected. After a couple of minutes futzing around, trying out various passwords, she gave up that mission as a waste of time and began leafing through the pile of papers on the desk. Most of them were junk mail, but about halfway down she came across a letter from the IRS. It was addressed to the Westovers. Never a good thing, Bernie thought, as she slid the letter out of its envelope and unfolded it.

"Oh dear," she said out loud as she read the contents.

It was a request for an audit. The IRS was demanding tax records for the Westovers' gallery for the past seven years. Bernie shuddered. This was her worst nightmare. She just hoped, for the Westovers' sake, that their records were in better shape than A Little Taste of Heaven's were. She and Libby really had to get their act together, Bernie decided, as she replaced the letter in the envelope and put it back in the pile where she'd found it. She and Libby kept saying they were going to get organized, but they never did. Their records were all over the place. Literally.

No more excuses, she vowed, as she started in on the desk drawers. The first two contained USB cables, takeout menus, a bottle of aspirin, a wrist guard, computer paper, stationery, staplers, scissors, and a large collection of pens and pencils. In other words, they looked like her and Libby's desk drawers—full of miscellaneous stuff. The third drawer, however, proved to be more interesting. It contained a checkbook ledger and several checkbooks. *Thank God, some people still did things the old-fashioned way*, Bernie thought.

The first thing Bernie noticed when she took out the checkbooks was that there were two different accounts. Even though Bernie wasn't good with figures—that was Libby's area of expertise—as she went through the checkbooks and the ledger, it became readily apparent to her that the Westovers were keeping two separate sets of books. And, even worse, they were keeping them badly. Really badly, Bernie thought.

She frowned. At least, if you were going to do this kind of thing, do it well. This was like amateur night, although Bernie supposed that the Westovers could always burn the checkbooks and the ledger if necessary. She wondered if there was an accounting program on the laptop that they were using as well. That would be harder to get rid of. They'd have to destroy the laptop to do that.

Not that it really mattered, because if she could figure this out, it would take the IRS guy less than two seconds to do so as well. Bernie shuddered again. *I wouldn't want to be in their position*, she thought as she took pictures of the two different sets of checkbooks with her phone, before putting everything back exactly where she'd found it. The IRS would not be amused if they saw what the Westovers were doing. They could do jail time for something like this. Then Bernie remembered what Clyde had said about the FBI having opened files on the Glassbergs and the Westovers. But had they closed them? Or were they still open? That was the question. And more to the point, how did this relate to Margo's killing? Or did it?

Bernie was wondering what her father would say, if she told him, as she went upstairs and looked through the three bedrooms, two bathrooms, and the attic, but unlike in the office, there was nothing in any of the rooms that didn't belong there. On her way out of the house, Bernie went by the hall closet and realized she hadn't looked through it. *I should*, she thought. After all, it would only take another minute or two, and who knew? Maybe she'd find something else of interest in there as well.

Apparently not, Bernie decided when she looked inside. The first thing she saw were seven coats hanging on bent-wire hangers. The coats looked old, the kind you put on to shovel snow or run out to get the paper or wore to walk the dog in the morning. Bernie quickly went through the coat pockets; there turned out to be nothing in them except old receipts, crumpled-up pieces of paper, and a few candy wrappers. Just garbage. Nevertheless, she stuffed the receipts in her pocket, then directed her attention toward the cartons. They were small packing cartons from Home Depot. She counted seven of them stacked on top of each other. They weren't sealed.

The flaps were open, and their contents were visible. Bernie could make out a couple of old lamps, and about a dozen books in the first one and a hodgepodge of old computer equipment in the second. The third carton contained a tangle of hangers, while the fourth one was full of board games. Bernie decided the cartons looked as if they were full of stuff that had been moved, stuffed in the closet, and forgotten about. She opened the flaps of two more cartons and found more junk. *So much for that*, she thought.

"Time to go," Bernie said to herself. She went to close the door, but when she started to push it closed, she realized she hadn't restacked the cartons properly and one of them had toppled over. She righted it and was bending down to pick up a pack of felt-tip markers that had fallen out when she spotted two picture frames jammed into the back. She pulled them out.

"Wow," she said. She couldn't believe what she was seeing. These were the two Eakinses, the ones the Glassbergs had been looking for, the ones that had disappeared from Margo's house. What were they doing here? Had the Westovers stolen them? That was the reasonable explanation.

As Bernie looked at them again, she realized why the frames had looked familiar. She'd seen Gilda loading them into her vehicle when she and Libby had pulled up to the Peterson Gallery in Nyack. Bernie clicked her tongue against her teeth while she thought. Did this mean that Rebecca, the owner of the gallery, was involved in this mess? She'd said she didn't know anything about the missing paintings. Had she been lying? It would be interesting to know.

Bernie was contemplating the possible ramifications of what she'd discovered when her cell rang. She took it out. It was her sister.

"Yes, Libby," Bernie said, answering.

"The Westovers are coming up the block. I can see their car. You'd better get out of their house now."

"Roger that," Bernie said, and she clicked off. *Time to put the Eakinses back where she'd found them*, she thought, but then she had a better idea. A much better idea.

Bernie smiled. This was going to be fun. Lots and lots of fun. Not that her sister would think so.

Chapter 35

Libby watched as the Westovers' Range Rover turned the corner and came up the block. Another moment or so and Harry and Gilda would be here. *Come on, Bernie,* she silently urged. *What's taking you so long? Move it.* She called her sister again, but this time Bernie didn't pick up.

"Great," Libby muttered to herself as the Range Rover drew up next to Mathilda and stopped. She was trapped. Even if she wanted to leave, she couldn't. *Bernie, I'm going to kill you when I get my hands on you,* Libby thought as she put on her best fake smile and nodded a hello to Gilda and Harry.

Gilda rolled down her window. "What's the matter?" she asked, momentarily recoiling from the heat. "Why are you here? Is everything alright?"

"Fine. Everything is fine," Libby lied, although it was anything but.

Should I stay in Mathilda or get out? Get out, Libby decided, as Harry started up the Range Rover and parked it in his driveway. *It would be too weird not to,* Libby thought. But before she got out, she checked her phone one last time. Nothing from Bernie. *The Westovers are here*, she texted her sister. *Where the hell are you?* Then she slipped her phone into her skirt pocket and exited the van.

"So what can we help you with?" Harry asked Libby after he and his wife had gotten out of their vehicle as well.

"Oh, we," Libby quickly corrected herself, "I mean I, just wanted to catch you up on our progress vis-à-vis Margo," she ad-libbed.

"Well, come in," Gilda said as she started walking toward the door of her house. "Where's your sister, anyway?" Gilda asked. "You two are always together," she noted.

"Oh, she had some stuff to take care of," Libby told her. It was the only excuse she could think of.

By now, the three of them were at the door of the Westovers' house. Harry had his key out and was just about to put it in the lock when the door swung open.

"Hi," Bernie said, smiling at everyone. "Glad to see you. Do come in."

Libby felt the blood rush to her head. She thought she was going to faint.

"What are you doing in our house?" Harry asked when he finally found his voice. At first, he'd been too stunned at the sight of Bernie to speak.

"Funny you should ask that," Bernie replied.

"How did you get in?" Gilda demanded.

Bernie's smile grew larger. "Through the rear kitchen window. You really shouldn't leave it open, you know. I understand why you did—ventilation is important, but it really is an open invitation, no pun intended."

"I . . ." Gilda spluttered, but Bernie cut her off before Gilda could finish what she'd been about to say.

"You should come in. We have things to discuss," Bernie told her, the smile on her face growing even bigger.

Harry flushed. His eyes narrowed. Then he drew himself up and reached for his phone. "I'm calling the police."

"I wouldn't do that if I were you," Bernie told him.

"You're not me," Harry replied. Bernie noted that his breath was coming more rapidly.

"Why shouldn't my husband call the police?" Gilda asked, her voice tight with anger. Or was it fear? Bernie couldn't tell.

"I'm glad you asked me that," Bernie answered. And she pulled out the two Eakinses that she'd stashed behind the front door. "This is why. We need to talk."

Interesting, Bernie thought, as she watched Gilda and Harry turn sheet white. She'd heard the expression that someone "turned sheet white," but she'd never seen it actually happen. And she hadn't even mentioned what she'd found in the desk drawer. Gilda and Harry would probably pass out if she did.

For a moment, the Westovers were silent. Then Harry turned to his wife. "I told you we should have just let it go, but you never listen, do you?"

Bernie cocked her head. "Let what go?" she asked.

Gilda ignored Bernie's question and shook a finger at her husband. "This isn't the time, Harry."

"It certainly looks like it is to me," Harry said. "We wouldn't be in this mess if it wasn't for you."

"How can you say . . . ?"

But Bernie interrupted before Gilda could finish her sentence. "How about we leave the bickering until later," she said to the Westovers, who were busy glaring at each other like two fighters getting ready to enter the ring. "Alternatively, you can explain things to the police."

"That's not necessary," Gilda replied, a quaver running through her voice.

"It certainly is not," Harry said, backing his wife up.

And with that, he, Gilda, and Libby stepped inside the Westovers' house.

"Now, do you want to tell me what this is about?" Bernie asked, nodding toward the two Eakinses.

Harry shrugged. "Ask my wife. She's the one with all the answers."

"We agreed, Harry," Gilda cried.

"Is that how you remember it?" Harry shot back. "Because it's not how I do."

Bernie held up her hands. "Enough! " she commanded, looking from one Westover to the other and back again.

"There's no need to yell," Harry protested.

Bernie took a deep breath and let it out. *Don't lose your temper*, she cautioned herself as she turned toward Harry. "Just be glad I'm not doing worse," she told him, although she had no idea what that meant. "Now, which one of you took the paintings out of Margo's house?" Bernie asked in the ensuing silence, as the four of them moved into the living room.

"We both did," Gilda promptly answered.

"Gilda," Harry squawked.

"What difference does it make, Harry? They already know."

Harry sighed. "I suppose you're right," he conceded as his wife continued to talk.

"The place was already a mess when we got there," Gilda continued. "Someone had gone through it."

Harry picked up where his wife had left off. "The back door to Margo's house was opened. We just took what was ours."

Libby wrinkled her forehead. "Ours? I'm confused. I thought these pictures were the Glassbergs'," she said.

Harry shook his head. "No. They're ours."

As Bernie leaned the two pictures against the wall by the fireplace, an idea occurred to her. "Are these even real?" she asked.

Harry nodded.

"So what were they doing in Margo's house?" Libby asked.

Harry and Gilda looked at each other.

"I think an explanation is in order, don't you?" Bernie said to them when Gilda and Harry didn't say anything.

Harry and Gilda exchanged another look.

"Did you steal the paintings and kill Margo, or just steal the paintings?" Bernie asked.

"How can you say that?" Gilda cried.

"How can I not?" Bernie replied.

"Margo was our friend," Harry said.

"So you say," Libby told him.

Bernie took her cell phone out of her dress pocket and held it up. "Do I call the Glassbergs? The police? Or you can talk to me. The choice is yours."

Harry sighed.

"Well?" Bernie said.

Gilda gestured to the sofa. "At least, let's sit down."

"Be my guest," Bernie replied.

For a moment, it was silent in the house, the only sound that of someone mowing grass down the street. Bernie fanned herself with the edge of her hand. She could feel a trickle of sweat work its way down her back. It was hot in the house. Too hot. She felt as if she were suffocating.

"Harry won't let us get central air," Gilda observed, even though Bernie hadn't said anything.

"It's bad for the environment," Harry replied.

"But I can't sleep in the heat," Gilda complained.

There was another moment of silence; then Harry began to talk.

"It's simple," he said.

"Somehow, I doubt that. It never is," Libby interjected, the comment slipping out before she realized it. She put her hand to her mouth. "Sorry I interrupted," she added. "Go on."

"We found the Eakinses at an estate sale last year," Harry began.

Gilda leaned forward. "And we bought them at a ridiculously low price." She smiled at the memory.

"These days, with the internet and all, most people know the value of their things," Harry said, continuing on with his explanation.

"But these people didn't," Gilda clarified. "And about a week later, I ran into Tom and Betsy at another estate sale and told them about what we'd found at the Posners'."

Harry looked at the Eakinses for a moment, then looked away. "And the week after that, they told us they had heard from one of their customers in Dubai or the Emirates or someplace like that. He was coming to the States and had expressed interest in owning an Eakins in the past, so Tom asked us if we'd be willing to sell them to this guy if he was interested, and if that were the case, they'd take a twenty percent finder's fee. So we said yes and gave them the paintings."

"Then we didn't hear from them." Gilda frowned at the memory. "Or rather we didn't hear about the deal."

"Every time I asked Tom, he said they were in the middle of working out the details," Harry said. "He always had some excuse."

Gilda leaned forward. "We didn't want to push. Sometimes things go like that. Anyway, two weeks later, I was at Stella's when I ran into Toni Musclow. Stella's is . . ."

"I know what Stella's is, Gilda," Bernie said.

Gilda nodded and continued on. "Evidently, she's the manager there while Jane is away dealing with her mom. Anyway, I mentioned what was happening with the Eakinses to Toni, and she got very flustered. It was a strange reaction, one that didn't make any sense. Finally, I wormed it out of her. Evidently, she had dropped by Margo's studio to pick up something, and there was Margo, copying the Eakinses. When Toni asked Margo about what she was doing, she told her that Tom had asked her to. Naturally, as soon as I heard, I called Margo. She told me she didn't know what I was talking about. That Toni must have misheard what she'd said. A moment after she told me that, she said that this was a bad time, that she had to go, and that she'd call me back in a few." Gilda took a deep breath and let it out. "But she didn't call back, and when I called her, my call went straight to voicemail."

"Did you believe her?" Libby asked.

"At first I did, but then I got to thinking about the way Margo had sounded on the phone," Gilda replied.

"How was that?" Bernie asked.

"Flustered," Gilda answered, using the same word she'd used to describe Margo a moment ago. She smoothed down her skirt. "She sounded really flustered. And then there was the fact that copying and repairing art was what Margo did for a living. And she was really good at it, too."

Gilda fell silent, and Harry took up the narrative. "And for the last couple of months, she'd been talking about how she needed money. Of course, now we know that wasn't true." He shook his head, more in a sorry than an anger gesture. "She was sick," he observed.

"She had issues," Gilda said, correcting him. "Margo had issues."

Harry waved his hand in the air. "Use whatever word you want, but it comes down to the same thing. It turns out the woman was a pathological liar."

"That's not true," Gilda protested.

"Then what would you say she was?" Harry demanded. "We didn't know she had those cars or that cash. Quite the opposite. If you listened to her, you'd think she was two steps away from being out on the street." Harry grimaced. "And the boyfriend. We didn't know about him, either. It's creepy."

"So she didn't want to discuss her love life with us—so what? After all, except for Lydia, we're all married. Maybe she felt uncomfortable," Gilda suggested.

Harry snorted. "Oh, come on! We've known her for years." He turned to Bernie and Libby. "But, as it turns out, we had no idea who she was. None at all."

"Does anyone ever know anyone?" Gilda asked.

"Oh, please. Give me a break," Harry snapped.

Gilda flushed. "Don't take that tone with me."

Bernie interceded before things went south. "Did you speak to Tom and Betsy after you spoke to Margo?" Bernie asked, endeavoring to get the conversation back on track.

"Of course, we did," Gilda replied. "They said Toni must have misunderstood what Margo was saying. They said they definitely hadn't told Margo to do that."

"So my wife called Toni back," Steve said.

"To clarify," Gilda explained. "She said she'd stand by what she told us. Then she said that she was wondering if the Benson the Glassbergs had sold her was a copy as well and she was going to have it checked out. She said she'd called Margo, but Margo hadn't called her back, at which point I told Toni we were planning on going to Margo's anyway because we needed answers, and I'd see what I could find out about the Benson. Only I couldn't ask Margo because she wasn't there."

"Like I said," Harry continued, "the door was open, and we went inside. The Eakinses were there, so we took them. After all, they were ours, even if the Glassbergs say different."

Gilda bit her lip. "Do you think that the Glassbergs killed Margo because they didn't want her talking about what she was doing? Maybe the Eakinses are just the tip of the iceberg? I mean, what if the Benson turns out to be a copy as well? Betsy sold it to Toni. That would be awful. It would mean they've been ripping off their friends, let alone customers, for years."

Bernie leaned forward. "Here's another possibility. Maybe Margo was doing it on her own. Maybe the Glassbergs didn't ask her to do it. Maybe Margo had another buyer for the works, a buyer no one knew about."

Gilda was silent for a minute, then she said, "That hadn't occurred to me."

"Me either," Harry replied. "I suppose it's possible."

Gilda nodded in agreement. "Anything is."

Chapter 36

"So what do you think?" Bernie asked her dad after she'd finished telling him about her conversation with the Westovers. "Do you think what the Glassbergs did could be a motive for murder?"

Sean corrected her. "If they did do anything."

"Hypothetically speaking," Bernie clarified.

Sean considered everything he'd seen in his years on the force and repeated what he'd said before. "I think someone looking at someone the wrong way can be a motive for murder," he told Bernie.

"So that's a yes?" Bernie asked.

It was dusk, and Bernie, Libby, and Sean were walking along the riverbank, trying to catch a breath of fresh air after the heat of the day.

"Well, it's not a no. But don't forget, we don't know if the Glassbergs did or did not do what the Westovers said they did," Sean replied as he watched two tugboats guiding a large barge down the Hudson.

"They said they didn't," Bernie replied, remembering what had happened when she'd called the Glassbergs. How angry Tom and Betsy had been, the phrase, "How dare you?" featuring prominently in the conversation. "They said the Westovers were lying and that they were the ones who had paid Margo to copy the pictures so they could keep the real ones and sell the fakes, and that they were shocked, absolutely shocked, that people whom they had thought of as friends would do something like that."

Sean laughed. "What else would they say? 'Yes, I did it. Now put the cuffs on and take me away'?" Then he added, "Moral outrage is a cheap commodity."

"So who do you think is telling the truth?" Libby asked as she took a sip of water from the thermos she was holding. She'd flavored it with sprigs of mint, making the cold water even more refreshing.

"Probably no one," Sean said. "Everyone has their dirty little secrets—in this case, forgery and tax evasion, just to mention two. From what you told me, Margo certainly wasn't the only one walking on the wrong side of the street." He thought about the FBI files. It certainly would be interesting to see what was in them, but the odds of that happening were about zero. "These people have met once a month for five years; they're all in the same business, and yet no one knows anything." Sean encircled the word "know" with finger quotes. "Amazing. What are the odds?"

"Pretty low," Libby said. "So who do you think killed Margo, Dad?"

Sean brushed a mosquito away. "Good question. At this moment, I'd award first place to the Glassbergs and second place to the Westovers, but that could change."

"Not exactly a definitive answer," Libby observed.

"True," Sean told her. "But it's the best I can do at the moment. There are just too many moving parts to this puzzle." Actually, Sean wasn't being quite honest. He did have an idea about who killed Margo, but it was just an inkling, really, improbable enough that he didn't want to discuss it yet, at least not until he'd dug around a bit more. "I think you should keep that question in reserve until you have more facts in your possession," Sean continued as they walked along.

A few minutes later, Bernie stopped and bought a lemon ice from a man with a cart. His name was Gino; he'd shown up at the park two years ago, and he made the lemon ices himself. They were just the right blend of sweet and tart. She held the white paper cup in her hand after she'd paid and took a bite. The taste of lemon flooded her mouth.

"This is so good," she told him.

"My mother's recipe," Gino said before he turned to the next customer in line.

"You think the book club was a cover for an illicit operation?" Bernie asked her dad after she'd taken another bite.

"If you're implying that everyone was in this together, then no, just the opposite, in fact, from what you told me," Sean remarked as the three of them continued their stroll down the Hudson River path. "I think everyone had their own little side operations going on."

"Margo's wasn't little," Libby protested.

"You're right," Sean allowed. "It wasn't. What it was was lucrative."

The Simmonses were heading toward the Boater's Club, half a mile away. There were a few benches there facing the water, and Sean liked to sit, feed the pigeons, and watch the boats coming in and going out. Lately, he'd been remembering the days when he and his wife, Rose, had taken the girls for rides in his motorboat. They'd had some good times. The boat was long gone, but the memories remained.

"What we need is some bait," Sean remarked, thinking of the fishing he'd done off the Boater's Club dock with the girls before they'd decided that worms were icky. "Something to lure Margo's killer out."

"That only works in Agatha Christie novels," Bernie said.

"Or sting operations," Sean replied as he thought about the Boater's Club.

The weathered, sky-blue building was a holdover from the days when Longely was a working-class community, the days before people with money had moved in and everything had been prettied up. The president of the town planning commission had been threatening to tear it down for years, but he could never muster the votes. Too many people had too many good memories of times spent there, having a beer or two on a summer's night. Sean was recollecting this when Bernie started to speak.

"I've been thinking," she said. "Maybe the pictures don't have anything to do with Margo's death. Maybe they're a whole other issue."

"I've been thinking that, too," Libby agreed. "Frankly, thinking it over, I can't see the Glassbergs killing Margo. Her murder was so cold-blooded. Maybe Tom or Betsy would have stabbed her in a fit of rage, but the way she died took planning."

"True," Sean replied. "I agree the Glassbergs don't seem like the kind of people who are capable of a thing like that, but you never know who is and who isn't capable of something. That's one thing I've learned over the years."

Libby took another sip of her water, then said, "You always say the simplest explanation is usually the correct one."

"I've found that's usually the case," Sean replied. "In all likelihood, Margo opened the door to her killer herself because she knew him or her."

"None of the doors were jimmied open," Libby recalled, confirming Sean's hypothesis.

"It could have been the man in the red truck," Bernie mused.

"Sounds like the Man in the Yellow Hat," Libby remarked.

Sean smiled. "You used to love *Curious George*."

Libby laughed. "I did, didn't I?"

The Simmonses walked another couple of feet, then Bernie said, "Or maybe Margo opened the door, and her killer disabled her and forced her into his vehicle. I can't see her leaving her door open otherwise—not given what we know about her."

"Or," Libby said, "Margo's killer could have told her there was an emergency, and she ran out of the house and forgot to lock the door."

"Also possible," Sean conceded. "Especially if that person or persons were her friends. Or they could have gone inside Margo's house and they had a drink and the person slipped something in Margo's . . ."

"Like a roofie," Bernie posited after she ate the last of her Italian ice. You had to eat it fast in weather like this or it melted. She licked the syrup off her fingers, then crumpled up the white pleated cup and threw it in the trash. The cup reminded her of the tortoni she used to eat as a kid. She'd loved the almond-flavored, egg-and-cream ice cream, but she didn't see it on menus anymore. She was wondering how hard it would be to make, when her dad started talking again.

"One thing is clear, though," Sean said. "Logically speaking, two people were involved in Margo's death. Had to be."

"You're right," Libby said after she'd thought through her dad's observation. "One of them drove Margo to the swamp in her vehicle, and the other person followed behind them . . ."

"Or met them there . . ." Bernie suggested.

"And then after Margo and the Camry were in the swamp, the two of them drove back in the second person's vehicle," Libby said.

"Which meant that Margo was out of commission when she and her killer got there," Sean said.

Bernie shuddered as she thought about it. It was a horrible way to die. "A bullet would have been kinder."

"I wonder what the perp used to wedge the gas pedal down," Sean mused. Clyde had told him that they hadn't found anything obvious, like a brick, when they had pulled Margo's car out of the swamp.

"They just left her there to die," Libby said. "That's so cold-blooded."

"They must not have expected her to wake up," Bernie said.

"But she did," Libby pointed out.

Everyone was silent again. Then Sean said, "With friends like that, who needs enemies?"

"But why the swamp?" Bernie asked.

"It's a good place to get rid of things," Sean suggested. "It doesn't get a lot of traffic. Except for the bird-watchers. The swamp is great for that. Or so I've been told," Sean said as he watched two swans swimming close to the shore. He knew that geese mated for life; he wondered if swans did as well.

"So her killers are local?" Libby asked.

"I'd say there's a high probability." Sean rubbed his knee. It was beginning to ache slightly.

"Somehow being a bird-watcher and a murderer don't seem to go together," Libby remarked.

"Not necessarily," Sean replied. "I once had a bird-watcher who killed his sister with a hammer. What a mess that was." Sean shook his head at the recollection. "Have you talked to Toni yet?" he asked, changing the subject as a biker pedaled past them.

Bernie replied, "I called her, and I texted her, but she hasn't gotten back to me."

"Interesting," Sean commented as he started walking again. The sun was going down, leaving ribbons of yellow and red in its wake.

"Maybe she just lost her phone," Libby suggested.

Bernie shuddered. "That would be bad," she said, thinking of the ramifications if that should happen to her.

"Not as bad as what happened to Margo," Sean noted.

"No, certainly not," Bernie had to agree.

Chapter 37

For the next five minutes, Bernie, Libby, and Sean were quiet. As they strolled along, they admired the last bits of color as the sun went down over the Hudson, and listened to the chatter of the people around them and the sounds of the tugs hooting back and forth.

"I always wanted to drive one of those," Sean said suddenly.

"A tugboat?" Libby asked.

Sean nodded.

"So what stopped you?"

Sean thought for a moment. "I don't know. I guess I didn't know anyone who did something like that. I didn't know how to go about it. And speaking of going about it," he asked, "what are you going to do about the paintings?"

"The Eakinses? Nothing," Bernie said. She didn't have to think about her answer. "Let the Westovers and the Glassbergs settle it themselves. Fake? Real? It's not my concern. If either couple wants to bring charges, I say have at it."

Sean turned to Libby. "Do you agree?"

"I do," she replied. "We weren't hired for that. What would you do, Dad?"

"As a cop?"

"No. If you were in our position."

"I'd do the same thing you are. You don't even know that a crime was committed. And, speaking of which, what's your next step in your investigation?" Sean asked, curious to hear what his daughters would say.

"Talking to Toni," Bernie promptly answered. She'd been giving the matter some thought. "I was thinking we can drop in on her place of work tomorrow and have a chat."

"At least we won't be climbing through any windows," Libby observed. Then she stopped because her sister was giving her the stink eye. "What? It's not like Dad didn't figure it out, Bernie," she protested.

"But you don't have to remind him, Libby," Bernie said.

"You think I've forgotten?" Sean asked Bernie.

"No, but I was hoping," Bernie allowed.

Sean sighed his long-suffering sigh. "You didn't listen when you were a kid, and you don't listen now," he remarked, recalling all the times Bernie had snuck out of the house when she was a teenager. "It's nice knowing that nothing has changed."

"What would you have had me do?"

"Oh, I don't know, Bernie. Maybe exercise some common sense for a change."

"I did. I didn't break the window, Dad. It was opened."

Sean raised his hands and let them drop in an "I give up" gesture. "I know. I know. You thought you heard someone yelling for help, so you went in."

"How did you get so smart?" Bernie said brightly, deciding to overlook her dad's sarcasm.

"You know, that only works if you're an officer of the law, and most of the time not even then," Sean said. "And you, my darling daughter, aren't even a licensed private detective, let alone police, so if caught, you could be charged with breaking and entering. And then let's get into the safety issue. What would have happened if one or both of the Westovers had had a gun, and thought you were an intruder and shot you?"

"Obviously, I wouldn't have gone in if they were home," Bernie told him. She was about to add that she could be a private detective if she wanted to; all she had to do was take classes and pass the test, and that maybe she would go ahead and do it, when Mike Crenshaw, one of A Little Taste of Heaven's customers, said hello. All three of the Simmonses turned and said hello back. They were now standing in front of the Boater's Club.

"We have to stop meeting like this," Mike joked.

Everyone laughed.

"It's a nice night," Mike said. "Good to get a breath of fresh air."

"Tell me about it," Libby said. Even though the shop was air-conditioned, the ovens made the prep room uncomfortably warm, and the two fans they'd brought down from upstairs didn't help much.

"Still working on your case?" Mike asked her.

Bernie and Libby both nodded.

"Any progress?" Mike inquired.

"We're getting there," Libby replied.

"Slowly," Bernie added.

Mike pushed his glasses up the bridge of his nose with his forefinger. "So no one is in your line of sight yet?"

Bernie replied, "Let's just say we're narrowing down the field."

"Anyone I know in the field?" Mike asked. Then he poked Bernie in the ribs with his elbow. "Just kidding. It must be gratifying to do that kind of thing," Mike reflected. "I was never very good at puzzles."

"Actually, neither are we," Libby confessed.

Mike laughed. "It seems as if you are to me."

"We're not," Bernie told him.

"So what's your secret?" Mike asked.

"Persistence," Bernie replied.

"Mostly, we talk to people and look for discrepancies," Libby answered.

"I wish you luck," Mike said. He swatted at a mosquito that was buzzing around his head. "Not to change the subject or anything, but I have to ask, is there any chance of your bringing back those vegan cinnamon scones, the small ones, with the powdered sugar on top."

"We can make some for you, if you'd like," Libby volunteered. They'd stopped baking them because they hadn't sold well. Hadn't sold at all, actually. Only one person had bought them.

"That would be great," Mike told her.

"Since when did you become vegan?" Bernie asked, thinking of Mike's standing breakfast order when he wasn't getting his cinnamon roll. Not to mention all the cream he put in his coffee.

Mike laughed. "I'm not. I just happen to like that particular item, and anyway, it's nice to give the cows and the chickens a rest once in a while."

"You've been watching PETA videos on Facebook, haven't you?" Libby guessed.

Mike grinned. "You got me." Then he smiled again, wished everyone a good evening, and continued walking in the direction he'd come from.

"He's like the invisible man," Sean observed as he plunked himself down on the park bench near him so he could rest his leg.

"What do you mean?" Bernie asked her dad.

"Just that that guy is completely unmemorable. You could put out an APB on him, and I'm guessing it would describe a third of the population in this town. He's Mr. Average: average height, average weight, average hair color, average eye color. There's nothing about his clothes that stands out, either. He disappears into a crowd."

"You're right," she said to her dad as she watched Mike stop and talk to someone. She squinted. "Is that Lydia he's chatting with?"

Bernie took a look. "I believe it is."

"Something's different."

"That's because she's changed her hair color, and she's lost weight."

"Ah," Libby said to her sister. "That's why I didn't recognize her at first."

Bernie nodded. *Not good changes, either*, she thought. *Not that she'd say it, but Lydia's new platinum-blond hair color made her complexion look pasty.* "We haven't seen her in the shop in a while," she noted. When she did come in, Lydia usually got some sort of salad and a piece of whatever kind of pie A Little Taste of Heaven was featuring that day. After all, as nutritionists like to say, balance is everything.

"Not since we found Margo," Libby remarked.

"She used to come in at least once and sometimes twice a week," Bernie said. "I wonder if anything is wrong."

"Your guess is as good as mine," Libby said as she watched Lydia chatting with Mike. After a moment, Lydia stopped talking to him and continued on her way.

"Hi," Bernie said to Lydia once she got closer. She took note of the deep circles under the other woman's eyes.

Lydia startled. Then she laughed. "I didn't see you there."

"Just trying to cool off," Bernie said.

Lydia nodded. "It seems as if the whole town is out trying to do that," she noted as a mother, father, and their two children walked by. "Or, at least, the people that don't have central air are."

"Comes from living in old houses," Bernie commented.

"I don't care. I like old houses," Libby said before turning to Lydia. "I didn't know you know Mike," she said.

"From standing on line at your shop," Lydia replied. "He seems like a nice guy."

"Yeah, he does," Bernie agreed.

"So how are you coming with the investigation?" Lydia asked, changing the subject.

"We're coming along," Bernie allowed. It seemed to be the question of the moment.

"Slowly," Libby added, saying the same thing to Lydia she'd said to Mike.

Lydia smiled. "That's good to hear because Betsy said you weren't making any progress at all."

Bernie raised an eyebrow. "Really? And what else did she say?"

Lydia opened her mouth to speak, then closed it.

"Tell me," Bernie urged.

"It's not nice," Lydia said.

"Tell me anyway," Bernie replied.

"Alright," Lydia agreed reluctantly. "If that's what you want."

"It is," Bernie assured her.

Lydia hesitated for another minute, then she said, "Betsy told me we should ask for our money back, that you and your sister don't know what you're doing. She said she was sorry she'd suggested getting you involved in the first place."

"Really?" Bernie said.

"Yes, really," Lydia said. Then she reached up and took Bernie's hands in hers. "But I'm not."

"Thank you," Bernie replied.

"People don't always have control over what they do," Lydia said, after which she continued on her way.

"Interesting lady," Sean commented as his daughters joined him on the bench.

"She is that," Bernie said to her dad.

For the next ten minutes, Libby, Bernie, and Sean sat there, watching the boats working their way up and down the river and enjoying the breeze coming off the water. Then they got up and started the walk back home, taking the path that wound around Antler's Hill and came out on Ewing Avenue. On the way, Sean decided to call Clyde once he got back to the flat. There were a few things he needed clarified.

Chapter 38

The next afternoon, Bernie and Libby made the trek down to Stella's to talk to Toni.

"We could have seen her at her house," Libby grumped as they circled the block for the third time, trying to find a parking space.

"This will be better," Bernie declared.

"No, it won't. You just want to shop."

"I cannot tell a lie," Bernie said as she spotted an empty spot and raced toward it. "There is that too."

She got to the space just before a man in a white Toyota did, and backed in. Spaces were hard to find for a van-sized vehicle, and she had no intention of letting this one go. It was hotter in the city than in Longely, and by the time Libby and Bernie had walked the five blocks to Stella's, they were both sweaty. As she picked up the smell of garbage from the trash bags that were piled in front of buildings, waiting to be picked up, Bernie reflected that, while she loved the city, she wouldn't want to live there during the summer.

"All I can say is that I hope Stella's is air-conditioned," Libby said as she wiped several beads of sweat off of her cheek with the back of her hand.

"It will be," Bernie assured her as she watched a group of kids in their bathing suits run in and out of a stream of water coming from an opened fire hydrant. It took every ounce of willpower Bernie had to keep from joining them. She and her sister reached the store five minutes later. It was long and narrow. At one point, it had been a travel agency, and the posters from its former incarnation were still up.

Toni Musclow didn't look surprised to see them when they walked through Stella's door. In fact, she looked as if she'd been expecting them.

"I thought you might show up," she said in a resigned tone of voice.

"A little conversation, a little shopping. Who can resist?" Libby replied.

"I don't want to talk about it," Toni said.

"Talk about what?" Libby asked.

"Funny girl. As if you didn't know," Toni replied. "Betsy and Gilda have been calling me and yelling at me nonstop. I couldn't take it anymore. I had to turn my phone off."

"Is that why my calls went straight to voicemail?" Bernie asked.

"Could be," Toni replied.

"Or maybe you don't want to talk to us, either," Libby observed.

"That too," Toni replied. She laughed. "Lighten up. I'm kidding."

"Good to know," Libby said.

Toni sighed. It was a sigh filled with regret. "I should never have said anything about what I saw."

"Well, I, for one, am glad you did," Bernie said as she walked over and studied the outfit on the mannequin that Toni was standing in front of. The top was an unremarkable tank top, but the skirt was stunning. It was a full skirt in a yellow-and-brown leaf print with the picture of a poodle outlined in small blue beads.

"You like?" Toni asked, referring to the skirt.

"I love," Bernie said. "How much?"

Toni named the price. Bernie whistled.

"I know," Toni said. "But it's from the fifties, it's in perfect condition, and Linda Lux wore it." Linda Lux was a TV star from *It's All in Your Head*.

Bernie whistled again. "Can I try it on?" she asked.

Toni smiled. "Of course." Then she lowered her voice and said, "Do you think what I saw at Margo's had anything to do with Margo ending up the way she did?"

"I don't know," Bernie confessed.

"Are you sure you did?" Libby asked.

Toni looked puzzled. "Did what?"

"See what you thought you saw."

"Of course, I'm sure, Libby. Are you calling me a liar?"

"Not at all," Libby assured her. "I was just wondering if you could have made a mistake. Maybe Margo was working on something else."

Toni sniffed. "I think I know an Eakins when I see one. I have two hanging in my bedroom. And, anyway, I saw the original ones."

Libby rubbed her arms. Now she was cold. It was freezing in here. "I thought you and Brad collected American primitives."

"We do, Libby, but my mom gave the Eakinses to me." Toni bit her lip. "I shouldn't have said anything to Betsy. Brad said I shouldn't. He told me to mind my own business and not meddle in other people's. And he was right. For once. Now everyone is at each other's throats." Toni lightly touched the base of her throat. "I thought we'd all work together to solve the mystery of Margo's death, you know. But that's not the way it turned out at all. Just the opposite, in fact."

"We saw Lydia last night," Bernie remarked. "She seemed really upset."

"That's because she is," Toni replied. "You know, she blames herself for Margo's death. She thinks she's responsible."

"No kidding," Bernie responded. "I never would have guessed."

"And all this fighting." Toni grimaced. "I find it upsetting, but Lydia really takes everything to heart. I know it's really bothering her. She's too sensitive for her own good. I told her she had to get a grip, but she's so emotional." Toni pointed to the skirt Bernie had been admiring and changed the subject. "Do you want to try this on?"

"Absolutely," Bernie said.

"So what does your husband think of all this?" Libby asked as Toni took the skirt off the mannequin and handed it to Bernie.

"Brad? He's like the rest of us. He doesn't know what to think. Although . . ."

"Although what?" Bernie asked, turning her attention away from examining the beadwork on the skirt.

"It's probably nothing," Toni replied. "He was really drunk when he told me."

"Tell me anyway," Bernie urged. "Please," she added when Toni didn't reply. "Any little detail could matter."

Toni didn't reply. Bernie could tell she was doing some sort of mental calculus. After a minute went by, she shrugged her shoulders and said, "Why not? I mean, it can't hurt, right? And it might even help, even though, like I said, it's probably nothing."

"We'd like to hear it anyway," Libby said.

"Okay, but I need to back up and put this in context,"

Toni said, looking from one sister to the other and back again. "You know Margo was a little . . . secretive."

"That's one way of putting it," Bernie said dryly, thinking of the money and the passport they'd found in the tree in Margo's backyard. "No doubt about that."

Toni touched her pearls. "If Margo was a character in a mystery we were reading, our book club would call her an unreliable narrator."

"Like in *Gone Girl* or *Rebecca*," Libby volunteered, naming two famous mysteries.

Toni beamed. "Exactly. I mean she made a big deal over certain things that weren't a big deal and then didn't mention other things that were." Toni took a deep breath and let it out. "Brad never had much patience for her stories," Toni reflected. "Of course, he doesn't have much patience with most things. Except his car." She laughed. "My husband has an old Bentley that he stores at Chung's garage," Toni explained as she led Bernie and Libby to the changing room in the back of the store. "It's the same place Margo stored her vehicles."

Bernie and Libby both nodded again, both unwilling to speak and interrupt Toni's tale.

"The Bentley has been there for a while. About ten years, as a matter of fact. My husband inherited it from his dad," Toni went on. "Brad takes it out in the spring and puts it back in in October. He loves that car. Sometimes, I think he loves it more than me. He certainly takes better care of it," Toni reflected as she stooped to pick up a sales tag from the floor. "Anyway, over the years, he's gotten friendly with Chung, the guy who owns the place."

"We know who he is," Bernie said. They were now at the changing room. Toni continued to speak as she pulled the yellow curtain aside and hung the skirt on the hook on the side wall.

"Brad and Chung go over to RJ's and have a couple of beers and shoot a game of pool a couple of times a month."

"Go on," Libby prompted when Toni stopped talking.

"Anyway, one night they're having a beer, and Chung starts telling my husband that Lydia was really spooking Margo, and that maybe he could tell Lydia to dial it back a few notches."

"Did Brad try?" Bernie asked.

Toni nodded. "So did I, but Lydia kept on anyway. Now, this is the interesting part: Chung told Brad he and Margo weren't getting along so good. He said that Margo was thinking of going away someplace for a while. He seemed pretty broken up about it."

Libby and Bernie both nodded. That jibed with what they already knew.

"Did Chung say where?" Bernie asked, thinking of the hidden passport.

"If he did, Brad didn't tell me," Toni replied. "But, then, I didn't even know Margo was seeing Chung before Brad told me." She frowned. "I asked him why he didn't tell me, and he looked at me as if I was nuts and asked me why I cared." She shook her head. "Men."

Bernie pointed to herself and Libby. "Do you think your husband would talk to us?"

"I don't see why not," Toni answered. "You try on the skirt, and I'll call him and see."

It turned out that Brad was willing to meet the two sisters. The three of them got together an hour later at Katz's Delicatessen. Because it was between lunch and dinner, the place was just crowded instead of packed to the gills.

"So you bought the skirt" were the first words out of Brad's mouth as he, Libby, and Bernie lined up at the counter to put their orders in. Brad got pastrami, while

Libby and Bernie got corned beef; all the sandwiches were on rye with mustard. Anything else would be heresy.

Bernie grinned. She'd worn the skirt out of the store. It went well with the dark blue tank top she'd had on.

"Toni would have bought it herself," Brad informed her, "but the waist was too tight."

"I feel bad," Bernie lied as the counterman handed her sandwich to her.

"No, you don't," Libby countered.

Brad laughed as he took his pastrami on rye. "You two remind me of my sisters."

"How many do you have?" Libby asked as she picked up the white plate with her sandwich on it.

"Five," Brad said, heading for the back. He chose a table that was empty and slid onto the bench. Libby and Bernie took the other side.

"That's a lot . . ."

". . . of hormones flying around the place," Brad said, finishing Bernie's sentence for her. "Tell me about it." Then he attacked his sandwich. "This is the first food I've had all day," he explained after he'd demolished the first half. He wiped his hands and took a long drink of Dr. Brown's Cel-Ray tonic. "God, that was good. Now, what do you want to know?"

Libby repeated what his wife had told them.

"If she said that's what I said, then I guess that's what I said," Brad answered.

Bernie put down her sandwich. "You guess?"

Brad laughed. "Truth to tell, my recollection of that evening is a bit hazy. Chung and I were lit, and we'd smoked a little weed in the back before we'd gone into RJ's. Not that we usually did that kind of thing—we usually just had a beer or two, but Chung was really upset—

so between the beer and the weed . . ." Brad smiled apologetically and shrugged. "It was one of those nights."

Libby put a dab more mustard on her sandwich before speaking. "Your wife said Chung and Margo were fighting, and that's what he was upset about."

Brad corrected her. "It was one of the things he was upset about, but money, or rather his lack of it, was the real thing. Evidently, he'd made some bad investments and was about to lose his business to the bank. Plus his house. He was mortgaged up to the hilt."

"That would do it," Bernie said, and she sat back and took another bite of her sandwich.

Brad went on. "From what he was saying, I gather he thought he was going to get bailed out, but the person he was counting on reneged."

"Did he say who that was?" Libby asked.

"Nope," Brad replied. "And that, as they like to say, is all she wrote. If you want to know any more, I guess you're going to need to talk to Chung."

"I guess we will," Libby said as Brad picked up the second half of his sandwich and started to eat.

Bernie and Libby did likewise. Once they were back in Mathilda, Bernie called Chung, but her call went straight to voicemail. They drove to his house next, but no one was home.

Chapter 39

"I guess Brad was right about Chung's money problems," Bernie said as they pulled up to Chung's garage. It had a CLOSED sign on it. Next they drove over to his storage facility, using the main access road, but that had a CLOSED sign on it as well, at which point they drove over to Pepino's Pizza Palace on the chance that Yuri, the owner, knew what was going on.

"I heard that the bank has the place now," he told them, looking up from taking a large cheese pizza out of the oven. He corrected himself. "Has both places. At least, that's what my friend at Chase says."

They chatted for a few more minutes and bought some chicken wings for their dad.

"I wonder what Chung's going to do," Libby mused as she and her sister walked toward their van.

"He's probably drinking himself senseless at the moment," Bernie guessed. "Boy, the stars are definitely not aligning for him right now."

Libby was about to say, "You can say that again," when she spotted a red pickup truck coming up the second, steeper path that led down to Chung's storage facility.

"Bernie, do you see what I see?" she asked, stopping dead in her tracks.

Bernie blinked. "The same truck we saw leaving Margo's house?"

"I think it is. Same color, same make and model, and it's got a dent in the center of the front bumper."

"What are the odds?"

"Very small," Libby replied as the truck headed for the strip mall exit. Then she saw something even more improbable. "Oh my God! Is that Mike Crenshaw driving?" She squinted because the sun was in her eyes. "And is Lydia in the passenger seat?"

Bernie took another look. "Yes, it is. What did Lydia say about just knowing Mike to say hello to?"

"Maybe it's true," Libby said. "Maybe he's giving her a lift."

"It's an odd place to be giving her a lift from."

Another thought occurred to Libby. "Do you think they were in there when we knocked?"

"They could have been," Bernie replied. She checked the time. "We were there, what? Fifteen, twenty minutes ago?"

The two women looked at each other.

"Are you thinking what I'm thinking?" Bernie asked her sister.

"Oh, yeah," Libby said. "I just wish our name wasn't plastered all over Mathilda," she added as she and Bernie ran for their van. "It makes following someone a tad more difficult," Libby observed as she jumped into the driver's seat.

Fortunately, there was a lot of traffic on Everheart Street, and Libby was able to keep a five-vehicle distance from the truck Mike Crenshaw was driving. She followed him through Fayetteville and Dewitt. At that point, Libby thought Crenshaw was going to turn into the Eastview Mall, but he didn't. He kept going. Then she thought he was going to stop at Costco, but he passed that as well.

"Where the hell is he going?" Libby muttered as he turned onto Bliss Street.

"Myer's Landing?" Bernie guessed.

"The swamp?"

"Yup."

"Why would he go there?"

"Good question," Bernie replied. The traffic had thinned, and Libby slowed down even more.

"We should call the police," Libby said.

"And say what?" Bernie challenged. "That Lydia and Mike lied about knowing each other? Exactly," Bernie said when Libby didn't respond.

"So now what?" Libby asked as she pulled back even farther. There was little traffic on the road now, and the chance that Crenshaw would spot them in his rearview mirror was becoming a certainty instead of a possibility.

"I have an idea," Bernie said.

"Never a good thing," Libby muttered.

"Ha ha," Bernie replied as she took her cell out of her tote, pulled up a map of Myer's Landing on her phone, and began studying it.

There were three entrances. The first was the main one, the one she and Libby had gone through when they'd gone there the first time; the second was the entrance off Euclid, which was the one Bernie was betting Mike Crenshaw was headed toward; and then there was a third, smaller path that intersected with the second road. Bernie showed the map to Libby and explained what she had in mind.

"Turn in here," Bernie commanded a few minutes later, pointing to what looked like a dead-end street.

"Are you sure?" Libby asked.

"Positive," Bernie said. The two-block street was lined with small, older houses that had seen better days. At the end of the street, there was a grassy area with a sign that read DEAD END, but as Libby and Bernie got closer, Bernie spied what looked like the beginning of a path.

"Are you sure this is an entrance?" Libby said, putting the van in park when she reached the grassy verge. "Because it doesn't look like one to me."

It didn't look like one to Bernie, either, which was why she consulted the map on her phone again. It didn't have dimensions. Next she tried the website for Myer's Landing. That map was more detailed. She showed it to Libby. "We should be able to get to here," she said, tapping her fingernail on the screen to indicate a bend in the path. "Then we'll have to walk."

"I hope you're right," Libby said as she put Mathilda in drive. She felt a bump as she directed Mathilda onto the dirt path. "This isn't helping the shocks," she noted, the van bouncing up and down as it went over the rocks in the road. Eight minutes later, they arrived at the bend in the road shown on the map. Bernie had been correct. This was as far as they could go.

"It's going to be fun getting out of here," Libby grumbled as she parked. There was no place to turn, which meant she was going to have to back up to get out of there, and she didn't like backing up. She had just turned off the ignition and was pocketing the keys when she heard a voice. "Is that Crenshaw?" she asked her sister. She couldn't make out the words.

"I certainly hope so," Bernie replied as she exited the van. The voice she was hearing sounded nearby, but it was hard to judge. She'd learned from past experience that sound traveled in funny ways.

She and Libby started walking along the path. Cattails blocked their line of sight.

"I hate this place," Libby groused as she swatted at an insect buzzing around her face. "All I can say is you'd better be right."

"I am," Bernie replied, with more confidence than she felt.

The path zigged and zagged, and it was a quarter of a mile before Bernie and Libby caught a glimpse of the red truck through the reeds. They walked faster. As they got closer, they saw Lydia. She was standing by the back of the truck, pulling at something lying in the truck bed. Then she stopped, straightened up, and started looking around. *She must hear us*, Bernie thought, as she noticed a red splotch on Lydia's pale pink T-shirt.

Libby put her hand to her mouth. "Is that blood?" she whispered to her sister.

"Maybe it's ketchup," Bernie whispered back. "Maybe she's a sloppy eater."

"And maybe I'm going to start going around in four-inch heels," Libby retorted as she looked for Mike Crenshaw. He was nowhere in sight.

"What are you doing?" Libby hissed as Bernie picked up her pace.

"Going to see if Lydia is alright," Bernie hissed back.

"I think we should wait," Libby cautioned. "Something doesn't add up here. Actually, nothing adds up." But it was too late. Bernie was trotting toward Lydia as the words left Libby's mouth.

Lydia heard Bernie coming and spun around. Her face went white when she saw who it was.

Bernie put on her biggest smile as she stopped in front of the passenger-side door. "Fancy meeting you here. Amazing how we keep running into each other."

"What are you doing?" Lydia cried.

"Enjoying nature," Bernie chirped, purposely omitting any mention of Mike Crenshaw. Instead, she pointed to Lydia's shirt. "Oh, dear. What is that? Did you hurt yourself?"

"It's nothing," Lydia answered, forcing a smile.

"It doesn't look like nothing to me," Libby said, coming up from behind. "It looks like blood."

"I cut my arm," Lydia explained.

"Really?" Bernie said.

"Yes, really," Lydia replied.

"That's odd, because I don't see anything," Libby told her.

"I meant my side," Lydia stuttered as she crossed her arms over her chest to hide the blood splotch.

"Make up your mind," Libby told her. "Which is it? Your arm or your side?"

Lydia swallowed. A vein began throbbing beneath her eye. "You have to leave," Lydia told the sisters. "You have to leave now."

"We can take you to a safe place," Bernie said gently as she took a step toward her.

"No, no," Lydia said, her eyes flicking to the truck bed and back again. "I'm fine. Just go. Please."

Bernie's eyes followed Lydia's gaze. She couldn't believe what she was seeing. "Because of what's in the back of the truck?" she finally managed to get out.

"Oh, that old rug." Lydia attempted a laugh, but it died stillborn. "I'm taking it to the dump."

Bernie raised an eyebrow. "Are they burying people there now?" she inquired as Libby craned her neck to take a look.

"Oh my God," Libby gasped. She put her hand up to her mouth. It was Chung. Or Chung's body, to be precise.

He'd been originally wrapped in the rug like a burrito, only the rug had come partially undone, revealing his face. "Is that where the blood on your shirt came from?" Libby asked.

But Lydia didn't answer. Mike Crenshaw did. He'd been so quiet coming around the bend that neither Bernie nor Libby had heard him approach.

"I'm sorry you saw that," he said to them. "I really am."

"Me too," Bernie told him. "How about we call it a day, and we'll forget all about this?"

"I'm afraid it's a little late for that," Crenshaw replied.

"Not really," Bernie replied. "Anyway, where are you going to get your cinnamon rolls in the morning?" Bernie asked. "Have you thought about that?"

"I guess I'll have to find somewhere else," Crenshaw replied. And then, before Libby or Bernie knew what was happening, Crenshaw had Libby in a choke hold. Libby tried to pry his arms apart, but she couldn't. He was too strong. "Lydia, get me the gun," Crenshaw ordered. "It's in the glove compartment."

"Don't, Lydia," Bernie cried.

"I'm sorry," Lydia said as she started moving toward the front of the truck.

"He'll kill you, too," Bernie warned.

Lydia shook her head. "He'd never do that, right, Mike?" Lydia said.

"Of course, sweetie," he replied absent-mindedly, his eyes on Bernie.

"He has to, Lydia," Bernie said. "He can't afford to let you live."

"No," Lydia protested. "We love each other, don't we, Mike?"

"Yes, we do," Mike said.

"You know what he did," Bernie said, nodding toward Chung while she moved a step closer to the passenger-side door.

"Stay where you are," Crenshaw warned Bernie, "or I'll kill your sister right now." And he tightened his grip slightly. Libby felt her vision begin to blur. Every cell in her body screamed out for air.

"No problem," Bernie said as she watched Libby gag. "Just ease up."

Crenshaw nodded and did. Libby took a deep breath. She never thought she'd enjoy breathing so much.

"I'd never tell," Lydia told Bernie. "Ever. Even if it were my friend."

"Why should he believe you?" Bernie challenged, trying to buy time for her and her sister.

"Because I've proved it, haven't I, Mike?"

Mike didn't say anything. He just nodded.

"Oh my God," Bernie said, Lydia having confirmed her suspicion. "You did kill Margo, didn't you, Mike? That's why you were always asking me how the investigation was going. And those scones you asked me about. Margo was the only one who bought them. You got them from her."

Crenshaw didn't say yes, and he didn't say no. Instead, he told Lydia to stop futzing around and get the gun.

This is it, Bernie thought. *This is our chance, and we're not going to get another one.*

"It's been fun, Libby," Bernie said, signaling her sister with an imperceptible nod.

"Maybe for you," Libby replied, "but not for me. I told you I hated this place," she added as she said a prayer. *Here goes nothing*, she thought, as she kicked Mike Crenshaw in the knee as hard as she could. She could feel her foot connect with Crenshaw's kneecap. She heard a crunch, and Crenshaw screamed and loosened his grip on her for just a moment, but that moment was enough to allow Libby to wiggle free.

She looked over at the truck. Bernie was trying to open the passenger-side door, but Lydia had grabbed her arm and was pulling her away. Libby ran to help Bernie as Lydia leaned over and tried to bite her sister.

"No, you don't," Libby screamed, grabbing Lydia's arm and pulling her off of Bernie.

"Thanks," Bernie said as she opened the door, leaned in, opened the glove compartment, took out the Glock, and pointed it at Mike. "Stay right where you are," she ordered.

"Or you'll what?" Mike demanded.

"I'll shoot," Bernie told him.

Mike snorted. "No, you won't," he said, taking a step back.

"Try me," Bernie told him. "I don't want to, but I will." Then she saw Lydia moving out of the corner of her eye. "And what I said to your boyfriend goes for you, too, sweetie," she told her.

Lydia froze, and Bernie turned her attention back to Crenshaw.

"Just one question," she said to him. "Did you drive Margo's car into the swamp with her in it?"

Crenshaw laughed. "No. I weighted the gas pedal down with a couple of bags of ice."

"And then the ice melted, leaving no trace," Bernie said. "Impressive."

Crenshaw bowed his head in acknowledgment as he took a third step back. Now he was standing in front of the reeds.

"Stop," Bernie commanded.

He smiled ruefully. "Sorry, that's not in the cards," he told Bernie. Then he turned to Lydia. "Too bad things worked out this way. I really thought we had a shot."

"Don't leave me, Mike," Lydia cried as Crenshaw took a fourth and a fifth step back and disappeared in the reeds. She heard a splash, and then he was gone.

"Watch Lydia," Bernie told Libby.

"What should I do if she tries to get away?" Libby asked.

"Deck her," Bernie said. Then she ran after Crenshaw.

But he was gone. Bernie could see the reeds moving as Crenshaw went through them. She started to follow him, then stopped as she felt herself begin to sink. *Oh my God, quicksand*, she thought as she heard a sucking sound. She hadn't believed her dad's story. She should have, she thought as she looked down. Yup. She was definitely sinking. With a great deal of effort, she extracted first one foot and then the other out, leaving her pink ballet flats in the muck.

When she looked up again, the reeds weren't moving, and the only sounds she heard were birds chirping. Crenshaw must be crouching in the reeds or sinking in the quicksand, she thought. She started in the direction he'd gone, took three steps, and stopped. Who was she kidding? She was barefoot, and there were snakes and probably more quicksand in the reeds. She should have shot Crenshaw when she had had the chance, she decided. But she hadn't.

"Guess your boyfriend isn't sticking around," Bernie observed as she walked back to where Lydia and Libby were standing, careful to avoid the pebbles in the road.

Lydia was sobbing hysterically. "He made me go along. I warned Margo," Lydia said, tears streaming down her face. "I did. Why did you come?" she moaned. "Why couldn't you two mind your own business?"

"Because you hired us," Bernie reminded her as she put the Glock back in the truck's glove compartment. Less chance of an accident that way. Let the cops deal with it and Chung. She'd call them when they got back to where there was service.

Chapter 40

"You two are really lucky you weren't killed," Sean told his daughters, grimacing at the thought of what could have happened.

"I know, Dad," Libby said. She was still having bad dreams.

It was a week later, and Libby, Bernie, Clyde, and Sean were sitting around a scarred wooden table at the Boater's Club, drinking beer and enjoying the view as the sun set over the Hudson. It was becoming an enjoyable habit.

Libby ate a potato chip. They made them at the Boater's Club from scratch and were addictive. "I still don't believe it," she said after a minute had passed.

"It's true," Clyde said.

Sean nodded. "It is."

"I'm glad they got him," Libby said.

"They wouldn't have if Crenshaw's rental hadn't broken down on the way to the airport and Andredi hadn't stopped his unmarked to help," Clyde said.

"Nice to know Andredi did something right for a change," Sean commented.

"Yes, it is," Clyde agreed. "Otherwise, Crenshaw would be in Belize right now."

"Why the UAR?" Bernie wondered.

"Because they don't have an extradition treaty with us," Clyde replied.

"And given what he does, he can work anywhere," Sean added.

"Nice perk," Bernie observed. "He probably doesn't get health benefits, though."

"That's the problem with the gig economy," Sean noted.

"I can't believe Mike Crenshaw is a professional hit man," Libby said, continuing on with her train of thought as she watched a squirrel snag a potato chip on the wood floor and scurry away.

"They don't call him the Exterminator for nothing," Clyde said. "At least, that's what my brother-in-law told me."

"Because Crenshaw has killed so many people?" Libby asked.

"No. Because he worked as an exterminator for ten years," Clyde informed her as he brushed some flying thing away from his ear. "But what you said, too."

Bernie frowned. "He doesn't look like I thought some-one in his line of work would."

"You expected him to look like a bad"—here Clyde bracketed the word *bad* with his fingers—"dude."

Libby nodded. "He's just so nebbishy."

"That's the secret to his success," Sean said. "Remember when I said he was like the invisible man. He can walk up to anyone . . . and then . . . blammo."

"And that whole getting the seven-fifteen Metro North every day." Libby shook her head. "Why go to all that trouble?"

"No. No. He did have an office to go to. I have to hand it to him," Sean went on. "He was a sales rep for a com-mercial water-filter company. What could be more boring than that? And, once in a while, he had to travel for business. No one would even think twice."

"Still, we should have seen it," Bernie said as she watched a sailboat docking.

"I don't see how you could have," Clyde said. "You were looking in the wrong direction."

"Yes, we were," Libby acknowledged. "All this time, we thought Margo's death was about an art deal gone bad, and it wasn't. It was about money."

"All that chat from Lydia about her warning Margo colored everything." Bernie shook her head. "I thought Lydia was nuts. Instead, she was saying those things to mislead us."

"I don't think so," Libby replied. "I think she wanted to be found out. I think she was consumed with guilt."

"Either that or it was a fantastic acting job on her part," Bernie said. She was still unconvinced by Lydia's protestations of guilt.

"Which do you think it is, Dad?" Libby asked.

"Honestly, I'm not sure," he replied. He turned to Clyde. "How's she doing?"

"They had to sedate her," Clyde answered after he took a sip of his beer. "She can't stop crying."

Everyone was quiet for a moment, then Libby said, "So I don't understand the Lydia thing. Did she know about Margo?"

"She says she knew afterward," Clyde said.

"Why didn't she go to the police?" Libby asked.

Bernie ate a potato chip. "Because love conquers all."

"Until it doesn't," Libby said, thinking of the scene between Lydia and Crenshaw at the swamp.

"Yeah," Sean said. "It's amazing what getting caught does to one's perspective in that regard."

"So how did Lydia find out about Margo if Crenshaw

didn't tell her?" Libby said. "I can't believe he would. That seems very uncontract-killer-like to me."

"According to Crenshaw, Lydia was looking through his desk for some stamps and found his ledger," Clyde said.

"He kept a ledger?" Libby said. "Jeez."

"What can I say? The guy is old school," Clyde answered.

"So Crenshaw knew that she knew?" Libby asked.

"He says he didn't know that she knew until after Margo's untimely demise," Clyde said

"And he let Lydia live?" Bernie said.

"I asked him that, and he told me they were in love," Clyde explained, "but I think he's lying."

"About being in love?" Libby asked.

"No. I think that part is true, but I think Crenshaw is lying about everything else. I think Lydia knew beforehand. I think she tried to warn Margo, but when that didn't work, she went ahead with Crenshaw's plan. I think she was driving the second car. I think she picked up Crenshaw afterward."

"Sometimes," Bernie reflected, "it's better to have no boyfriend than the wrong one."

"Very profound," Libby observed.

Bernie shrugged. "It's the truth in this case. But how could we not know about Lydia and Crenshaw? It's impossible to keep secrets in this place."

"I knew," Sean confessed. "Well, kinda."

Bernie turned to him. "And you didn't tell us?"

"I didn't realize. I never connected the dots."

"When did you know?" Libby demanded. "How did you know?"

"I saw Crenshaw and Lydia over at Hyde's in White Plains once in a while."

Libby's eyes narrowed. "What were you doing at Hyde's, Dad?" Libby asked.

"Uh . . . getting coffee."

"And doughnuts," Libby said. Hyde's was famous for their freshly fried doughnuts. "Dad," Libby remonstrated when Sean didn't say anything, "you're supposed to be cutting down on that kind of thing."

Sean gave her a defiant stare. "You know what? At my age, I think I can eat whatever I want."

"But your doctor . . ."

"It's my body, and I'll do what I want," Sean told her.

"Let him," Bernie said to her sister.

Libby whirled around. "You knew he was eating doughnuts?"

"Brandon told me," Bernie confessed.

"And you didn't tell me?" Libby snapped.

"And this is why I didn't," Bernie said. "And anyway, he's eating the strawberry shortcake that we make."

"Doughnuts are worse."

Clyde clapped his hands. "Ladies, leave your poor father alone. Now, do you or do you not want to hear the rest of this?"

"The rest," both Libby and Bernie promptly replied.

Then Bernie said, "Okay. So we have a conflicted Lydia."

Clyde nodded. "Exactly."

"One part of the mystery solved, but why did Crenshaw kill Margo?" Bernie asked. "You haven't explained that."

"Now that's the interesting part. Because Chung hired him to do it," Clyde replied, and he went on to fill Libby and Bernie in on the why before they could ask for an explanation. "You know Chung was broke, right? Well, he thought he had an ace in the hole—Margo. He knew she had money, and she had said she'd loan it to him, but then she caught Chung fooling around with one of his customers. She walked in on them."

"A definite deal breaker," Bernie commented.

"At least, that's the story Crenshaw told me. Chung apologized and promised never to do it again, and Margo said she forgave him, but Chung didn't believe her. He was pretty sure she was planning to leave him. He was going to lose everything, so he decided to get rid of Margo. He knew she kept cash in the house, and he thought he could sell the vehicles Margo had stored in his facility as well. And there was her will. She'd told him she'd left everything to him—which, as it turned out, wasn't true because she'd changed it."

"He couldn't find the money," Libby guessed.

Clyde nodded.

"But he still had the vehicles," Bernie pointed out.

"Two of which he promised to Crenshaw as payment," Clyde replied.

Bernie whistled. "Not bad."

"But then, after Crenshaw did what he did, Chung got a bad case of the regrets—at least, that's what Crenshaw told me. He said he got a strong feeling Chung was going to have a chat with the police."

"And implicate himself?" Bernie asked. "Would he really?"

"Sometimes people do. Sometimes people can't live with the guilt." Clyde ran his finger around the rim of his beer stein. "Or maybe Crenshaw found out that Margo had donated her vehicles, that they weren't Crenshaw's to sell. In any case, Crenshaw decided Chung had to go."

"And he brought Lydia along with him when he killed Chung?" Bernie asked. "That seems like an epically bad idea."

Clyde replied, "According to Crenshaw, Lydia walked

in on him when he was rolling Chung up in the rug. She'd come to discuss buying one of Chung's vehicles."

"And you believe that?" Libby asked Clyde.

"No, I don't, but that's what Crenshaw said," Clyde replied.

"And she didn't run screaming out of the place when she saw that?" Libby countered. "I would have."

"Like I said," Clyde told her, "love conquers all. Or at least it's supposed to."

"That old saw about never mixing business and pleasure is true," Sean observed. "It usually doesn't turn out well."

Bernie thought of something else. "Was Lydia the reason Crenshaw's marriage broke up?"

Sean nodded. "That's what Crenshaw said. He told Clyde he thought he'd found his soul mate."

"But isn't she's going to testify against him?" Libby asked.

"That's my understanding," Clyde said. "Let's say she had a change of heart."

"I guess true love only goes so far," Sean said.

"Dad, would you have left Mom?" Bernie asked.

"Never," Sean said. "No matter what the circumstances."

For the next fifteen minutes, the four of them sat there watching the boats going up and down the river.

"One last question," Bernie asked Clyde after she'd finished her beer. "How did Chung find Crenshaw?"

This time Sean answered. "On the dark web, of course."

"Of course," Bernie murmured. "Why didn't I think of that?"

"Now I have a question for you guys," Clyde said to Bernie and Libby. "What's happening with the Longely Mystery Book Club."

Bernie answered. "They're meeting again. It seems that Margo had a client for the two Eakinses and she was copying them for him."

"So apologies all around?" Clyde asked.

"Exactly," Libby responded. "They've gone back to meeting again, only they've changed the day to Wednesday and switched their order. Now they want a chocolate cheesecake and a small pear tart. And Betsy said they were switching to reading science fiction and fantasy. They've had enough of mysteries for a while."

"I can see that," Sean said, after he'd finished off the last of his beer. He held out his hand. It had begun to sprinkle. The storm the weather forecaster had predicted this morning had arrived. It was time to go.

Recipes

I have been a member of a neighborhood book club for a number of years. Our book club meets every six weeks, and I have to confess we gossip more than we talk about the book we've read. Most of the time, our snacks consist of cheese, crackers, fruit, and wine, although occasionally someone gets ambitious and bakes something like muffins, cookies, or banana bread. Here are three recipes that have proven to be successful. The first two are from my good friend and excellent baker Linda Kleinman, while the third is from my daughter-in-law Betsy Baum, also an excellent cook and baker.

GLUTEN-FREE CRANBERRY BREAD

2 cups gluten-free flour with ½ tsp xanthum gum
2 tsp baking powder
½ tsp salt
1 tsp ground cinnamon
¼ cup butter
1¼ cups sugar
1 tsp grated orange rind
1 large egg
¾ cup orange juice
2 cups fresh cranberries
½ cup chopped nuts (I use pecans, but walnuts work as
  well)

Preheat oven to 350° F. Line bottom of 9 × 5 × 3-inch loaf pan with wax paper. Grease paper. In a bowl, thoroughly sift together flour, baking powder, salt, and cinnamon. In another, larger bowl, cream together butter, sugar, and orange rind. Beat in egg and mix well. Combine dry and wet ingredients, a third at a time. Mix in cranberries and nuts. Turn into prepared pan and bake for about 55 minutes or until tester comes out clean. Let cool completely on wire rack. Wrap tightly in tinfoil, and store for two to three days in refrigerator before using.

Note: You can double the recipe and make three 8 × 4-inch loaves or use a 10-inch tube pan.

PUMPKIN BREAD

3⅓ cups flour (if using gluten-free, add ¾ tsp xanthum gum)
2 tsp baking soda
3 cups sugar
1 Tbs cinnamon
1 Tbs nutmeg
½ tsp ground ginger
4 grade-A large eggs
1 cup canola oil
⅔ cup water
1 15-oz can unseasoned pumpkin purée

Preheat oven to 350° F. Sift dry ingredients together. Combine all wet ingredients, including pumpkin purée. Add wet mixture to dry mixture in thirds. Pour into two 9 × 5-inch or three 8 × 4-inch oiled pans lined with wax paper. Bake for 60 minutes or until tester comes out clean. Cool on rack, wrap in tinfoil, and refrigerate for four days before using. Can be frozen.

ORANGE-CARDAMOM MORNING MUFFINS

2 cups unbleached all-purpose flour
⅔ cup sugar
2 tsp baking powder
½ tsp baking soda
Pinch of salt
¾ stick of butter
Grated zest of 1 orange and 1 Tbs juice
1 tsp cardamom seeds, divided in half
⅔ cup Greek yogurt or buttermilk
2 large eggs
1½ tsp vanilla extract
1 cup semi-sweet chocolate chips (optional)
1 Tbs brown sugar
½ cup walnuts (optional)

Preheat oven to 400° F, and place oven rack in center. Grease 12-cup muffin tin. Sift together dry ingredients. Melt butter with orange juice and orange zest, then add ½ teaspoon cardamom. Take butter off stove, and slowly add yogurt. Let sit for a couple of minutes, then transfer to medium-size bowl and add eggs and vanilla. Make a well in the middle of dry ingredients, and slowly add wet ones, using spatula and mixing just until everything is combined. Add nuts and chocolate chips, if using. Pour batter into tin, then mix brown sugar and ½ teaspoon cardamom together and sprinkle on top of muffins. Bake for 18–20 minutes or until tester comes out clean. Cool in pan for five minutes, then turn out onto rack to finish cooling.